DROWNED MAN'S KEY

Also by Ken Grissom

Drop-Off
Big Fish

DROWNED MAN'S KEY

A JOHN RODRIGUE NOVEL

Ken Grissom

ST. MARTIN'S PRESS
NEW YORK

For Matthew

This novel is a work of fiction. All of the events, characters, names, and places depicted in this novel are entirely fictitious or are used fictitiously. No representation that any statement made in this novel is true or that any incident depicted in this novel actually occurred is intended or should be inferred by the reader.

DROWNED MAN'S KEY. Copyright © 1992 by Ken Grissom. All rights reserved. Printed in the United States of America. No part of this book may be used or reproduced in any manner whatsoever without written permission except in the case of brief quotations embodied in critical articles or reviews. For information, address St. Martin's Press, 175 Fifth Avenue, New York, N.Y. 10010.

Editor: Jared Kieling

Production Editor: David Stanford Burr

Design by Glen M. Edelstein

Library of Congress Cataloging-in-Publication Data

Grissom, Ken.
    Drowned man's key : a John Rodrigue novel / Ken Grissom.
       p.   cm.
    ISBN 0-312-06955-3
    I. Title
    PS3557.R5366D77   1992
    813'.54—dc20   91-39135
                                                            CIP

First Edition: April 1992

10 9 8 7 6 5 4 3 2 1

*Don't be afraid to jump for treasures (like
keys) that appear in awkward locations.*
—Instruction manual for a computer game

1

Blindingly white against the blackness of space, the aging orbiter *Columbia* whizzed along on its starboard side at 298.22 miles per second. Its payload bay doors were open and the mechanical arm—the remote manipulator system, or RMS in NASA initialese—was deployed on the port side, holding a convex dish toward the fierce orange sun.

In the middeck of the crew compartment, Mission Specialist Marsha Janke was having lunch. She had Velcroed herself to the lockers on the forward bulkhead and was in the semifetal position the body favored in microgravity. Her long blond hair floated above her like a mermaid's. Empty foil pouches waved like sea fans from the aluminum tray strapped to her thigh. Her sandwich was thermostabilized chicken salad on wheat.

Other figures hovered nearby, feminine figures clad in baggy blue IVA pants and navy pullovers. Mission Specialist Roberta Anderson was also eating. Mission Specialist Amy Simmons had just finished and was cleaning her tray with a wet wipe. Pilot Betty Kim had already stowed her tray and was fiddling with the new high-resolution video camera.

On the flight deck, Commander Alicia Burton was in her seat, preparing to roll the orbiter back upside down over the luminescent blue curve of the Pacific Ocean.

As Marsha absently chewed her sandwich, she gazed at a framed eight-by-ten color photograph Velcroed on the waste-management compartment next to the airlock. It was a photograph of a tiny tropical island, just a spit of white sand not much larger than a suburban yard, with an airy grove of a dozen or more coconut palms in the center. It looked like a cartoon island where a shipwrecked sailor could be happily marooned.

It also had the quality of a really nice watercolor with a lot of greens—dark and blue-tinged in the shade, glinting like tarnished brass where the sun shone on the fronds. Even the shallow water surrounding the island was a mottled green, pale lime over patches of sand and a rich emerald where coral heads dimmed the reflected sunlight.

Marsha had no idea where the island was exactly, although she assumed it was down in the Caribbean somewhere, or maybe off Florida. The photograph had belonged to an old man who had lived—and died—aboard a large sailboat at one of the marinas on Clear Lake, near the Johnson Space Center south of Houston. There were no family members or even friends close enough to claim his effects, so the marina's management had put everything up for sale, displayed on a table by the parking lot, with strips of masking tape for price tags.

She had been bicycling around the lake that Sunday and cut through the marina. Always a sucker for a flea market or a garage sale, she dismounted and squeezed in with the rest of the browsers. The photograph seemed out of place with the nautical gear and sparse bric-a-brac. It was framed in black wood, like a diploma, and it seemed somehow impersonal, as though the photo had come with the frame and hadn't yet been replaced by whatever the dead man had intended to display.

It might've been impersonal to him, but it sang like Bali Ha'i to Marsha.

She was thirty-two years old, with a Ph.D. and a dream career because she had known what she wanted early in life and had gone after it. She had a creamy complexion because she had always watched her diet and used sunscreens. Her smile was perfect because she had endured braces. Her body looked soft, but it was hard because she exercised. People liked her because she listened to them. She had a big hollow place in her gut because . . .

Because she had slowly and instinctively realized that you could take cause and effect just so far, that around the solid little blocks of achievement we build for ourselves flowed currents of mystery. Whispering, seductive currents . . .

It was getting dangerous. She had almost maneuvered a fellow astronaut into trying to impregnate her. Why? That was the scary part. There *was* no reason, or at least no rational one. Thank God he was a rational man. Very rational—a systems freak, in fact. Marsha had broken it off delicately because she still had to work with him.

When she found the photograph, she began to suspect that she simply needed a vacation. It was like a poster in a travel agency—with no one there to sell her a ticket. That made it all the more attractive. But then when she went to change frames (she had bought a more suitable one of bamboo), she had discovered a handwritten inscription on the back of the photo: *Drowned Man's*. And her scalp bristled with instant, irrational fear.

It was like a message from a ghost, as if the dead man were claiming his property. That was absurd, of course, and sure enough, the people at the marina said the man had not drowned at all but, rather, had shot himself.

The dread vanished, if not the tingling sense of the surreal. Marsha changed the glass pane for one of Plexiglas and—hinting to the crew that it had been the site of some torrid romance—packed the photo along on the flight as a sort of good-luck talisman.

Certainly she couldn't have called it that. You can't hope for good luck without admitting the possibility of bad luck, and everybody in the shuttle program was already edgy enough as it was.

A certain amount of bad luck had led to the unprecedented all-female crew in the first place. The original commander had been grounded for reckless operation of one of the T-38 trainers while giving his girlfriend a ride to Disney World. That bumped Alicia, who would've been pilot, into the commander's seat. Then they had had to reach up to the next mission to get a pilot, and that happened to be Betty. Marsha and Roberta had already been scheduled for this flight, but Amy replaced a male mission specialist whose wife had had a premonition of disaster and threatened divorce if he took the flight—and survived it, of course.

NASA had tried to inject the rumor that what she had really objected to was her husband being the only man with four women for seven days in space, but the damage had already been done.

Another source of uneasiness was Marsha's own popularity with the media and with the aerospace community. She figured she owed it more to her bra size than to her fitness for the mission, but whatever the reason, there hadn't been that much affection invested in an astronaut since *Challenger*.

So Marsha pretended there was more to the photo than there was and endured the other women's teasing about it. And as it turned out, they seemed to appreciate it as much as she did. After six days spinning around a big blue sphere, wearing blue, crawling into a blue sleep restraint at "night," the astronauts had developed a real hunger for the color green.

As she wiped down her food tray, a calm male voice suddenly filled the crew compartment.

"MurTech says bakeout is complete," said CAPCOM from his console at JSC. (CAPCOM meant "capsule communicator," a holdover from those wild splashdown days. The position was being held by a veteran astronaut.) "Resume vacuum operation."

"Affirmative," came Alicia's bored jet-jockey voice from the flight deck. She was a handsome woman, raven-haired, with high cheekbones and big eyes that were beautiful even when they squinted in her cigarette smoke. Marsha would've loved a chance to pluck the eyebrows a little, though, and bleach the few dark hairs on her lip.

The primary RCS thrusters hissed and the orbiter rolled ninety degrees.

"Just in time for the show," commented CAPCOM.

Marsha hurriedly stowed her tray and flew up to the aft flight deck, where two windows overlooked the payload bay and two larger ones overhead looked up on earth.

Betty came up with the video camera through the

starboard interdeck hatch, on an entirely different mission from Marsha's.

Marsha was working on the gallium-arsenide thin-film experiment, a commercial payload for MurTech Engineering. Gallium arsenide (GaAs) is a crystalline material that can be formed into an extremely thin film in a vacuum. The use of GaAs in computer chips was expected to result in radically smaller and faster computers.

MurTech had gotten very close to developing a workable GaAs thin-film recipe using earthbound vacuum chambers. But the process was so dirty, it made quality control very difficult inside the small chamber.

Even in near-earth orbit, there was too much cosmic pollution floating around. Then MurTech came up with the wake shield, a fourteen-foot disk like a huge Frisbee at the end of the orbiter's mechanical arm. Positioned exactly perpendicular to the flight path, the shield blocked gas molecules and other particles, creating in its wake a clean ultravacuum ideal for growing GaAs thin films in commercial quality and quantity. And the residue that so quickly gummed up a vacuum chamber could be burned away by the sun just like a self-cleaning oven—the bakeout operation *Columbia* had just completed.

There really wasn't a lot for the crew to do. The experiment—actually just fine-tuning the times and temperatures involved in growing GaAs thin-film wafers—was being controlled by MurTech personnel in the Payload Control Center at JSC. And the arm was programmed to reposition the wake shield automatically with the aid of the inertial measurement units or IMUs, a system of gyrolike sensors that fed information about the spacecraft's attitude relative to earth into the on-board computers. Marsha's role was simply to twist a knob on the upper left of the RMS control panel to AUTO 1 and push the ENTER button.

She hovered at the windows, watching the arm slowly rotate inward, her thumb on the rocker switch that would halt the process if necessary. The arm jamming so they couldn't get the bay doors closed for entry would be a good example of bad luck.

Betty ignored the maneuvering arm. She hooked the video

camera into the S band for instantaneous transmission to Mission Control.

"Here it comes," said Alicia.

The raven-haired commander floated out of the seat for a better view through the overhead ports. Roberta and Amy appeared at the interdeck hatches, craning to see past their colleagues.

Meanwhile, the mechanical arm locked into position. The payload computer, satisfied that the wake shield was exactly perpendicular to the flight path, began telemetering data back to Payload Control Center at JSC.

The mainframe computer in the Payload Control Center responded, and immediately things started going wrong. Rogue impulses sped through the orbiter's position sensors and into the on-board computers—all five of them.

The astronauts were crowded in the aft flight deck, staring though the overhead observation ports, waiting to witness what was already the most powerful Atlantic hurricane on record. Betty started operating the video camera as *Columbia* streaked over Acapulco. Where the Gulf of Mexico should've been was a huge white dome, fluffy, like meringue, with a gentle ridge coiling into a small cone-shaped depression in the middle.

Alicia shouldered between Betty and Marsha for a better view.

"*My God,*" she said.

In the panel of warning lights behind them, the one labeled IMU flashed red, unnoticed by the commander or her crew.

2

When the controllers in the Mission Control Center saw *Columbia*'s avionics program go haywire, they took it in stride. Computers could fail. That was why there were five of them aboard the orbiter, any one of which could do the job. CAPCOM's voice was calm, almost bored as he informed the flight crew of the problem. Although the orbiter was only about 800 miles to the south (and 269.29 miles up), they spoke via a complex hookup that involved two communications satellites and the NASA ground station at White Sands.

Meanwhile, not more than a half a mile away from where CAPCOM sat, a local businessman named John Rodrigue was frantically trying to reach a handful of employees on a small marine radio mounted on his desk.

"Any RYS crew, come back!" he called. "*Any* RYS crew, come back!"

He was a big man, rough-looking, and he spoke with a faint Louisiana-French accent. He wore a garish tropical-print shirt and he had a faded tattoo of an anchor on his tanned right forearm.

The office looked like Philip Marlowe had relocated in Papeete: A gray government surplus desk, file cabinet, and metal wastebasket shared the storefront room with a high-backed wicker chair, a couple of arreca palms, and a faded red plastic ice chest with four cans of light beer floating dejectedly in cold water.

The other eight cans from the twelve-pack were in the wastebasket, empty, the top ones crumpled.

The view through the tinted picture window was of docked sailboats, cabin cruisers, and houseboats—and beyond, open water and a far stretch of wooded shoreline, deceptively calm.

"Any RYS crew, come back!" Rodrigue said angrily at the microphone.

They were just college kids, and they were at the other end of the lake in aluminum pontoon boats, diving to scrub moss and barnacles off the bottoms of yachts.

Hurricane Jeanette had suddenly formed in the southeastern Gulf from the remnants of a cold front that had petered out over South Florida. One minute, it had been an area of low pressure at the end of a frontal trough, and the next, it had a name and was growing rapidly. Now they were saying it would probably reach category 5 by landfall that night. That meant winds over 155 miles an hour and a storm surge—the real killer—of around twenty feet.

The phone rang and Rodrigue glared angrily at it. All afternoon people had been calling. Business was too good. He started to let the answering machine handle it, but impulsively he reached for the phone.

"¡Hola! Tío Johnny!" It was Neesay, the daughter of an old friend from his days in Venezuela. She was all grown up now, an anthropologist studying aerospace workers at the Johnson Space Center. She was, she had explained, under contract to the Instituto de Pesquisas Espacias, the NASA of Brazil.

Neesay had appeared out of the misty past when Rodrigue had become infamous for his part in a very public drubbing of the U.S. Justice Department. She and Rodrigue had been living thirty-five miles apart without knowing it until she had seen him on "Eyewitness News" one evening. She called him up while the broadcast was still on, and they arranged to meet in Galveston the next day.

He had been astounded to see little Neesay all matured into a beautiful, confident, and, God help him, thought-provoking woman. But her timing was lousy. Then, Rodrigue had a girlfriend. Now, a girlfriend was the last thing he wanted. Anyway, Neesay was like family.

"Hey," he said, pleased to hear her voice. "You escaping to Houston?"

"I'm escaping to the Nassau Bay Hilton. And you?"

"Are you crazy? This hotel's right on the goddamned water!"

"And you?" she repeated.

He shook his head, grinning. "Yeah, me, too. Buy you a drink tonight?"

"*¿Cómo no? Hasta pronto.*" She hung up.

Something suddenly blocked part of the window, deepening the gloom in the office. Outside, a pair of amiable illegal aliens hammered nails around the edges of a sheet of new plywood. One looked past into the glass and grinned. Rodrigue had gotten them their jobs.

The beat-up radio crackled. "Kelly back to Rod," said a feminine voice. Kelly was one of Rodrigue's college students. She and a girl named Lynn operated one of the boats stationed at the far end of the lake, about three miles away at a marina called the Seabrook Shipyard.

"Where are you—come back?" demanded Rodrigue.

"Watergate. We just finished Mr. Allwyn's boat. Over."

"What about Clifford and Murphy? Come back."

"Supposed to be on a job at Lafayette Landing. Must be both down if they didn't answer. Over."

The lake was a brackish estuary joined to the much larger Galveston Bay by a short, twisting creek. It was a narrow lake, less than a mile from north to south. At the eastern end, where the creek exited, two big marinas straddled the channel—the Seabrook Shipyard on the north shore and Watergate Yachting Center on the south. Inside the creek, just under the tall Highway 146 bridge, was the marina called Lafayette Landing.

"Kelly, one of you can go. The other one go over to Lafayette and tell Cliff to quit—unless they're just about finished, anyway. Put the boats in the slips and get the hell out of Dodge. Do you read me?"

"Aye-aye," Kelly said cheerfully. She was a tall, cinnamon-haired thing with green almond-shaped eyes and high cheekbones, an education major at the University of Houston's Clear Lake campus. She could've revived every crush Rodrigue had ever had on a teacher, if he would've let it happen.

But the red hair reminded him too much of a former girlfriend, Ann Eller. He wondered about Ann briefly, suppressed the urge to call. She would be safe enough way up on the northern end of Houston. Besides, he had business to attend to.

To his credit, he didn't start worrying about the boats until he had sent the kids scurrying. But now, how in the hell was he going to get the boats gathered up by himself?

Like everyone else, he had been caught off guard. His partner, Leyton Mills, had the day off. Leyton was a young black lothario who by now would be ensconced in the apartment of whatever girl or girls he had picked up on Galveston's East Beach. Anyway, Leyton didn't have a car, and there wasn't much he could do stuck on the island.

Rodrigue's hurricane contingency plan—every coastal businessman had one—was to have the boats pulled out of the water and set them on one of the soccer fields at the county park, just a few hundred yards across NASA Road 1 from the big public boat ramp. But Rodigue only had one trailer for the six pontoon boats, and there simply wasn't time now for him to haul them out one at a time and dump them onto the grass.

There wouldn't have been time if he had had the ramp all to himself, and he knew without stepping outside that the crowd around the ramp would look like Dunkirk. A hurricane roaring back out of a cold front had caught everyone by surprise.

At least he already had four of the boats rafted up here at the Hilton Marina. He could run them up the creek and around into a sheltered drainage canal if he could just figure out how to get back to his truck.

The phone rang.

"RYS, Rodrigue," he said in a deadpan business voice.

"An' dis is you illegitimate son. You gonna let me perish doan here, maan?"

It was Leyton in his Pan-Caribbean accent, which Rodrigue hadn't bought from the first moment he'd heard it. The accent was credible enough, but Rodrigue had a very talented ear for language. And he himself lived half the year in the

Caribbean—or had until this year. The masquerade didn't bother him, though. Leyton was a good hand and a jolly soul.

"You at home?" Rodrigue asked.

Leyton didn't have a phone at home, which was an old apartment house built during the boom of the late forties and now shared by beach bums and medical students. But there was a pay phone at a convenience store down the street, and that was where Rodrigue meant.

"Yaas, but ah'm packed."

Packed! Leyton could carry all his belongings in a pillowcase.

"Ah'm gwine to de yacht basin and gat de *Queen* rady."

Rodrigue's personal boat, the *Haulover Queen*, was at the yacht basin, about a mile away from where Leyton was calling. Rodrigue would put it on its trailer and drag it back up to Clear Lake.

"Okay, I'm going to secure these boats here, pick up some stuff at the house, and then I'll meet you at the yacht basin," said Rodrigue.

As he hung up, a man he knew only as Sid, who kept a large motorsailer in the marina, opened the door and leaned in.

"Hey, can I keep a dinghy in here?" Sid asked urgently. "I don't know what else to do with the son of a bitch."

"Can you *get* it in here?" Rodrigue got up and peeked around Sid; sitting on the winding brick walk outside was a little yellow inflatable boat with a five-horse outboard motor.

Rodrigue stroked his jaw and peered at Sid in a comical one-eyed squint, a faithful imitation of actor Robert Newton's Long John Silver. "Mind if I uses 'er first?" he asked in his husky Long John voice.

Sid shrugged, then his eyes narrowed. "What the hell for?" He didn't care that much about the dinghy, but he couldn't imagine anyone going out in the teeth of the biggest hurricane in Texas history—especially in a little rubber tub.

"I'm going to run my pontoon boats into that drainage canal up to NASA One. Run 'em into the bank and anchor 'em the best way I can. I could sure use that dinghy to get back here to my truck."

"Sure, sure, don't worry about it," said Sid. "I just didn't want it blowing around doing damage in the marina."

Sid left. Rodrigue popped open another beer and followed, not bothering to lock the door.

The Nassau Bay Hilton was built on a steep bank at the western end of the lake. The main entrance was on the landward side, adjacent to the southeastern corner of the Johnson Space Center. On the lake side, the marina entrance was a full story lower. That level, which had a tile floor and echoed like a basement, contained a few offices—a travel agency and a vessel-documentation service—and a meeting room. A wide flight of steps led up to the lobby.

Looking at the Hilton from the lake, there was a wing of storefronts—including Rodrigue's—to the right, topped with a small parking lot. There were cement stairs between the hotel and the storefronts. To the left was a swimming pool, and beyond that, a stately old yellow brick mansion that now served the hotel as extra meeting space.

The marina itself was formed by a pair of wooden breakwaters that enclosed the rows of pleasure boats like embracing arms. Rodrigue's four pontoon boats were in the farthest row. Rather than drag the dinghy along the curving breakwater walkway, he launched it right in front of his office and puttered across the small harbor.

With the pontoon boats and the dinghy tied in a string, he piloted the lead boat out of the breakwater and onto the open lake.

Clear Lake had actually been clear once, when only Indians and pirates lived on its banks. Then settlers had come, families who raised crops and kept livestock. The creeks drained muddy water from the fields and biological wastes from the pastures, and the water turned brown. Now the low prairie to the north was a patchwork of upper-middle-class neighborhoods with Tudor houses and Old English street names, and the creeks drained water enriched with Ferti-Lome and the droppings of thousands of well-fed dogs and cats. Municipal sewage systems were strained beyond capacity, too, with the overall result that Clear Lake could grow moss on a duck's butt.

And in this rich biological soup sat hundreds of sailboats, many of which belonged to people who were too busy to sail. The area was an enclave of engineers and technicians who tended to look to science to deal with mundane problems like the slimy green beard growing below their waterlines. And for a while, science seemed to have found the answer with tributyltin-based bottom paints that lasted two full years even this near to the Tropic of Cancer. But tributyltin was killing more than just barnacles and moss, so the EPA banned it. Now that the yachtsmen were back to using copper paints, they tended to wait too long between haul-outs. It was a bird's nest on the ground for a fox like Rodrigue.

He had bought a dozen pool-cleaning Descos, full-face masks similar to his old navy Jack Browne, and hired certified scuba divers, of which there was no shortage at the nearby university. The work was simple enough—the pneumatic scrubbers operated like upside-down floor polishers. But shallow-water diving was still dangerous. Like a nagging mother, Rodrigue stressed that a diver should never, never, never hold his breath. Shooting up from under a boat without exhaling, he warned, would be like trying to keep a scared rat in your lungs.

When Rodrigue finally got back to the Hilton, Kelly was standing on the breakwater. Her flawless face was pulled into a frown and she was hugging herself unconsciously.

"What the hell are you doing here?" Rodrigue growled as he climbed out of the dinghy.

"I thought you might need some help," she said.

"What am I gonna do with you," he said, wrapping one strong arm around her waist and giving a squeeze.

She blushed as she thought of a retort. When he had come through the breakwater and spotted her, he had thrown up both arms in a sort of Gallic resignation. She found things like that about him very attractive. Even though he was twice her age, he was in some ways more youthful than the bored rich kids in her classes. Maybe it was the glass eye, which often caused him to cock his head exactly like a playful puppy.

"What about the honey barge?" she asked hopefully.

Rodrigue laughed. "The honey barge can only benefit from this, Kelly," he said. "Martyrdom."

The honey barge was a big aluminum flatbottom he had fitted with a fiberglass tank for receiving the thin mush of raw feces, urine, and dissolved toilet paper from the holding tanks now required by law in most yachts. But the only customers the honey barge had were the yachtsmen who hadn't yet figured out how to bypass their holding tanks and flush their toilets directly overboard. Now the flatbottom was tied up with the Vietnamese shrimp boats in the winding channel between the lake and Galveston Bay. None of the marinas would have the honey barge for a tenant.

"Hey, where do you have to go?" he asked suddenly, letting the dinghy slide back into the brown water. "Where are you staying? Not at home, for sure."

She shook her head. "South Shore Harbour Hotel. My father's on the ride-out crew."

She didn't say at JSC. Everyone knew her father worked for NASA.

"Who're you staying with? Your mom?"

"That's the plan, but—" She bit her lip. "She wouldn't worry if she knew I was here with you—if I got caught, I mean. I could call her—I mean, we could go get the other boats, you know?"

Rodrigue thought he knew what she meant, and it stunned him. Of the four girls working for him, she had probably flirted the least. It was probably the storm. Impending catastrophe did something to the hormones. Even he was feeling those old familiar urges. She *would* be a joy to have slithering naked across. . . .

Nah. Leyton would be with him.

And besides, he was expecting to see Neesay. Of course, there would be nothing between them except maybe a couple of seafood platters—if they could even wrangle a table somewhere—but a temporarily enamored college kid might throw the conversation out of kilter.

He looked at his watch. "I've still got to run down to Galveston and pick up a few things, not the least of which is Leyton," he told Kelly. "Still—"

He looked over at NASA Road 1, which followed the north shore of the lake. All of the traffic was headed west, toward the main evacuation corridor on the Gulf Freeway.

"Be quicker for you to run around the east end of the lake, against the flow of traffic. So you want to drop me off at Seabrook Shipyard on the way?"

"You going to move the other boats? I can help."

"Not necessary. I'll stop in here on my way back and pick up the dinghy, and use it to come back for my truck."

Kelly drove a five-year-old gold Porsche. Her pert breasts jiggled threateningly as she shifted through the gears. It was one time he was grateful for his diminished peripheral vision. He said good-bye with a pat on the little car's roof in the parking lot of the other marina.

"Be safe," he told her.

He wheeled and jogged for the pontoon boats now nodding nervously in their slips. Seabirds twittered high in the pale bronze sky like flakes of ash rising from a crackling fire. The atmosphere was charged with majesty.

3

At the Hilton, a bicyclist in bright neon-yellow shoes pedaled up the steep front drive and stopped under the covered entrance. He dismounted and folded the high-tech bike. He was wearing a black polo shirt and gray casual slacks with the legs wrapped in Velcro straps to keep them from getting caught in the bicycle chain. A NASA badge clipped to his collar identified him as one Cordell Pritchett.

He had just driven his wife, Claudette, and their twelve-year-old son, Timmy, to Hobby Airport in the family's Grand Wagoneer. Then he had come back to the Johnson Space Center, and left the station wagon in the employees' parking lot to avoid the unbroken stream of traffic on NASA Road 1. The bike had been stored neatly behind the rear seat.

Now with the folded bike under his arm, Pritchett squeezed into an elevator with baggage-laden guests. He pressed the button for the top floor, fourteen. Actually it was the thirteenth floor, but, like most hotels, the Hilton acquiesced to triskaidekaphobia.

The people in the elevator were chatty, almost giddy. They were mostly refugees from the low-lying coastal areas, no doubt, but they acted more like madcap conventioneers. Of course, it took a special class of refugee to flee a category 5 hurricane no farther than the first hotel. The elevator stopped on a floor and two people got off, and Pritchett could hear talking and laughter down the hall.

With more breathing room, he glanced around him. A man in a business suit was looking at Pritchett's feet. He sneered. "Nice shoes."

"They fit into the pedals of the bike," said Pritchett.

The man nodded and winked at a companion, and everyone laughed nervously. Pritchett self-consciously sneaked his left hand up and unclipped the identification badge from the collar of his shirt. He stuffed it into his pants pocket. He hadn't quite gotten the hang of being a spy.

By the time he reached the top floor, he was alone. The doors opened and the party sounds that had echoed around the corner on the lower floors smacked him full in the face here. These were the luxury rooms, and opposite the elevators was a large suite set up for entertainment. Through the phony French doors, Pritchett could see a crowd milling around divans and card tables. An L-shaped bar on the right held dozens of bottles of booze, but most of the people were grouped around two large picture windows on the left.

Another window was at the end of the hallway between the suite and the elevators. Pritchett pulled the curtain aside and peeked out: It looked down on NASA Road 1 curving westward toward the Gulf Freeway. The lanes of traffic moved so slowly, they seemed to slither, bronze sunlight dancing on glass and chrome. It was like a huge funeral procession.

Doors were open all down the hall. The rowdy clatter of tiny ice cubes in plastic glasses punctuated the urgent drone of TV news. All this desperate gaiety disturbed Pritchett. It seemed foolhardy to tempt fate with a hurricane party. Didn't anyone remember Camille in 1969? Gulfport, Mississippi? All those dead partygoers?

Pritchett found room 1422 and rapped lightly. A balding white-haired man jerked open the door. His eyes whipped down to Pritchett's shoes, then he turned back into the room without a word, drawn by the blaring TV.

Naturally, the news was on. News and weather were all that had been on all day. All furrowed brows and no happy-talk.

The man in the room was about Pritchett's height but wiry, with skin that had long since lost its tan but still looked weathered. He was probably in his early sixties. Pritchett knew him as Andres Weizman, but he could've been anybody. He assumed Weizman worked for the government of Israel and that eased his conscience about what they were doing, although he didn't know why. Pritchett had been raised a Presbyterian.

Pritchett set the folded bicycle down and said hello, but Weizman impatiently flashed a palm for silence. Pritchett, too, stared at the TV: A creamy swirl of clouds filled the screen—video from the orbiting *Columbia*.

"It's a real woolly-booger," drawled the voice of Commander Alicia Burton. "It eclipses the entire Gulf of Mexico."

Pritchett had to hand it to her, the woman was cool. At the Space Center, Alicia was almost as beloved for her cool toughness as Marsha was for her bouncy personality and bouncy breasts—almost.

Half of the men who worked at JSC had a secret crush on Marsha Janke. The other half worshiped her openly. Either way, it was a strange kind of affection, part wholesome lust and part brotherly pride. She was the cheerleader-astronaut, golden-haired, compact, curvy, and brainy. The most charming thing about her (after the pair of cantaloupes rolling around in her IVA shirt) was that she didn't even seem aware of her attractiveness. She could light up a conference room just by walking in, yet she was unassuming, one could almost say shy.

Marsha was single and lived in Seabrook, right on the bay. Who would be seeing to her things? No shortage of volunteers, Pritchett guessed. Besides, what could she have? Her preflight group photo, books, a wallful of diplomas . . .

And a bicycle—he knew she had a bicycle. She had participated in some of the group rides, but, to his disappointment, she had never joined the club.

On television, the newscaster was describing in hushed tones *Columbia*'s progress around to the other side of the world, where the breezes were gentle and people weren't fleeing for their lives. Pritchett sensed a new wedge of clouds had been driven between mere mortals and the astronauts—or at least these five, who had sat like goddesses, viewing the most dangerous storm of the century as though it were a billboard for some roadside attraction.

The esprit de corps spinning off this flight made Pritchett sick. It wasn't just this flight. He no longer had the sense of mission that drove many of his fellow workers. All that remained was an exhausting sameness about the days, the endless picking of very complicated nits.

Claudette pretended not to notice that he was sick of his job, sick of the mentor-driven bureaucracy, sick of the smug sense of superiority that had settled over the whole community like the poison spewing out of the chemical plants around the bay. But she was hard that way. She had said good-bye in the crowded and anxiety-charged airport as though she and Timmy were merely going away for a visit, or at the most escaping the discomfort of the inevitable power outage. And all the while they were making small talk, waiting for the call to board, Pritchett had been crumbling inside. They were waiting for the last plane to The Way Things Should Have Been. There was an air of finality about it.

Maybe she *was* escaping more than just a storm. Maybe she wouldn't be coming back. It was, after all, his fault they were in such a mess. He had done it for her, partly—and certainly with her encouragement—but *he* had done it.

And then in trying to undo it, he had made it so much worse.

He should have been a jock to begin with. He had the timing and the reflexes for it. Trouble was, he had the looks for it, too—he looked like a Neanderthal, with his prominent brow ridge and merged bushy eyebrows. His looks had so appalled him in junior high that he had joined the Slide Rule Club to compensate. From then on, it was like being stuck out there on NASA Road 1, stuck in the flow of traffic.

Then one day, he quit denying his physical self. It was because his physical self was getting flabby and listless in his sedentary lifestyle. He started jogging in the muggy early mornings, and switched to cycling when he discovered the exhilaration of the sport, and the practical advantage of being able to outrun the mosquitoes.

It was a fairly self-indulgent sport because it was so

19

expensive and time-consuming. But it was good for the family, too. An afternoon of pumping his legs against the Texas wind cleared his mind of all the shapeless little anxieties caused by doing technical work in a highly political environment, thus making him a nicer husband and dad. He had tried involving the family more directly, but Claudette and Timmy weren't up to pedaling marathons through the countryside, and loafing around the block in the evening didn't satisfy his growing need for speed and burn.

Then Pritchett suddenly thought he saw a way off of the NASA treadmill: He decided to open a bicycle shop.

Claudette loved the idea. Cycling was trendy. Besides, everyone they talked to about it agreed it would be a damned gold mine. And while Pritchett wanted only to make enough to quit his job, Claudette had visions of all that money being piled on top of his present salary. She wasn't being greedy. Like any good woman, she only wanted the best for her family.

She had changed over the years, but all women did that. She had been a freckle-faced hippie, tall and bony and carefree, when they married. Her idea of furniture were cinder blocks and barn doors. The miscarriage took a lot of her gaiety, just as Timmy's infancy gave her strength. The long straight brown hair evolved into short blond curls, and the angular body became almost voluptuous and then just heavier, and Pritchett accepted every change as a new lover. Claudette, for her part, placed ever-increasing importance on the PTA and Little League, and the Taylor Lake Village Garden Club, and in keeping a nice home.

The bicycle shop was an immediate success, spawning first group rides, then a club, then club races. It didn't bring in enough to live on, but Pritchett believed it eventually would—especially if he was successful in getting the chamber of commerce behind a public velodrome. Clear Lake could become the Indianapolis of bicycle racing, he told the executive committee. Some of them really liked the idea.

But then the chamber busied itself with the hydroplane races on the lake, then the Christmas boat-lane parade, and then Spring Fling. Then someone opened an Ivy League–style rowing club, and soon all the people who had been pedaling were streaking across the glassy surface of the lake in the still mornings. Sales at the cycle shop fell off drastically, and the gold mine turned into a millstone.

Pritchett had squandered his savings and still owed on inventory he couldn't sell. Claudette blamed him, and life at home became tense. And that was the situation when Andres Weizman walked into the shop the first time and stood bemusedly looking over the rows of gleaming spokes.

"Yes, sir, may I help you?" Pritchett had called out. This was a disagreeable part of his dream he hadn't forseen, being a damn store clerk.

Weizman had regarded him with an ironic twinkle. "Perhaps. I have a cruising yacht and I need some form of stowable transportation. There are small motorcycles, of course, but their oil and noise seem somehow out of place aboard a sailing yacht, don't you agree?" And then Weizman had smiled at Pritchett as though he were seeing into the middle of his brain.

Pritchett sold him a folding bike. A week later, Weizman was back, this time just to talk—and to listen. Pritchett extolled the benefits of bicycling for its own sake, and he tried to sell Weizman a racer.

By now, he had dropped all the self-delusions about being this fitness guru who wanted only to help others tone their bodies and clear their minds. He *had* been that once, maybe, early on. But his life was being choked into the center lane, and for too long he had been one of the good-intentioned slugs who merged left and crept along in a responsible, orderly fashion while the cheats continued to whiz by on the right and then wheedle or force their way in at the last minute. That was all the hell life was, a big yellow RIGHT LANE CLOSED AHEAD sign, a game of musical chairs, odd man out, survival of the fittest. No, not the fittest. The most autonomous. All suckers merge left.

At first, Weizman seemed to be the perfect sucker. He wasn't interested in buying another bike; he wanted the whole *store*.

Or no, as it turned out, just a piece of it.

But no, that wasn't it, either.

Somewhere along the line, their relationship flip-flopped.

Weizman became the predator and Pritchett the prey. But it happened so slowly that Pritchett didn't notice. What was worse, he actually enjoyed it. As prospective business partners—and even, briefly, as friends—they had spent a lot of time together aboard Weizman's sailboat, seesawing leisurely over the open bay. Pritchett found that he enjoyed the man's talk. The Israeli was positive, aggressive. He made it seem all things were possible.

"The money is an insult, of course," he had said that day as they ghosted into the wind toward Red Fish Island. "It is an insult to offer money to you for such a thing, and it is an insult that it is not enough money."

Maybe it wasn't enough, but ten thousand dollars would enable Pritchett to catch up on some delinquent bills. All he had to do was steal some data from a private experiment in an upcoming shuttle flight.

"We should say it is industrial espionage," said Weizman, smiling like a wise, sad grandfather. "It is, of course. The chief business of nations today is industry, to paraphrase your President Coolidge. Not long ago, when it was the defense industry that fueled both our economies, it was a matter of give-and-take between governments. . . ."

Weizman breathed a sigh and assumed an expression of deep sorrow. "Now, instead of weapons, it's computer technology," he continued. "And the private sector holds sway."

The U.S. State Department had indirectly sponsored legislation that would've required NASA's payload clients to share information with Israel, but the anti-Zionists in Congress killed it, Weizman had said.

Now, looking back on the way Weizman had sucked him into the plot, Pritchett wasn't sure he believed any of it. But now it didn't really matter. He was in it up to his chin. . . .

The TV weatherman, looking grim, flashed back on the screen. Weizman switched the set back to NASA Select, a local cable channel with a direct feed from Mission Control. *Columbia*'s ground tracks undulated soundlessly across a blue background.

Weizman turned and, looking down at Pritchett's feet again, smiled with cruel thin lips.

"The shoes—quite colorful."

Pritchett looked down at his yellow cycling shoes. "Yes, I suppose. The soles merge with the bike's pedals."

"Intelligence operatives generally avoid apparel that attracts attention." It was a good-natured rebuke, but a rebuke nonetheless.

"These were a pair I couldn't move in the store," Pritchett said with a flash of irritation.

"Yes, I quite imagine." Weizman changed the subject. "Are we safe here?" He asked it without any show of anxiety, an academic question.

"It depends," said Pritchett, who was dog-tired of having to be precise about things.

"Upon what?"

"How well this foundation was engineered."

Weizman nodded and turned to the dresser.

"I have left plenty of room for you to set up," he said.

On the dresser, Weizman had already arranged some of the gear he had removed from his boat: his personal computer, modified Israeli army field receiver, and a new DAT (digital audio tape) recorder. A cable from the radio ran out to a small balcony. Pritchett went to the sliding glass door and peeked out.

With metal hose clamps, Weizman had fastened the antenna at a right angle to the top of the balcony rail. It could pass for miniature VHF elements, as though here was a fellow with a battery-powered TV who intended to tune in the broadcast stations after the power and cable went.

"That antenna's not going to stay there," Pritchett predicted.

Weizman shrugged. "If it blows away, I'll set up another. It cannot be helped. There are no windows in this hotel that face Building Thirty."

The top floor was the only one on which the rooms opened to the outside. Pritchett slid the door open and stepped onto the tiny triangular balcony. The wind sucked at him, flapping his clothing. He had to lean out over the rail to see the cluster of beige concrete buildings a half a mile away and, among them, Building 30, the windowless structure housing the Mission Control Center.

Weizman stepped into the door behind him, and Pritchett's gaze darted to the pebbly, tarred lobby roof far below. His mind suddenly flashed on an image of his own body crashing through the arched skylight to the horror of the guests relaxing by the potted palms. After all, Weizman didn't really need him now. . . .

They were stealing the data from MurTech Engineering, a private company growing gallium-arsenide wafers in a payload experiment. The results of the experiment were being beamed to earth along with regular orbiter telemetry in a single radio downlink. Once in the MCC, the individual signals were separated in the PDIS—the payload data interleaver serializer—which was Pritchett's baby. He had helped design it, and now he helped to keep it operational. And with a little inspired head scratching, he had been able to figure out how to bug it.

Bugging the PDIS itself was a piece of cake. Weizman had all the right spy tools. Pritchett hid a small wideband transmitter inside the cabinet and ran wires to the backplane to intercept data from the proper circuit board and also to leech power for the transmitter. The backplane was a mass of wires and connectors, and two more wouldn't be noticed.

The problem was how to send the data out of the building. Building 30 was almost bugproof. Its walls were steel-lined, and emerging land lines were heavily shielded—both of which had been done to prevent innocent electromagnetic interference rather than bugging, but the effect was the same.

The solution had been an ordinary pay phone in the visitors' gallery overlooking Mission Control Center. One night just before lift-off, when his colleagues were preoccupied with their own tasks, Pritchett went into the maintenance area and picked up the running list for under-floor cables. He found the unshielded wire from the pay phone and installed a receiver that would pick up the signal from the bug in the PDIS and relay it onto the phone wire via induction clips that wouldn't leave a trace once they were removed. Then he went up to the visitors' gallery and taped an OUT OF ORDER sign over the coin slot of the pay phone so the line would remain clear.

Someone in Weizman's employ—Pritchett didn't know

who, nor did he want to—had climbed the utility pole outside, identified the pay phone's line, and clipped on another wideband transmitter like the one in the PDIS. Before the storm blew up, the signal from this one had been picked up by the antenna high in the mast of Weizman's boat, anchored in the lake.

The data—groups of digits representing time and heat values—were electronically scrambled. But because Pritchett was responsible for the output of the PDIS, he had been issued a MurTech crypto-key, a circuit board housed in a plastic container, with the connector end open. It plugged into the equipment like a kid's computer game. Using the crypto-key and recorded test signals he had been able to sneak out before the flight, he had programmed Weizman's computer to unscramble the data. And as a safeguard in case the program didn't work on the real thing, he had rigged another PC to physically accept the crypto-key, just like the payload computer in Building 30.

But the program was working fine, so Weizman didn't really need him any longer.

Pritchett remembered something; sudden panic squeezing at his guts, he shoved past Weizman into the room.

"Acrophobia?" asked Weizman nastily.

"Where's the other computer?"

"Here," said Weizman, opening the closet.

Pritchett took it out and turned it over, and then he felt the tumult in his stomach again.

"Where's the crypto-key?" Even as he spoke the words, he knew damn well where it was; it was still on the boat. He had put it in a plastic freezer bag to keep out moisture, and he had stowed the bag in the big chart drawer. His own voice echoed in his ear: *Where is the crypto-key?*

"You do not have it?" said Weizman accusingly.

"I—I must've left it at home!" he lied.

Weizman shrugged. "Do we really need it now? Can't you verify the data off the tape?"

Pritchett felt as though someone had him by the throat. The crypto-key had a serial number. He was responsible for it. Worse, if it was found aboard Weizman's boat somehow, it could be linked to him.

"I need the crypto-key," Pritchett said. He improvised: "In case they change the data run because of the propagation changes. The storm—"

Pritchett had the door half open now. Weizman shut it again and said in a low voice that was almost a growl, "Calm down. You will draw attention to yourself."

Pritchett nodded soddenly.

He forced himself to walk out, walk calmly through the revelers. But he paced frantically in the hall while the crowded elevators inched their way floor by floor to the top of the Hilton.

Outside, the lake rolled northward relentlessly, lacing the Hilton breakwater with explosions of dirty foam. Pritchett squinted into a gust; glowing white against the dark water was Weizman's yacht, bobbing gently in the choppy chocolate-colored lake.

Two swarthy workmen were carrying a sheet of plywood, holding it parallel to the wind to keep from being bullied around.

"Hey!" Pritchett yelled.

The men looked at him but kept going with the plywood until they reached the storefront of a boutique that specialized in Jet Ski and Hobie Cat wear.

"*Hey!*" he insisted. "Do you have a launch?"

One man smiled uncomprehendingly. The other pointed up to the unboarded glass wall of the restaurant, two floors above the marina level.

"Not lunch, you idiot! *Launch!* Boata!"

"Ah, *lancha!*" said the smiling workman. "*Para allá.*" He jabbed his thumb over his shoulder in the direction of a line of plywood-covered offices. A sign over one read, RODRIGUE YACHT SERVICES, INC.

Pritchett reached for the door, but a gust of wind buffeted him back a step. He was about to try again when it opened and a big, rough-looking man in a loud Hawaiian shirt slammed into him. Although he was coming out of the building, the man was drenched, hair streaming down his forehead.

"I'm sorry!" said the rough-looking man in a surprisingly civil voice. "Are you all right?"

"I'm all right," Pritchett said when he recovered his breath. "But I need to rent a boat."

The man stepped back and cocked his head quizzically. "Rent a boat? In a fucking hurricane? Look—look at me!" He stepped back and spread his arms. There were puddles where he had stood. "I just got out of a fucking boat!"

"Look, I've got to get out to that boat out there!"

The rough-looking man turned and looked in the direction Pritchett was pointing. "Yours?" he asked.

He had a trace of an accent—Cajun, Pritchett supposed. At any rate, he was hardly the type to be an FBI agent or anything of the sort.

"It belongs to a friend of mine. I've left something aboard—" He improvised again, something he was getting good at. "My—my heart pills. Can't get in touch with him. Gotta have them!"

The man looked at his wristwatch.

"Tell you what, there's an inflatable dinghy in my office here. You're welcome to it if you can handle it by yourself. I've got to go. Just put it back. Don't worry about locking the door."

"What about the motor? Do I need a key or anything?" Pritchett was unfamiliar with boat motors.

"It's a little outboard," the rough-looking man said. "You pull the rope. Lever on the side is the gearshift."

He squinted suspiciously, looking at Pritchett with one eye.

"You gonna be all right out there?"

"Yes, yes."

The man hesitated, then shook his head and headed for the outside stairs to the parking lot.

A light, whirling rain began as he finally eased down into the little yellow boat. The motor started instantly, and he puttered uncertainly, experimenting with the twist throttle in the tiller handle as he found his way around the piers and out the marina.

In the lake, the water was rough, pounding the boat and soaking him. Halfway out to Weizman's yacht, Pritchett realized he had made a big mistake—that his whole life had been one stupid mistake after another.

But it was too late to turn back now.

4

In the Mission Control Center, the branch chief stared at the monitor in the console as the flight controller changed the display. At each change, the screen flickered but returned to the identical image.

"One through five," said the controller in a voice tight with restrained emotion.

The branch chief blinked with disbelief. What the monitor was telling them was that all five of the general-purpose computers in the orbiter had taken a hit somehow. Which was not possible—unless the flight crew had for some reason been using all five simultaneously to run the payload software.

"Ask her to read panel six again," he said to the CAPCOM.

"Alicia, Houston," said CAPCOM in his pilot's monotone. "Uh, give me the GPC switch positions again."

"Roger, Houston," answered Alicia Burton in *her* monotone. "One: Run. Two: Run. Three: Standby. Four: Run. Five: Standby."

"Uh, thank you, uh, *Columbia*," said CAPCOM.

The branch chief knew the astronauts, including the one serving as CAPCOM, were ticked off at him for questioning the flight commander so closely. They figured he was doing it because she was a woman. Well, fuck them, he thought. He had every right to be suspicious. He had no authority over operations, but when something went wrong with the equipment, it was *his* ass in the sling.

Even with three of the GPCs running, only two at the most would've been used for primary avionics, the program called guidance, navigation, and control, or GN&C. Another would be handling systems management and payload operations. That would still leave two as backup in case of program or hardware failures.

One GPC was all it took to get the orbiter safely home, but right now *Columbia* had none.

And since it was evidently a glitch that had come from somewhere in the bowels of Building 30, it was up to the branch chief to find out where.

"Okay, dump three and five, and let's upload the new program."

CAPCOM relayed the instructions to Commander Burton, who would take the two "freeze-dried" computers off standby, and then order someone in the crew to twist a switch on the aft flight deck that would scrape the memory from each one in turn like dead coals from a firebox.

Mission Control had never furnished an orbiter with a new GN&C program in midflight before, but that didn't mean they didn't know how to do it. The program was really nothing but a high-tech means of dead reckoning, only in this case it wasn't *where* the orbiter was that was critical. It was *how* the orbiter was, its attitude relative to terra firma.

There were three gimballed sensors called IMUs in the nose of the orbiter that had kept track of the vehicle's attitude since the moment of lift-off. The computer used the data in a continuum to calculate with typical NASA precision the orbiter's relative attitude at any given moment. And it was this continuum the glitch had somehow eliminated from all five general-purpose computers at once.

Normal drift of the IMUs was corrected on board with a computerized star-tracking system that served as a spacegoing sextant. For larger errors—and this one certainly qualified—the task could be accomplished manually with an optical sight. But that wasn't the branch chief's responsibility. Keeping the orbiter tethered to its stream of telemetry was.

Fortunately, Mission Control routinely monitored and recorded all of the orbiter's avionics data, so all they had to do was recreate the continuum up to the point the on-board computers took the hit. It was like push-starting a stick shift—get it up to speed and you're off and running again. No problem.

But it was scary all the same. It was also a bit like pulling the ripcord and nothing happening. You know you've got a reserve chute, but *shit*. . . .

The shuttle had to enter the atmosphere at precisely the right attitude or it would burn up. It was as simple as that.

It would be damn tragic, losing *Columbia*, the branch chief thought glumly as he trudged back down to his office on the first floor. NASA was under heavy pressure by Congress to consolidate, and without Jim Wright up there to fight for JSC, the likelihood of the whole shuttle shooting match going to Kennedy Space Center would be pretty strong in the wake of a Houston-centered disaster. LBJ would be logging some rpm in his grave.

One of the MurTech engineers was waiting in the branch chief's office.

"It wasn't us," he said.

"Bullshit," said the branch chief. "The IMUs lit up the second the experiment started back up."

"I'm telling you, we ran the program twice and it's clean. I think you've got to look somewhere else."

A NASA engineer, one of the branch chief's employees, stood at the door, listening in.

"You hear that?" the branch chief asked him.

The NASA engineer shrugged. "We're independently re-creating every stream of information in the uplink. Nothing so far."

The branch chief cursed. It *had* to be MurTech. That goddamned payload was an Achilles' heel because *it*, unlike every goddamned thing *else* on the orbiter, did not have redundancy built into it. Yet because the wake shield had to be so precisely aligned with the orbiter's flight path, the *one* on-board computer being used for payload had to interface with all *three* IMUs, which in turn interfaced with all *five* GPCs. It was like tying all your lifeboats to the sinking ship.

The phone rang on the branch chief's desk. He picked it up. "Yeah," he said dully.

"This is Bain," said another of his employees. "You'd better get up here."

"Problem?"

"The program we just uploaded is garbage. Looks like we've got a problem in the NOM."

"We've got *three* fucking NOMs! Use a backup and try again!"

"I don't want to tell you what to do," said Bain carefully. "But we just made the number three and five GPCs considerably more confused than they were."

"So what are you saying?"

"That maybe we can bounce a telemetry link off a TDRS into Goddard and let them read what we're sending first. When we can get it clean to them, then we'll uplink with *Columbia* again."

Goddard Space Flight Center outside Washington was the heart of NASA's space communications system, as well as having a backup mission control center. The TDRSes were communications satellites used along with their ground terminal at White Sands, New Mexico, to link the orbiter to Mission Control.

"Good idea," growled the branch chief.

And I'm damn glad I thought of it, he thought nastily as he hung up the phone.

5

From the hotel parking lot, Rodrigue turned right on NASA Road 1. It was a wide four-lane that ran from the Gulf Freeway eastward toward the bay, bordering the south side of the Johnson Space Center, then skirting the north shore of the lake. Rodrigue's old black Chevy Blazer was one of the few vehicles traveling east, but the oncoming traffic was bumper-to-bumper and crawling. At the first intersection, the signal light was being ignored. A cop in a yellow slicker had stopped the traffic to let cars in from a side street. He looked back in time to give Rodrigue a perfunctory wave.

The road wound past boat dealerships, marinas, restaurants, and condominiums sitting on the lakeshore. In Seabrook, with the wide bay just ahead, Rodrigue turned right onto Highway 146, the old bayside highway that would take him south. He came immediately to a high bridge that spanned the channel connecting Clear Lake with the bay. On the other side was Kemah and the start of Galveston County.

The bridge was relatively new. Before, there had been a drawbridge that held up motorists while sailboats filed in and out of the lake. The new bridge helped the motorists, but it didn't do much to speed up boat traffic. There was still a hundred-year-old railroad trestle crossing the creek below. The trestle was unused and the swing bridge stayed open, but there was room for only two boats to pass, and then only very slowly and very carefully. On sunny weekends, boats were lined up thirty or forty deep on each side, waiting for a turn. Progress, Rodrigue had decided, did not go on like a smooth coat of paint.

On the other side of the bridge, a Galveston County sheriff's car was parked sideways, all but blocking the southbound lanes. Rodrigue stopped and showed his driver's license, and the deputy waved him on. One of the problems with a massive evacuation like this was keeping looters away from the abandoned homes and businesses. They had to assume a resident was on a legitimate errand, but they would keep out all nonresidents.

Rodrigue was stopped twice more on 146, once at Dickinson and again at Texas City. And then after he had merged onto the Gulf Freeway and was approaching the Galveston Causeway, he saw a whole line of emergency vehicles—police and sheriff's cruisers, ambulances, and a fire truck—blocking the freeway. He rumbled to a halt, elbow resting on the open window. A deputy walked up suspiciously. A gust of wind forced him to grab his hat.

"Island's been evacuated, bub."

Rodrigue handed him the license. Looking at the name on it, the deputy's right eyebrow arched in recognition.

"Where ya goin', Rod?" he asked in a friendlier tone. Rodrigue was something of a legend on the island.

"Pick up some stuff at home, and at the yacht basin, then I'm outta here."

"Better get a move on," said the deputy, handing back the license. "We're cleaning everybody off this time—us included. You get hung up, there ain't gonna be nobody to help."

The causeway was a mile and a half long, with a hump in the middle to let the tall inland tugs on the Intracoastal slide under. It spanned an arm of the bay that separated Galveston Island from the mainland. On the east end of the island were ferries that carried traffic across the main ship lane to the Bolivar Peninsula. And on the west end, there was a bridge over San Luis Pass. But whether you went east or west, you would find yourself on a low-lying road right on the Gulf beach—no place to be in a hurricane. Very soon this causeway would be Galveston's only route to safety.

Galveston was a barrier island, the principal geographic

feature of the Texas coast. Essentially, they were sandbars that had emerged offshore and become more and more substantial as they moved landward. In an eon or two, they would merge with the land and a new sandbar would rise from the sea. East of Galveston beyond Bolivar Peninsula (an island in the act of merging), the coast began to take on the marshy character of Louisiana. But stringing westward and then southward as the coastline curved were Follet's Island, Matagorda Peninsula, Matagorda Island, San Jose Island, Mustang Island, and Padre Island. In Mexico, the process continued for another hundred and fifty miles, two-thirds of the way to Tampico.

Human history had caught Galveston in its prime, with terrain high enough to support a live oak forest that sheltered inhabitants and anchored the drifting sands. Centuries of Indians sitting in the shade shucking oysters had left shell middens that would later become part of the foundation for the Gulf Freeway. Jean Lafitte built his famous red house and some wharfage for his pirate ships. Then came the Texas Revolution and a flood of settlers from the United States. For a time, Galveston was second only to New Orleans as a Gulf port, but then business interests in Houston got the upper hand and built a ship channel through the bay that routed most commerce past the island.

Now Galveston relied on tourism. Mainly, there was the beach, blue-green water that tumbled onto the khaki sand in rows of gentle breakers. The seawall protecting the city was topped with a broad walkway that linked curio shops, carnival rides, and fishing piers. In between were long stretches of open beach for sunbathing and volleyball and girl watching. A cruise ship docked where the banana boats used to, and the old redbrick warehouses of the harbor district were one by one being turned into Yuppie bistros. The stately Victorian mansions rising from the subtropical vegetation along Broadway attracted old couples with cameras. Fishermen flocked to the yacht basin, where they could book a trip for speckled trout or blue marlin.

The fishermen and other boaters had been the reason Rodrigue had moved to Galveston. There was always a way an enterprising diver could pick up a few bucks around a busy seaport. And a few bucks had been all Rodrigue thought he needed until that last visit from Ann Eller. Now he was a CEO with a forty-five-mile commute to work.

Rodrigue took the Sixty-first Street cutover to Seawall Boulevard. The seawall extended from the eastern tip of the island westward for nearly ten miles. It had been built after an unnamed 1900 hurricane shoved Gulf waters completely over the city, erasing most of what had been built and drowning some six thousand residents.

Past the seawall, the island was lower, with just a narrow strip of land between the Gulf beach and the marshy coves that lined the bay side. Rodrigue drove through several small resort communities until he reached his own, Sea Isle, at the far west end. He backed up the drive and hitched onto his boat trailer.

His house was on the beachfront. Like most houses on the unprotected part of the island, it was built high on piers, so that the house itself served as a carport. Steps up the side took him to a wide deck overlooking the beach.

The angry Gulf caught his attention and drew him to the smooth wooden rail. The tide was already raging and the first line of glinting olive green breakers were crashing way offshore. Rushing shoreward, tumbling, boiling up sand and foam, they produced a monotonous roar that he felt as much as he heard.

Rodrigue had always been soothed by the raging surf, a feeling he only half-understood. Maybe, because his ancestry was so intertwined with the sea, some kind of genetic memory was involved. Certainly, though, he had his own memories. They flooded back into his mind almost like a vision.

The sea had been raging then, too, pounding so hard they could feel it on the damp sand where they sat, watching the sun climb out of the thick storm haze. They were all wet and cold and elated.

Their shrimp boat had capsized and sunk in rough seas and they had clung to a wooden hatch cover half the night, miraculously winding up on a barren stretch of Mexican beach about eighty miles south of Brownsville, Texas.

Sooner or later, Papa would have to think of something to

do, but there didn't seem to be any hurry. They just sat in a row—Papa, Uncle Maurice, Reuben with the bad complexion, and him—gazing at the waves, which at first seemed to roar and snap at them like some caged animal denied its meal.

At some point that day, though, the pounding surf lost its malevolence for the young Rodrigue. It was still awesome, but it made him feel good to bask in the harmless violence a few yards away while at the same time soaking up the warmth of the rising sun.

About midmorning, Papa and the others started talking about how to get back to civilization and what they would do when they got back. For them, the euphoria had worn off.

But Rodrigue carried the feeling into adulthood, past many encounters with a frisky sea.

Now, this thundering ocean scared him. Rodrigue was a changed man, no question about it. He shook his head disgustedly and went into the house.

He hurriedly packed a seabag with clothes and hustled it and a few other belongings downstairs. Back in the kitchen, he loaded an ice chest with most of the fresh fruit from the refrigerator, put some canned goods in one cardboard box and the contents of his liquor cabinet—mostly rums of widely varying quality—in another. He put the rest of the contents of the refrigerator into a garbage bag to be chucked, and used the emptiness to give the inside of the fridge a quick scrubbing. At the very least, the electricity would be off for days.

At the *very* least.

He pulled a new fifth of dark Jamaican rum back out of the cardboard box, cracked the lid, and sloshed some of the coffee-colored liquor into a plastic tumbler. He scooped up some ice cubes and found a wedge of lime in the ice chest. Satisfied with the drink, Rodrigue leaned on his breakfast bar and let his gaze drift around the room. The furniture, even the TV, had been here when he moved in. Even the Starving Artists seascapes on the wall, which were pleasing to him, had been hung by the former owner.

Easy come, easy go.

6

Up in Clear Lake, Weizman's boat was yawing in the steep waves, rolling over the deep, narrow troughs, jerking violently as each peak raised the bow and tightened one of the anchor lines.

Squatting in the inflatable dinghy, Pritchett approached the yacht. He cut the engine, but too late; the dinghy slid down the back side of one wave just as the boat, heeling precariously, rose on another. He found himself looking up at the slimy, barnacle-dotted bottom.

In an instant, the waves marched on and the positions were reversed—Pritchett now hovering above the sailboat's slanted deck. He jumped or fell—he couldn't have said which—but in the next instant he was aboard the sailboat and holding on for dear life as it rolled steeply and fell back into a trough with all the gun-wrenching dynamics of a roller coaster. At least he'd had the presence of mind to hold on to the dinghy's rope. Lose the dinghy and his life wouldn't be worth spit.

The boat kicked up sharply at a new angle and he felt his stomach contract sickeningly. He got to his knees and tied the dinghy off to the little cable fence around the boat. Gingerly, he crawled to the cabin. The heavy wooden hatch cover was closed and latched, but not locked. He unlatched it and slid it forward, then—carefully timing his actions with lulls in the boat's motion—he removed the wooden slats that formed the door. The boat jerked viciously at an anchor line, and Pritchett used the next instant of stability to plunge down the ladder into the dark cabin.

The crypto-key was where he had left it, in the drawer of the chart table, sealed in a Ziploc bag. As he reached for it, the boat heeled again and threw his body against the table, slamming the drawer shut on his hand. Tears filled his eyes and the pain added to his nausea. He threw up on the Plexiglas-covered chart table.

He was in bad trouble. He was in a hell of a fix, and nobody knew about it. Claudette was flying to her mother's house, not even thinking about him. Nobody was thinking about him. Everybody had their own problems. He was like one of those accident victims smashed and bleeding by the freeway, and the radio telling people which exits to take so they won't have to slow down. He was definitely out of the fast lane.

If Claudette was leaving him, what was it all for? He didn't need any of the things that had cost so much. He could've lived in a little efficiency on the lake and ridden his bike to work.

Work? He could've *been* the cycling guru. He could've started a long time ago instead of wasting so much time. He could've opened a smaller shop and let it grow naturally instead of desperately trying to pump it up to meet a payment schedule.

These thoughts didn't come progressively in Pritchett's mind but, rather, expanded like an explosion and were gone in an instant. Then all that was left was a terrible longing for Claudette and Timmy.

Sudden fear nearly buckled his legs. He stuffed the crypto-key into his hip pocket and grabbed for the ladder. As he made his way up, the boat jerked violently at the anchor again, and the hatch cover slid rearward and hit him squarely on the back of the head.

Pritchett fell back into the cabin, unconscious.

7

At the Galveston yacht basin, a lone figure paced the concrete wharf. He was a handsome young black man with God-given muscles, a smoothly shaved head, and a close-cropped beard. A gold hoop dangled from his left earlobe. His name was Leyton Mills.

The sky had darkened with the threat of rain coming from the Gulf. The wind had been blowing hard for some time, filling the empty boat sheds with clouds of dust.

There were only two boats left on Pier B. One was an aged wooden Chris-Craft motoryacht, now mightily pitting its tired buoyancy against taut nylon dock lines. The other was Rodrigue's *Haulover Queen*, a twenty-five-foot fiberglass boat with a high pilothouse and an aluminum lifting boom, like a miniature shrimp boat. It was sitting in broad slings above the water—although not nearly as far above as normal—and it swayed unnervingly in the wind.

Leyton paced between a spot where he could keep an eye on the hanging boat and one where he would see Rodrigue pull up at the boat ramp.

When did this quit being fun? he was asking himself. The wind dipped between the piers and ruffled the water in the slips. It was frightening.

But he hadn't expected this to be like Dartmouth, had he? Not when you're dealing with a rogue elephant like this Rodrigue.

Leyton had collected a lot of information about Rodrigue before he had ever spoken with him. Unfortunately, much of what he had learned couldn't be proved and seemed too fantastical to be true. Knowing the man personally didn't help, either. He was surprisingly civil and yet there was a darkness behind his wide white grin.

They said he had killed a man right there in the yacht basin some years back. Self-defense, supposedly. And then not too long ago, he had been involved in some cocaine-smuggling ring somehow, but he had evidently turned against the ring and avoided prosecution. Some kind of shady deal with the FBI, people said. But Leyton was hardly in a position to check up on the FBI.

You certainly couldn't count on what people said. People said he was a womanizer, when in fact he avoided women. It seemed more caution than misogyny, though. Layton could tell that Rodrigue liked them well enough—always gave a hardbody a thorough going-over with that funny cockeyed stare—but he always went home alone at night.

And then there was the matter of Central America. People said Rodrigue dropped everything in the winter and went down there to hang out in the jungle. Now here it was October and he showed no signs of getting restless. Instead, he was buckling down to business up in Clear Lake, apparently intent on becoming the Earl Scheib of barnacle removal.

One thing people said about him was true, however: He certainly drank a lot.

Speak of the devil and there he was, backing the trailer down the flooded ramp. Rodrigue got out of the Blazer and sauntered over to the trailer tongue, his Hawaiian shirt billowing in the wind. Leyton spun and raced for the *Haulover Queen*. He leapt aboard and lowered the boat enough for the outboards' lower units to be submerged.

When both Evinrudes were blubbering steadily, the oily exhaust ripped away by the wind, Leyton lowered the slings all the way, settling the *Queen* into the lively water. He cast off the one dock line and steered the boat out of the slip. A gust heeled the boat slightly and made Leyton's skin crawl. The wind in the high metal roofs on each side sang just below a howl, and ahead, the channel was a mass of churning whitecaps. This was no place for a small boat, Boston Whaler or no Boston Whaler.

Leyton rounded the fuel dock, feeling suddenly the full force of the wind blowing across the vacant parking lot and down the twin ramps. He overcorrected the helm, making the boat seesaw toward the submerged bed of rubber rollers on the trailer. Rodrigue motioned for him to fall back again. He looked almost bored, leaning there on the side of the Blazer.

This time, Leyton looked back to assure himself the Evinrudes were pointing straight . . . they were straight enough. He gunned both throttles simultaneously and the *Queen* leapt forward—three hundred horses were more than enough power for this little workboat. He hit the trailer more or less head-on, and before the boat could lose momentum, Rodrigue had reached out with the cable and snap, and was winching the bow snugly against the trailer post.

Leyton stood aft, hanging on to the stubby mast, as Rodrigue pulled the boat and trailer across the lot, finally coming to a stop at the yacht basin's exit.

"I t'ought you were gonna mek me ride in de baat all the way to Clear Lake, maan," Leyton joked as he bounded down to help Rodrigue secure the boat on the trailer.

"Rum'd go further," said Rodrigue, pretending to consider it.

They slung a nylon strap over the gunwales and Leyton pulled it tight while Rodrigue fastened it to the trailer with an expert flurry of motion.

They jumped into the Blazer; Rodrigue threw it into gear—and it died. Now it wouldn't start.

"Oh *no*, maan!" entoned Leyton.

"Hah! Fucking fuel filter," said Rodrigue. "I got bad gas at one of those little tourist traps down on the west end."

"You have a new filter? Yes? Tell me yes, maan."

"Yes. Unfortunately, that's it." He looked at Leyton and shrugged helplessly. "I just put it on last week."

"What are we going to do?" Leyton felt panic grabbing at his throat.

"Aw, relax. Just take a minute to flush the gunk out. Ever use a coonass credit card?"

"What's a coonass credit card?" asked Leyton suspiciously.

He knew it wasn't any kind of a racial slur—*coonass* meant Cajun, and Rodrigue *was* one.

Rodrigue grinned slyly and opened his door. He motioned for Leyton to follow him outside.

Leyton had to hold the door tightly to keep it from being ripped away from him by the wind. An aluminum beer can pinged past them like a frightened rabbit. Rodrigue was already at the tailgate, pulling out a four-foot length of garden hose and a greasy one-pound coffee can.

"Coonass credit card," he said, handing the hose and can to Leyton.

The Blazer's hood wobbled noisily in the wind as Rodrigue groped around below. Leyton bent to the unfamiliar task of siphoning gasoline from the tank. When the first hearty suck produced nothing, he tried again—and suddenly got a burning mouthful. He gagged and spat, but he remembered to direct the flow from the hose into the coffee can.

Rodrigue came with the filter, laughing. "Run over there and rinse your mouth out with one of the dock hoses. Go on; I've got the can."

The nausea left, but the bitter gasoline taste wouldn't go away. Back at the Blazer, Rodrigue was swishing the filter in the amber fuel. It started raining, just a light drizzle, but it felt like sand in Leyton's face. Rodrigue straightened, smiling confidently. He carried the can to a nearby fence and carefully poured its contents on the weeds growing at the bottom. Then he returned and disappeared under the wildly rattling hood.

The Blazer coughed and Rodrigue pumped the accelerator. Finally, the engine started.

"Whew!" said Rodrigue—and Leyton realized just how dangerous their situation had been.

In a plastic tumbler, Rodrigue mixed himself a rum and soda, squeezing in a wedge of lime from a bag in the cooler. He offered the bottle to Leyton.

Leyton declined. He needed to keep his wits about him.

8

At the Hilton, a massive hurricane party was in full swing. Conversations and the constant whir of blenders merged into a merry din that overpowered the urgent whispering of the wind. The crowd spilled out of the second-level restaurant and lined the rail of the mezzanine overlooking the lobby. In the cocktail lounge, below the restaurant and off the lobby, another crowd had formed.

The lounge was meant to be an inviting place for conventioneers and lonely travelers. It was completely open to the adjacent hall, and the bar was a low horseshoe affair that didn't restrict a passerby's view of the happy people gathered around small tables, nor of the pleasant view of the lake.

Now, with standing room only, bodies blocked the view—and it was the view Andres Weizman wanted more than he wanted a drink in cheerful company. The fury of nature pleased him, as long as it didn't get in the way of his work.

What damage control could be done had been done. The data were still being recorded. Security hadn't been compromised that much. He might put off housekeeping service for a while, but the chambermaids were all half-illiterate Mexicans. What would one of them think about a radio set? Who would she tell about it?

Security around the Johnson Space Center was halfhearted

at best. From where Weizman stood in the hall, he could count a half a dozen NASA identification badges dangling carelessly from partygoers. He could jerk one off, have it duplicated, and have it on the floor under a table in time for the morning cleanup crew. In normal times, of course, not now.

There was no reason to think anyone was on to him. The people he had were all well placed, beyond suspicion. His key man, Pritchett, had just now shown some sign of stress, but that was probably tension because of the approaching storm.

If there was a vulnerable spot in the network, it was Eunice Cara, simply because of her high visibility at the Space Center. But she was a legitimate anthropologist on a legitimate mission. Anthropologists are often suspect in Third World countries, usually because they are at odds with government-fostered conditions. In an enlightened nation like the United States, however—and especially in a community of scientists and engineers—there shouldn't be any innate distrust of anthropology. Disdain, perhaps, for being inexact and even a little shamanistic in comparison to aerospace technology, but not suspicion.

Besides, no one could establish a link between him and Cara. They communicated mostly via a message drop at Baybrook Mall. He would write in code on a regular piece of notepaper, crumple it, and throw it into one of the potted palms. She would come along later, pick it up, and pretend to throw it in a trash bin. Their infrequent telephone calls were brief and cryptic, usually just establishing a new code key.

There was nothing to worry about, Weizman told himself.

He worked his way as near to the bar as he could get. The mingled smells of colognes and perfumes, fresh sweat, damp wool, and the vinyl of cheap new raincoats was pleasantly exciting. He stood on tiptoes and craned his neck to search for a likely victim. Through the milling bodies, he noticed a man in a seersucker business suit seated at a small table right beside the window.

None of the windows above the marina level were boarded. It would've taken two men on a scaffold a week to do it—and besides, they were supposed to be hurricane-proof.

Weizman was determined to have a seat by the window,

where the view was certain to be spectacular as long as the light held. He edged deeper into the crush of bodies and found a tall man standing at the bar. He pulled at the man's arm and the man twisted around with a boozy grin.

"See that man sitting over by the windows?" asked Weizman.

The tall man had to rise on tiptoes himself. "I see several. Which one?" He smiled, as though he saw a joke coming.

"The striped suit. Seersucker, I believe." His demeanor remained serious.

The man took another look. "Yeah, in the seersucker suit. What about him?"

"He has a message to call the sheriff's office, pronto."

The clumsy Texanism was even more so in Weizman's accent.

"Would you ask the bar girl to inform him?" His thin lips formed a cruel smile. "You are nearer, after all."

The man made an okay sign with his fingers and turned to wave at the barmaid. Weizman squeezed on through the crowd.

The man in the seersucker suit was talking animatedly with another man. Weizman eased behind him, pressing himself against the window and pretending to be fascinated by another conversation nearby. The barmaid took nearly twenty minutes to deliver the message. She stooped and spoke in his ear, nearly losing a tray of promised drinks. The man in seersucker asked her a question, but she was already moving on to deliver the drinks. The other man was curious. The man in seersucker shrugged and rose, squeezing into the crowd.

Weizman settled into his place as rightful heir.

"Hey, that chair is taken," barked the man across the table. He was quite a bit larger than Weizman, a rubbery-faced fifty or so, with oiled and neatly parted hair. A NASA badge hung from his shirt pocket.

"Don't be an ass," said Weizman, smiling. "You cannot reserve seats in a crowded place like this."

They were nearly yelling, but so was everybody else in the lounge, just to be heard.

The man glowered, his elastic jowls growing red. "Listen,

fella. He's just gone for a moment. And when he comes back, he gets his chair back. You got it?"

Weizman leaned forward, grabbed the man's left middle finger and pried it backward. The man shrieked noiselessly and then looked down with bulging eyes at his hand. Backs and buttocks and elbows hid them from view like a wall of dirty laundry.

"You cannot reserve seats in a place like this," Weizman repeated patiently.

When Weizman released his finger, the man lunged to his feet and disappeared into the chattering revelers, not looking back.

It was perhaps foolish of him to risk calling attention to himself this way—and after he had chastised Pritchett for wearing yellow shoes! A military man by training, Weizman had come into intelligence work rather late in life. His temperament was better suited to action than stealth, which was why he was no longer with the Mossad. Mutual dissatisfaction, he liked to think.

A laughing young woman sat in the abandoned chair. Weizman was both pleased and irritated—the company of a laughing young woman was always to be treasured, but he had wanted time with his thoughts, to plan.

When the woman ignored him, continuing to talk and laugh with her companions standing around her, Weizman felt a flash of disappointment, and then anger. He was not, he supposed, an unattractive man, even at his age. Certainly many women had found his worldliness appealing. But what was she? A silly young girl. He had contingencies to think through.

He turned his gaze to the window, which was flecked with rain—or was it spray from the waves that now dashed skyward at the breakwater? There were no clouds to be seen, just the thickening haze, greenish charcoal through the tinted glass.

What was it Pritchett had said about changing the "data run"? Because of radio-wave propagation? Weizman was no technician, but he didn't see how changing propagation could command changes in the text of a radio signal—the carrier, yes, but not the text. Whatever it was, the prospect seemed to have deeply disturbed Pritchett. People like Pritchett were professional worriers, anyway. Not Weizman. Oh, he was careful, all right. But there was a time to stop calculating the odds and play the game.

He dismissed his misgivings with a wave of his hand, and he looked around for the barmaid. Here she came, holding a tray of empty glasses and bottles above the crowd with both hands. Soon she would be near enough, and he would be able to order.

And soon the hotel would be in chaos, very probably out of electricity. With his battery-powered equipment, he could continue to operate, very quietly, unnoticed, the least of anyone else's worries. Meanwhile, he would settle back, a drink at hand, while the tropical weather raged outside.

He looked across the lake at his boat yawing in the confused chop. It was a Cheoy Lee Offshore 41—forty feet, nine inches overall, ketch-rigged, beamy and comfortable, with the warmth of teak everywhere. He had convinced the Brazilians to buy it, and rightly so, as the perfect cover for the intercept station. The little wideband antenna looked like a TV antenna up on his mast, and nobody would think anything of a pleasure yacht anchoring in Clear Lake—less than a mile from Building 30.

In the back of Weizman's mind was the idea that maybe he would buy the boat himself—or, no, graciously accept it as a bonus for a job well done—and sail her down to South America. Not to Brazil, though. It was fine to do business with the Brazilians, but he didn't want to live there. Maybe it was because so many former Nazis had sought refuge there, or because of the centralist background typical of Latin America. In any case, Weizman sensed the country was drawn to fascism.

Maybe Barbados. It would be only a base. Weizman expected to do a lot of traveling in the coming years. Maybe even to the Far East, to China. If he successfully completed this mission, he might find quite a warm welcome for him there.

The Chinese and the Brazilians had been in a joint venture to launch satellites since 1989. China had extensive experience in launching the vehicles, while Brazil, chiefly through its bustling trade in arms, had developed international marketing tentacles. It also had some satellite-tracking capabilities and was developing two launch complexes. But it was that ability to operate as businessmen in the West that the Chinese valued most. They contracted with Brazil's Instituto de Pesquisas Espacias—who, in turn, contracted with him—to obtain the data from the gallium-arsenide thin-film experiment.

Once the Chinese had the correct time and temperature values, they could launch their own unmanned thin-film labs at Xichang, and then intercept the returning space labs with fixed-wing aircraft equipped to grab the parachute cords the same way they retrieved their spy satellites.

The Chinese were not bound by the natural constraints of capitalism, which encouraged hoarding to drive up profit. With their labor pool and nationalized resources, they could leapfrog over the United States and Japan in microcomputer technology. In Weizman's grandest vision, China would replace the Soviet Union as the military and industrial counterbalance to the United States. The old race to arm client states would be back on, and the trade in weapons—and in men who knew how to use them—would blossom once again. In any case, China would certainly have entered the commercial technology race.

Brazil, meanwhile, would have enhanced its reputation for providing hardware, domestic or otherwise, for the emerging Third World space effort.

And he, Andres Weizman, would have at least earned himself a place at the table in the new tough, energetic Brazilian economy.

Suddenly, he noticed something bobbing alongside his boat. He pressed his face to the window, cupping his hands around his eyes to shut out the inside light. It was a small rubber dinghy. Nobody in sight—but the cabin was open! Someone was aboard!

For an instant, Weizman thought it must be the FBI. He sat back quickly, forcing himself to examine a table tent advertising the lounge's tropical drinks, while his mind dizzily ran through the possibilities. One kept popping up out of sequence: Only a computer wizard would be stupid enough to take a little rubber boat out in a hurricane.

The crypto-key! Pritchett must've left the crypto-key on the boat! How stupid to go groveling for it now. Certainly he wasn't risking his life for some remote contingency; after all, they didn't really need the crypto-key to record the data.

Pritchett had programmed Weizman's computer to descramble the data before they were recorded. The only conceivable use for the crypto-key now was in the event his computer went on the blink and they needed Pritchett's as a backup.

No, it had to be something else. Probably Pritchett was afraid the boat would sink, and some salvager would come along and find the crypto-key and turn it back in to MurTech or NASA. They, in turn, would want to know what it was doing aboard an Israeli national's yacht.

Weizman looked out at his wildly yawing yacht, at the gaping doorway to the cabin, and he had a chilling thought—something a lot worse than a crypto-key aboard an Israeli's sunken boat.

What if the salvager found a drowned NASA computer wizard?

Abruptly, Weizman abandoned his ringside seat and pushed his way through the crowd, accidentally jostling the barmaid with the tray of empties. The tray teetered, and for a long instant, all the faces in the immediate vicinity were trained on the desperate balancing act. Some looked horrified, some amused, and many others were expressionless.

The barmaid lost in the end, and glasses shattered on tabletops and tepid beer sprayed the crowd. But Weizman was already out in the hall, heading for the elevators.

In his room, the DAT recorder was grinding away, but the level meter on the receiver was still—no data coming over. Weizman checked his watch; the experiment should still be going on. He switched off the recorder, fighting panic. What had happened? Maybe they had found the transmitter.

If they found any of the intercept equipment, it could quickly lead to him—it was all of Israeli manufacture. But what could they prove? In this country, the authorities needed more than circumstantial evidence.

He was losing his grip. In all probability, the coming hurricane had caused them to shut down the experiment, maybe to evacuate the MurTech personnel. At any rate, this was no time to engage in wild speculation. He must deal with what was known.

Now his military training engaged in his thinking. He would assume the worst had happened and take steps to allay the situation. What was the worst thing? The boat had sunk and Pritchett had drowned aboard her. The first thing to do would be to remove the body *before* raising the boat—quickly and quietly.

He would have to hire someone to do it. He had neither the proper equipment nor expertise himself. It shouldn't be that difficult to find a diver, though. Deep-sea diving was a popular sport in Texas. The trick was to pick someone who would keep his mouth shut. Of course, he did have some expertise in shutting mouths.

Attacking his problem in a logical fashion gave Weizman back his confidence. He walked to the telephone and punched in a number.

"Hi," said a sultry female voice. "This is Neesay. You can reach me at three-three-three, three-six, zero-zero." The number of the Nassau Bay Hilton.

Weizman's thin lips formed a smile. Hundreds of hotels up in Houston and she had come to this one right on the bloody water. He broke the connection with his finger, the handset still cradled on his shoulder. It was to be expected, he supposed. People with the moxie to be involved in espionage would be reluctant to stray far from the action. He rang down to the desk and asked for Eunice Cara's room.

"Yes?" she answered pleasantly, almost expectantly.

"Have you been on the Rio Orituco lately?" he asked in a low drawl.

He always disguised his voice during their telephone conversations, just in case. So that she would be sure to recognize him, he prefaced by mentioning a river beginning with the same letter as did the current month. There were rivers enough in her native Venezuela to make it sound like a private joke between old friends.

"Not lately. What have you been up to?" This time her voice was cool. She didn't like him very much.

"I have lost a book. I wonder if you might have seen it?"

"What is the book about?"

"Salvage diving."

She laughed unexpectedly. "And what is this book's name?"

"*Pegasus*." He spelled it.

"I might not be able to get it to you until after the storm."

"Perhaps you could suggest the proper library designation."

"Designation?" She said it again— "Designation?"—and her voice was incredulous.

"Yes. I'm familiar with the Dewey decimal system, of course, but the university I believe uses different designations of mostly letters?"

"Ah, yes, of course. One moment."

It was a horrendous lapse of security to give the code and the key in the same telephone call, but it was better than taking a chance on being seen together. He needed to get her working on it right away, while the telephones were still functioning. And there wasn't time to scout for a new drop here in the hotel.

Neesay came back to the telephone. "Depending upon which university library you go to, it might be under one of several. Do you have a pencil?"

"Yes, yes, go ahead," he said irritably. Did he have a pencil!

She spoke and he wrote: RIOTE DHLRE TISUO GH.

He hung up and took out another sheet of hotel stationery, on which he wrote out the key and, under each letter, its numerical ranking in the alphabet:

$$P \quad E \quad G \quad A \quad S \quad U \quad S$$
$$4 \quad 2 \quad 3 \quad 1 \quad 5 \quad 7 \quad 6$$

It was a primitive columnar transposition, the like of which a NSA cryptoanalyst could solve on his coffee break, like a crossword puzzle, even without the key. Hopefully, no one was listening.

Or if there was someone, he was a bloody dunce.

Neesay's message had seventeen characters, and the key had seven. Seven went into seventeen twice, with three left over. Thus there would be three characters in the first three columns, two in the rest. Starting under the 1 (two characters), then moving to the 2 (three characters), he filled in the first group of the message:

```
P E G A S U S
4 2 3 1 5 7 6
    O   R
    T   I
    E
```

He should try to be more pleasant to her, he thought. She was, after all, invaluable. Two years of interviewing aerospace workers about their hopes and frustrations had made her a peerless headhunter for spies. How she could have found a deep-sea diver this quickly was a mystery to him, however.

He finished decrypting the message:

```
P E G A S U S
4 2 3 1 5 7 6
R O D R I G U
E T H I S H O
T E L
```

9

In a small windowless room on the first floor of the Hilton, two FBI agents sat at a desk, wearing earphones. On the desk, a small black box winked a red digital readout: 8888888.

"Jesus, why didn't he just take out a billboard?" said the other man, whose name was Phil Seidenhaur. He was young, trim, and well groomed.

"He's desperate," said Special Agent Roy Wilson. "Something's going down."

Wilson was a burly blond, middle-aged, newly overweight, and his white dress shirt strained around his middle like the skin of a boiled sausage. His suit coat lay as it had been tossed on a roll-away bed, next to a small suitcase.

The office belonged to the hotel's accounting staff. The manager had moved them in with the salespeople and turned the room over to the agents. The single roll-away bed had been brought in (the agents anticipated sleeping in shifts) and there was a rest room just out in the hall.

The important thing was that the room adjoined a storeroom bristling with switching circuitry on one wall. That had greatly facilitated the bugging of Eunice Cara's phone on such short notice.

The bureau had placed a court-ordered tap on her home phone two weeks ago, when agents felt they could no longer ignore her activities. During the months previous, no fewer than a dozen NASA employees had independently come to the

FBI with their suspicions. Most had been apologetic, saying they were "sure it was nothing," and most had not confided in anyone else at the Space Center. Some were afraid they might seem paranoid. After all, it was probably her job as an anthropologist to probe for feelings of resentment about NASA or the government or society in general. Others had a better reason. One of Cara's activities had been to lure her subjects into romantic entanglements—very brief ones. The bureau firmly believed that where there was that much smoke, something was cooking.

The readout of the little black box wouldn't quit flashing 8888888.

"It keeps coming right back," said Seidenhaur disgustedly. His clothing, including the coat of his expensive blue suit, was in a hanging bag on the door.

"Whoever he is, he called her from another hotel phone," Wilson said tiredly. He reached into an open briefcase and drew out a Radio Shack laptop. "Let's see if we're still on the same page, at least."

He handed the telephone book–size computer to Seidenhaur, and he rose and poured himself another cup of coffee from the stainless carafe on the hot plate. It was too hot to drink, so he blew into it.

Seidenhaur entered the probable key, Pegasus, and then he typed in the text. If the key was wrong, or if they had switched to another method of encoding, it could be hours before the computer jocks in D.C. could figure it out. But the plain-language text soon appeared on the small liquid-crystal screen.

"Yeah, they're still using the same one," he said. He wrote the message on a yellow legal pad.

Wilson peered over his shoulder and poured his coffee down Seidenhaur's back.

"*Yow!*" yelled Seidenhaur, twisting out of the chair and to his feet. He threw his shoulders back to loosen the steaming cloth.

"Sorry," said Wilson distractedly. He reached for one of their phones and rang the front desk. He frowned at it as it rang and rang.

On the pad, Seidenhaur had written:

"Front desk, how may I be of service?" sang a feminine voice.

"Get me Pfluger," Wilson barked into the phone.

"I'm sorry, Mr. Pfluger is not in at the moment. Can someone else help you?"

"This is Wilson, FBI. Who am I speaking with?"

"This is Alice Garcia, Mr. Wilson. Is everything all right? Mr. Pfluger left strict instructions to give you and Mr. Seidenhaur every consideration."

"You have a John Rodrigue registered here?"

"He has an office at the marina," came the instant reply.

"He does? What kind of office? I mean what does he do?"

"I—I'm not sure." The woman was starting to balk. "Something to do with boats."

"First thing I want you to understand, honey, is that this doesn't go past you, you understand? Alice, is it?"

"Of course, sir." She sounded insulted.

"Okay, Alice. I want you to discreetly check and see if Rodrigue is registered as a guest. Go ahead; I'll hold on."

Seidenhaur had taken off his shirt and was sadly examining the coffee stain on the back. He unfolded another shirt from the hanging bag and put it on.

"I'm just going to slip out and run some water on this," he whispered, holding the stained shirt under Wilson's nose. Wilson looked up and impatiently waved him away.

He sat holding the phone and glowering.

"Mr. Wilson?" said Alice tentatively. "Mr. Rodrigue *is* registered, but he hasn't checked in yet."

"Fine. But there is a room reserved for him?"

"Yes, sir."

"The number?"

She told him and he wrote it down.

"Thank you, Alice. Would you locate your phone man for me and send him back here?"

"Yes, sir."

"And Alice? Do *not* say anything to Rodrigue. I'm sure Mr. Pfluger has explained that our national security is at stake here."

Seidenhaur came back in and eased the door shut.

"What about this Rodrigue character?" he asked. "You know him?" He hung his damp shirt over a chair back.

Wilson nodded. "Soon as the phone man gets here, we'll put a tap on his phone."

"Are you kidding? We'll never get a court order in the middle of a hurricane. You know that."

"Too bad about that court order," said Wilson, leveling his eyes meaningfully at his partner. Meaning, Who the hell's in charge here?

"What're the chances of turning him?" asked Seidenhaur. "Maybe we can get to him before our boy does."

"Son of a bitch is trouble. Were you on board during the Ferguson thing?"

"Un-uh. But I heard."

Mike Ferguson had been a popular Houston journalist killed in the course of a politically sensitive investigation. The bureau had kicked sand over it, but it had all come out eventually—and rather brutally for the careers involved.

"Rodrigue's the one we had in Maxwell," said Wilson. "Nearly killed a psychiatrist, a contractor. Damned good man, too, but he would never work with us again after that."

Wilson's cheek twitched as he remembered.

"Rodrigue's the one who sicced the newspapers on us. I'd be in Denver by now if it wasn't for him."

"So? You stay out of it. I'll work him."

Wilson glared. "No way. The son of a bitch is dirty. He skated out of the Ferguson thing, and he may not be involved in this—yet. But take my word for this: For every one thing he's innocent of, he's guilty of ten we don't know about."

He ripped the page from the yellow pad and crumpled it.

"When the girl leads us to her controller, Rodrigue falls with them."

10

Down on Galveston Island, rain hit Rodrigue's windshield like pebbles. They could see huge frothy waves leaping skyward at the seawall. Rodrigue wanted to go down for a closer look, but he knew better. The waves crashing down on Seawall Boulevard were rushing back to sea with enough power to drag truck, boat, and trailer along with them. Sensibly, he turned on Strand for the inshore route to the causeway.

Leyton was smacking his mouth distastefully. Rodrigue looked over at him with his one-eyed Long John Silver squint.

"Open yer hatch, matey" was his gravelly advice. "Let the petrol evaporate."

"Seriously?" Leyton was understandably skeptical.

"Aye, sez I. Gasoline don't mix with water—ye wouldn't hose down a fuel fire, would ye? What it mixes with is air, matey. That's why it's so volatile—it fumes."

Leyton stretched his mouth wide and rolled his eyes dolefully at his ridiculous predicament.

The redbrick buildings and creaking warehouses of the old waterfront district shielded them from the brunt of the wind until they came to an intersection. Then the wind bashed against the broadside of the truck and flexed its springs. Rodrigue looked in his side mirror and saw the boat rocking alarmingly.

The next intersection was worse: Debris from the beach

park was being funneled down the cross street. A chaise lounge slammed into the side of the truck with a startling bang, then flipped over the windshield and hung there, a leg firmly grappling the side mirror. Rodrigue cursed and slammed on his brakes. The wrecked chair ripped loose and flew off into the darkening sky.

Overhead, the traffic lights swayed and bobbed, dutifully cycling through the changes. Alternating streaks of yellow, red, and green glistened on the oily surface of the empty street. The buildings were fading, as if being scrubbed away by the metallic swirls of rain. And the wind howled in the emptiness like some triumphant beast.

Rodrigue liked it, and because he liked it, it scared him. He no longer trusted his instincts.

There had been so many false starts in his life already. Detours. But what forty-five-year-old man was what he had thought he would be back in high school?

What Rodrigue had wanted to be was a shrimper. He had not disguised his contempt for his father, uncles, and brothers for selling out to the oil-field jobs, which provided hospitalization insurance and retirement but stole their independence. But then in the summer between his junior and senior years, when he'd had girlfriends and wanted a car—and shrimping was terrible because of flooding that spring—he had sold out himself and crewed on a supply boat. After high school, he'd gotten his captain's license and ran crew boats until he became disgusted with himself. Then he'd joined the navy.

He had stayed ten years in the navy, taking a medical discharge after his river patrol boat ran over a Vietcong mine and he lost an eye. Then he had gone to work as a diver in the oil fields, did that for another ten years. But the old anger toward the oil industry resurfaced and he had to walk away from it.

And ever since, walking away had been his forte.

November had come, rainy and cold, and Rodrigue had been restless. He hadn't endured a northern Gulf winter in years.

"Look," he said, grasping her hand gently. "Why don't you come with me? Take a leave of absence."

Ann Eller gave him an exasperated look. "I can't take a leave of absence to go lie around on the beach. You have to have a *reason* for a leave of absence."

"Well, quit then. I have plenty of money."

"John!" Her pale brow was furrowed, and the frown lines bracketing her mouth showed her age. "That's not the point. Money is not the only reason we work."

"No?"

"You're trying to be funny and I'm serious. I don't understand you. What do you want out of life?"

"Warmth."

"Come on, John, be serious! Why can't you stay here?"

"Well, okay, you want to put it in economic terms. In the summer, there are things I can do here to make money that I cannot do in the winter—tow boats, recover lost objects, and so forth. But in the winter, there's a good flow of scuba divers through Belize City, and I can make money taking them out to the reef."

"But, John, these things are beneath you."

He stared at her for a long while, waiting for the sting of insult to subside before speaking.

"You flatter me," he said finally.

He came back by to see her as he passed through Houston on his way south. She was cold, but she cried silently, the two thin streaks glistening on her cheeks as she waved from her door.

His journey took a week, Rodrigue in the process of getting drunk or sobering up as he drove precariously though the vast milo fields of Tamaulipas (not far from where he and his father and the others had been cast upon that lonely beach so many years before) into the hills of Veracruz and the swamps of Tabasco, through the dense rain forests of Campeche and Quintana Roo, and finally arriving red-eyed and wasted in the steamy, exotic Caribbean city of Belize.

Standards of behavior were somewhat more relaxed in the teeming, isolated backwater founded by British pirates—it was truly a jungle down there—and Rodrigue tended to grow a keener edge when he was among his own kind.

He, too, was the descendant of a line of pirates, beginning with a Rodriguez who in the dim 1600s had fled the Spanish

Inquisition to the island of Tortuga, off the north coast of Haiti, and ending with Captain Dominique Rodrigue, who regained the family's legitimacy alongside Lafitte at the Battle of New Orleans. Except in John Rodrigue's case, the legitimacy sometimes wore thin.

Two weeks after he was back in Belize City, a rich kid with a gold Rolex on his wrist that cost more than Rodrigue's Blazer came swaggering along Haulover Creek with a sassy sorority type on his arm, looking for adventure, both of them—but in different ways.

They wanted to dive a wall. The kid was more experienced than his girlfriend, so Rodrigue buddied with her while the kid went off on his own.

No reputable divemaster would allow someone to dive a wall by himself. It was too easy to get too deep too quickly—get caught in a down current, or just simply have his head up his ass and lose track of his depth. It's a goof-up with a nasty acceleration factor. He goes deep and loses buoyancy, so he goes deeper. Then nitrogen narcosis—the poetically termed "rapture of the depths"—kicks in and he believes he can breathe seawater.

But if Rodrigue had wanted to be reputable, he would've stayed in Galveston.

Besides, he thought he sensed something in the looks the girl was giving him. She was a pretty thing, with honey brown hair and big brown eyes. She was tall and slim-hipped. Her high, pointy breasts destroyed the logos on her T-shirts.

She refused to wear dive skins, despite Rodrigue's warnings about the pain of coral scrapes. She dove instead in a T-shirt and string bikini bottom. Rodrigue was pretty sure he knew what that meant, and he lingered behind with her when they hit the water.

Sure enough, after her boyfriend disappeared over the edge of the reef, she tapped Rodrigue on the shoulder and spoke to him in sign language: formed a circle with the thumb and forefinger of her left hand, thrust the index finger of the right hand in and out of it.

Mais oui! thought Rodrigue, returning the okay sign.

She was a better diver than her boyfriend had given her credit for. She hovered gracefully, knees crooked, one arm outstretched and rotating with a minimum of motion. With her other hand, she dug into a pocket of her BC—buoyancy compensator, part flotation vest and part tank harness—and came out with a condom in a foil envelope. Smart girl. Never know what you might catch from the locals. Rodrigue anxiously popped the buttons on his Levi's cutoffs.

The girl peeled off the envelope and conscientiously stuffed it back into her BC pocket. Then she peeled off her bikini bottom, rising slightly with the effort and giving him a gynecologist's-eye view of her crotch.

Rodrigue was definitely a crotch man. He knew he ought to be as rigid as a tire tool, but he couldn't feel anything. He had to remove his scuba regulator to lower the field of view sufficiently through his old-fashioned oval mask. *Thank you, God!* he thought as he watched her carefully unroll the condom down his stubbornly vertical erection. Then he had to have air in a hurry.

She grabbed his BC and lowered herself onto him. Her warmth was almost startling. But it was an altogether unsatisfactory coitus. Hovering there a foot or two above the jagged coral, it was impossible to create the resistance to one another that makes for good sex. Plus, they had to regulate their breathing. If they both exhaled too much, they would sink into the coral. If they gulped air, as people tend to do when they're enjoying themselves, they would rise to the surface. After a few minutes of just being coupled, the girl looked at her watch and lifted herself. Coitus fucking interruptus.

Or was it reservatus?

She rolled up her condom again and stuffed it back into her pocket. Her wisp of a bathing suit slid on easily, and she hovered there watching as he struggled to button the Levi's over his unyielding hard-on.

She made the surface sign and he nodded.

The boyfriend surfaced before they got into the boat. Rodrigue took them to a little sand cay for a picnic. It was an idyllic place, rustling palms and warm sand. The boyfriend kept boasting about his adventure on the wall. The girl smiled patiently and turned knowing glances on Rodrigue. This was going to be an interesting week, he thought.

It was indeed—Ann was waiting for him at the dock.

She just had a couple of days, she said, but she had missed him. That night, they had the most rollicking time in bed ever, both driven by an almost-angry lust. The next day, he had to take her to Ambergris Cay to one of the tourist resorts. She had not been able to abide Belize City, which was to her a slum packed with overly familiar black men with long hair. But she seemed to enjoy the remainder of her visit, and granted him a grateful hug and a peck on the lips before she walked out onto the steaming tarmac at Belize International.

Rodrigue had not enjoyed himself at all. Ann had been a tonic for his atrophied sense of nobility. But now the feeling was gone. . . .

On Port-Industrial Road, the thoroughfare across the back side of Galveston, the landscape opened up and the Blazer was being pelted and whipped around frighteningly. Orange fishing floats, trash cans, thousands of beer cans, whole sheets of galvanized metal roofing, ghostlike scraps of clear plastic sheeting, gallon varnish cans, asphalt shingles—even branches now—and hundreds of things Rodrigue didn't recognize were all sweeping across the road in a single-minded evacuation of the island. There wasn't another car in sight.

"Hell, I wonder if we were supposed to turn out the lights," said Rodrigue.

"We're cutting it close, maan," said Leyton.

Once they turned onto the freeway, more or less with the wind, it was better going—until they reached the causeway: The crests of the steep waves were dashing against the rail, sending cascades of luminescent foam and dark water that glinted like ribbons of steel in the Blazer's headlamps. They could feel the span shudder with each blow. Ahead, a single set of taillights winked uncertainly.

"Good thing we brought a boat," said Rodrigue through gritted teeth. He shifted the Blazer into four-wheel drive and plunged into the boiling mass of foam.

Halfway to the mainland, a huge unseen wave hit and the causeway swayed and seemed to dip. Rodrigue cursed and downshifted, juggling—but not spilling—his drink. The Blazer plowed on. The orange overhead bridge lights winked on suddenly, illuminating a car that had been washed against the inside rail by the wave. The taillights were still burning and the car's head beams reflected a thousand silvery raindrops dancing on the blackness of the sky.

It was a sheriff's cruiser, and the deputy was standing beside it, shielding his face from the needles of rain.

Rodrigue stopped and honked the horn. Another wave shook them and twisted the boat and its trailer sideways behind them. The deputy hung on to Rodrigue's bumper, then pulled himself around to the passenger door.

Leyton climbed over the console into the backseat to make room. The deputy was almost swept into the car by the wind. Rodrigue had seen him around. He was a big former center for the Longhorns, whose days of glory were behind him. An island native, he was under somebody's political patronage.

He knew Rodrigue, too, of course—recognition showed on his broad, freckled face.

"Son of a bitch hasn't even *hit* yet!" he said with a mean grin. "How ya doin', Rod. I'd be dead if you hadn't come along."

Rodrigue laughed. "You may be dead yet."

The side mirror was ruined. Rodrigue twisted around and watched the boat and trailer straighten satisfactorily as he pulled slowly past the patrol car.

"Anyone left on the island?"

"No sir," said the deputy. "This motherfucker's too dangerous."

"How'd you come to be the last one off?"

"Well, I wasn't—thank God."

"I mean the last cop."

The deputy grinned sadly. "A bad motherfucker like this comes along only once every hundred years or so. It was kinda hard to leave."

Windshield wipers were useless against buckets of saltwater. Rodrigue steered by the overhead lights, holding as far to the right as he dared in order to keep from being washed into the left rail the way the deputy had. Below, the bay became shallower and the crashing waves diminished. But the awful shuddering of the causeway did not.

"Drink?" offered Rodrigue.

"Aw, I can't, man. I'm on duty. Besides, it's against the law to drink and drive in Texas."

"This is not driving. This is more like surfing."

The deputy shook his head, chuckling.

Soon the wipers were slapping at tiny sparkles of blue and orange and red, smearing them across the windshield. Gradually, the smears grew larger and brighter.

"Pass that drink back to your partner until you get through here," said the deputy.

Rodrigue obliged. He slowed down and gratefully eased through the roadblock of emergency vehicles on terra firma.

The deputy shook Rodrigue's hand. He started to get out, but then he reached back and stuck his hand into the backseat.

"Good luck, man," he told Leyton. "You're in dangerous company."

Rodrigue couldn't tell whether it was a joke or not.

Going more or less with the wind up the Gulf Freeway, the storm didn't seem nearly as threatening. The trailer still tugged stubbornly as the boat rocked behind them, but at least the road itself was steady.

Traffic thickened as they approached the NASA Road 1 interchange, and from there a wide ribbon of red lights flowed slowly northward. A somber line of headlights, weak against the glistening sheets of rain, fed the flow from the east. Rodrigue and Leyton had the eastbound lanes to themselves.

"God, I can't believe people are still on the road," said Rodrigue.

Leyton eyed him coldly. "I can't, either."

Rodrigue laughed. "Relax, we're home."

The Hilton loomed ahead, its stylized red *H*'s and cheery lighted windows holding back the purple-black sky. The constant drumming of rain on the Blazer's windows fell startlingly silent as Rodrigue pulled into the covered drive. The bell captain stepped to Leyton's window. His yellow poncho ballooned in the swirling gusts that found their way around the building.

"Do you have reservations, sir?" he asked Rodrigue.

"Yes indeed."

"I'm afraid there's no parking left. Some of the guests have parked on the shoulder and the median of NASA Road One. I'm afraid I'm going to have to ask you to move your, er, car as soon as you've unloaded."

"Aye-aye," said Rodrigue playfully, stepping out of the Blazer. He civilly left his nearly depleted drink in the console, but as he pulled the ice chest from the backseat, he stashed the bottle of rum inside. He carried the chest to the front desk.

"Alice," Rodrigue said with roguish charm as a plump, pretty Hispanic woman stepped up to serve them. "If you've given my room away, I'm moving in with you. Me and Queequeg, here—right, Queequeg?"

"Right," said Leyton, distracted by the twinkle of feminine laughter coming from the party on the mezzanine.

The desk clerk was looking at Rodrigue with wide, frightened eyes. It was almost the same look some Vietnamese peasants had given him when he had regained consciousness and staggered onto the road after floating on a raft of river debris all night, half his face a bloody pulp, so many years ago.

"Something wrong?" he asked gently.

"Er, no. No, nothing." She turned to the computer screen. The storm had her spooked, Rodrigue decided.

It took six trips apiece for them to haul up what was haulable from the truck and boat—diving gear, two toolboxes, booze box, another big box of canned goods and condiments, a duffel of clothes each, and Rodrigue's old sea chest with his treasured black beret and the other shabby keepsakes of a squandered youth. Finally, Rodrigue left Leyton in the shower while he went down and moved the Blazer.

He drove back westward toward the higher ground of the Space Center—the traffic had thinned out dramatically—and parked on the grass in the lee of a tall bank building. It was quiet and almost dry there. From the glove compartment, he drew a large pistol wrapped in an oily red mechanic's rag, and he put it in his waistband, under his shirt. As an afterthought, he removed the tie-down strap from over the boat and disengaged the dog on the trailer winch. Let the poor son of a bitch have a fighting chance, he thought.

The hike back to the hotel was like wading in the surf; the gusts bullied him around and soaked him to the skin. When he finally made it to the hotel, he was panting with exertion. The air inside was chilly, giving him goose bumps. As soon as he hit the room, he piled his sopping clothes on the bathroom floor and had a hot shower.

"Wo-maan named Neesay called f'you," said Leyton when he emerged. "Soun' int'restin'."

Rodrigue took his pistol from the dresser and removed the wet rag. It was a government-issue .45 auto. He wiped it dry with the towel he was using.

"See this thing? I'm gonna shoot you with it if you mess with that girl. She's like a niece to me."

"Neesay, Neesay . . . dat Spanish for niece? Nah, nah—at's *sobrina*. But she am Spanish, eh?"

Rodrigue took long khakis and another Hawaiian shirt from his duffel and shook out the wrinkles.

"Venezuelan," he said. "Her daddy was the sort of mayor of a town we built right at the edge of the jungle way up the Orinoco where we were putting in a barge terminal some years back."

He smiled. "It was some place—jaguars getting into the garbage at night, monkeys screaming, these huge snakes slithering in the trees. Neesay is short for Eunice—*aay oo NEE say*, it's pronounced in Spanish. She uses an Anglicized spelling so people don't call her *nice*."

He smiled a threatening shark smile. "But she is. So wachit."

After he dressed, he dissembled the .45 and carefully oiled it, well aware of the effect it would have on Leyton. He wasn't doing it for effect, though.

Rodrigue had been taught that if you took care of your tools, they would take care of you.

11

The phone rang in Neesay's sixth-floor room. She came out of the bathroom, wearing only sheer bikini panties, to answer it.

"Good evening," a young male voice said hurriedly. "This is the front desk. We're calling everyone to warn them to please stay away from the windows. Thank you." He hung up without waiting for a reply.

Neesay went to the window, opened the drapes, and quickly stepped back so no one could see her from the parking lot below—as if anyone who happened to be out in this weather would take the time to window-peep. The view from her window looked to the west, upon dim lights sprinkled in the blackness that had enveloped Nassau Bay and Clear Lake City. Mostly, she saw her own reflection.

She was a tall woman with good childbearing hips, her mother had always said. She was twenty-eight now and childbearing still didn't interest her.

The good childbearing hips were proportionally supported by long legs with trim thighs. Her high breasts angled apart enticingly, and the brown nipples were erect in the air conditioning. Eunice Cara was well aware of just how sexually appealing she was. Sometimes it aided her in her work. More often, though, it was a hindrance.

Her image seemed to shimmer as the double panes flexed

ever so slightly. The wind produced a low hum. Funny how she was drawn to dangerous things.

Like Johnny Rodrigue.

She had been in Clear Lake a year when she learned that Rodrigue was also living in the area. He had been involved in cocaine smuggling but somehow emerged a big hero—same old Johnny. She had gone to the phone to call the Galveston information operator while he was still on the television screen, being badgered by newspeople.

She had found him older and heavier, but he still had that same deadly smile and that way of making love with his eyes, though only one of them was real. She had been a little unnerved to find that the old crush was still there.

Of course, all the teenage girls in Nueva Yavita had been in love with the divers—they, even more than the jaguar hunters they had replaced, were the local heroes. Even then Neesay hated North Americans, but Johnny was not at all like a North American. His Spanish was flawless and he had a dark, sort of Mediterranean visage. He had been especially fascinating because of his dangerous dealings with her father.

Her father was a merchant from Puerto Ordaz who had been invited by the mining company to set up a store, restaurant, and movie theater—the "Shopping Center," the North Americans called it—in the company-built town. He was the consummate entrepreneur, and in Venezuela, being an entrepreneur often meant dealing outside the law.

Being an outpost of civilization in a pristine wilderness, Nueva Yavita was the perfect base for hunting expeditions. Even the clientele was assured—the rich *yanqui* mining bosses who came to oversee the construction of the terminal.

There had been two problems, however. One was that the high-powered rifles with telescopic sights the *yanquis* preferred were not allowed in the country. (The locals used old single-shot shotguns.) And the other was that U.S. law did not allow the *yanquis* to bring home the skins of the jaguars they killed. Spotted cats were in danger worldwide, although they were certainly plentiful enough around Nueva Yavita.

Johnny had solved both problems. Nobody knew how—or at least her father had never known exactly how—but by some means he had smuggled the rifles straight into Nueva Yavita, and smuggled the skins to New Orleans.

Neesay had flirted shamelessly with the roguish diver and he had always playfully fended her off. But she wasn't a skinny child any longer. When she discovered him here in Texas, she tried to bring the old flirtation back to a boil, just to see whether he could still be so cavalier. But then he had been deeply involved with some woman. And lately he was working so much. It was not the kind of thing she needed to be doing, anyway.

She wondered what kind of job Weizman had for Rodrigue. The Israeli kept his affairs so rigidly compartmentalized that nobody in the network knew exactly what another was doing unless it was necessary for the performance of his own job. Most of them didn't even know the others. She alone knew who they might be, since she had supplied dossiers on the raw talent.

"Talent" meant first that they were in a useful position. Weizman was interested in land-line communications, microwave communications, and, of course, Mission Control. What the Instituto de Pesquisas Espacias was interested in as an end product, she could only guess. Probably the gallium-arsenide thin-film experiment. If successful, the resulting data could give a developing nation like Brazil a tremendous boost into the so-called Information Age.

The second criterion for recruitment into Weizman's network was vulnerability to compromise. Some of it was already there: disenchantment, greed, and—surprisingly enough for such a well-educated community—debt. Yet in some she had to create vulnerability. That was where her sexual appeal came in.

She wondered what her father would think if he knew he had sent her to Rio de Janeiro to become an educated whore? And would it have been any different, really, if she had come to the States, the way he had wanted?

It had to be one or the other—serious degree programs in anthropology were practically nonexistent in Venezuela, as they were in most of Latin America. She had chosen the Federal University of Brazil because she had seen what happened to Venezuelans who went to the United States for their educations. They became just as greedy and ruthless as any North American she had ever known. Worse, they became disdainful of their own country and its heritage.

Looking back, now, she could see how her decision to take what she considered the high road had led to other dangerous, even despicable choices. When the INPE invited her to study aerospace workers in the United States but then added the proviso that she must also work for Weizman with no questions asked—Weizman about whom it was whispered that he was an arms merchant and a spy—she could have refused, as probably most anthropologists would have done. Certainly those trained in North America would have refused.

But North American anthropologists hadn't grown up with the kind of poverty and injustice Neesay had witnessed. She herself had been well nourished because of her father's skill in manipulating the system created by North American hegemony. But how well she remembered the anguish of her best friend, Elena, whose father was killed in the strikes, and who afterward grew dirtier and more gaunt and distant until she was like a small animal pinned beneath the wheels of a big oil truck, still alive, still alert in that passive way of the dying, but beyond help.

There was greed in Brazil now, too, but it was a righteous greed, a Third World greed awakened after centuries of withering off the path of commerce between Europe and North America, the *favored* America. So when she was introduced to Weizman shortly after accepting the INPE grant, Neesay didn't demur.

Even when he made the most outrageous demands on her, she didn't demur. Each time he came with a new demand—to make him privy to the most intimate of her interviews with her subjects, to pump them for information, and finally to seduce them—she could simply have packed her bags and flown home to Venezuela. Yet she did not.

She did what she did to avenge the millions of emotionally crushed and helpless little girls like Elena. And there was satisfaction in it—some of the North Americans were as personally odious as their culture. But there was also a perverse fascination to looking for soft spots in her subjects.

It was the dark, forbidden side of anthropology—finding out what makes a person do evil.

For Johnny, it would be money. No, that wasn't quite right. Johnny *took* money, but he committed illicit acts for some other reason, which he might not have understood himself.

But what act was he now to commit for Weizman? What could Weizman need recovered from the sea? Neesay worried for a moment that maybe she was leading her childhood idol into trouble that even he could not avoid. But that was ridiculous. Weizman was a snake, but Johnny was like the big black eagle of her homeland. She should be worried for Weizman.

Neesay stepped to the window and drew the drapes. She switched on the television for company while she finished making herself up in the bathroom.

Something disturbing eased into her consciousness. More serious talk, of course, but with a new lilt of urgency. It was something about *Columbia*.

Neesay ran back into the room just as the picture flashed to a reporter live in the pressroom at the Mission Control Center:

". . . inertial measurement units, or IMUs in NASA parlance, are basically gyros that tell the on-board computers how the space shuttle is positioned. Because of the precise alignment necessary for the wake shield, the IMUs were interfaced with the program used to run the gallium-arsenide thin-film payload, and somehow, it is feared, a glitch in that program bled through the IMUs back into the shuttle's computers. It would have occurred, Ron and Jan, when the experiment was being controlled from the ground, from a room here in Building Thirty adjacent to the Mission Control Center."

The reporter paused to look back and establish his surroundings.

"The IMUs also interface with the computers' guidance, navigation, and control function, and that has become impaired, as well. That's all we have at this point. Ron. Jan."

Anchorman Ron Stone's grim face flashed on the screen.

"But if the problem is *not* fixed, then the prognosis is what, exactly?"

The reporter smiled. "Well, Ron, there is a backup system aboard the shuttle that will enable them to recalibrate the IMUs by noting the position of the stars—basically the same way Columbus found America—should the efforts to reprogram the computers fail. But however they do it, they must assume the correct attitude upon entry."

Neesay shivered as she heard him say, "Otherwise, the shuttle would simply burn up."

12

Building 30 at Johnson Space Center was insulated against both the ravaging heat of Texas summers and the penetration of stray radio waves. What news there was of the storm came from network television reports piped in to the handful of reporters riding it out in the Space Center. Earlier, there had been a stream of curious MCC workers into the pressroom. Now it had slowed to a trickle.

Hurricane Jeanette scarcely scratched Joe Bain's consciousness as he puzzled over stacks of figures on his computer screen. He didn't even notice the presence of the branch chief until the man slapped both hands down on the desk. Bain looked up, dazed from the sudden scrambling of his concentration.

The branch chief had his fingers spread apart, and he was supporting himself with them as if he was about to do a push-up. Bain studied the fingers, absently calculating the percentage of stress allotted to each and marveling anew at the miracle of creation.

"This is getting embarrassing," said the branch chief.

"It's getting dangerous," said Bain.

He was a small blond man, balding, almost elfin, and he had long ago reached a plateau in his career. He was deeply religious—which in itself was annoying enough, he knew. Coworkers had to watch what they said around him or suffer his "for they know not" look. The killer, however, was that

Bain did not believe in the ultimate supremacy of science. It probably made him less than aggressive in tackling the stickier problems. Like now.

"Look," he said, standing in a vain effort to be on a par with the branch chief. "All I'm saying is that we can't count on finding it in time."

The branch chief rolled his eyes.

"We *can't*," insisted Bain. "We have switched out half the circuit boards in all three NOMs and we're still uploading the same garbage." He offered the unintelligible mishmash on the screen as evidence.

A NOM—network output multiplexer—was an apparatus that wove different strands of telemetry into one radio signal to be beamed up to the orbiter. Apparently, there was something on the order of a computer virus in all three NOMs.

Normally, such a virus being uploaded to the orbiter would've been isolated in the payload computer and at most one of the other GPCs. But since the payload program was tied into the IMUs, which of course interfaced with all the on-board general-purpose computers, the virus had bled back into the GN&C programs in all five GPCs simultaneously, like a bridge of misinformation.

"Probably it's one species of chip, possibly UARTs, and we will eventually find which one," said Bain. UARTs were universal asynchronous receiver-transmitter chips, and they were in the NOMs by the double handful.

"But whatever it is, what if every one that we've got like it is flawed?" Bain demanded. "We're going to do everything we can, but all I'm saying is we better be gearing up to switch MCC to Goddard."

The branch chief shook his head. "We had to cue the new GN&C program from the moment the GPCs took the hit, so Goddard doesn't have the right software."

Bain nodded glumly. It was true—the GN&C program was nothing more than a continuum of flight data from T minus zero. Goddard had Mission Control capabilities, but it had not been monitoring this flight. Only JSC had recorded the flight data, so only JSC could write a new program.

"With the NOMs all screwed up, we can't link it to Goddard any more than we can to the orbiter," the branch chief was muttering. "Phones are down. We're looking at flying the program up to Andrews, but Jesus Christ, there's a fucking hurricane out there!"

Bain folded his arms and stared. Gotcha.

The branch chief sat on the desk and assumed a tone of confidentiality. "Besides, think of what else's at stake here, Joe. If we have to pass the baton to Goddard, we could damn well lose JSC."

"What are you trying to do, scare me?" said Bain icily. "What good do you think that's going to do? We've got every mainframe on the place tied up running tests chip by chip. We'll find the problem, but I can't tell you when. You can threaten to move me to Guam, but we still have to test the chips systematically. I can't *divine* which one it is."

"No, of course not." The branch chief smiled weakly. "Pressure. Name of the game around here these days."

Bain stared at him. The branch chief didn't know what pressure was. Bain would have loved to move—to someplace civilized like Goddard, preferably, but Guam didn't look that bad.

Joe Bain had had an affair. It was not something he had contemplated—he was certainly no womanizer. But this woman was unlike any he had ever met. She might as well have come from Mars. And sex with her had been unlike any he had ever experienced. It had been so—well, informal. Hot, sweaty, wild, literally breathtaking, but—what? There was no commitment? No, that wasn't it. He knew what it was—there was no guilt. It wasn't as if he was taking something, and she giving. They were just having fun together.

Or so he had thought. The FBI had suspected differently. The woman was an anthropologist from South America doing a study of aerospace workers in the United States. Apparently, one of her interview subjects had thought her line of questioning was inappropriate. Or—why couldn't he face it?—perhaps she had initiated an affair with him, too. At any rate, the man, whose identity was unknown to Bain, had gone to the FBI with his suspicions. And then the FBI, simply going down the long list of interview subjects cleared by NASA, had come to Bain.

Not knowing what it was all about, Bain confessed the affair to an Agent Wilson, a big doughy blond with an impassive bulldog face, and his Yuppie partner, whose name Bain could never remember. They made him say it into a tape recorder.

Wilson promised not to tell anyone at NASA unless it became germane to their case against the woman. But Bain went ahead and told his wife. He had to—they had had too honest a relationship for too many years to let her hear about it on the evening news. And to his surprise, the crisis seemed to break down the wall that had grown between them during their child-rearing days, with her the mother first and foremost, in charge of this, and him the father in charge of that, and never the twain shall meet in any other context.

Still, she felt violated, and she blamed the community—or specifically that freewheeling, hard-charging element that was the legacy of the Apollo days. Mrs. Bain wanted to live somewhere where there were no astronauts for everyone to emulate.

Bain seized upon her determination to move as a sign from God, which meant he was due and could wrangle a promotion. Certainly he was trapped in the strata here at JSC. Perhaps he needed to seek a smaller pond.

But flirting with another disaster was not the way to a promotion.

13

Rodrigue found Neesay alone on a small sofa in the hotel lobby. She was staring, fascinated, at the people around her. He sat beside her and remained silent.

There were crowds around the two TV sets, now tuned to coverage of the crippled shuttle *Columbia*. Up on the mezzanine, partygoers leaned over the rail, craning for a glimpse of one of the screens or simply watching the faces of those who could see. Meanwhile, in the depths of the first-level cocktail lounge, the party continued with loud laughter and the clinking of glasses.

The TV news switched back to the hurricane. There was an overturned eighteen-wheeler on the Gulf Freeway and hundreds of motorists were trapped in the resulting traffic jam. Emergency personnel were using school buses in an attempt to evacuate them via the feeder roads, but locally heavy rains had already led to flooding on some of these auxiliary routes. People wandered away from the TVs, back to the parties. The people noise increased, only occasionally overridden by a mournful howl from the side door at the end of the hall, the one facing the lake.

"I can't help wondering what's at play here, what kind of demographics," she said.

She looked around with a detached fascination, like a visitor to the zoo. "About half the people here seem properly stunned by what is going on. The other half are delighted."

"Demographics," Rodrigue said with a derisive chuckle. "More like alcohol. Besides, I don't believe it's quite that clear-cut," he said.

"What do you mean?"

"See that guy right there?" He aimed his Long John Silver squint at a man in his midthirties who sat on another of the small sofas across the narrow lobby. Next to him was a woman also in her midthirties. She had captured the man's right hand as though it were a bird and held it in her lap. They both frowned at the TV, but she put muscle into it, especially in her brow, while his frown was lax, flat-mouthed.

"He belongs in the other group," said Rodrigue.

Neesay stared at him for a long while, far longer than she needed to consider the cynical remark. She had decided that Rodrigue's responses were strictly visceral. She had been raised in a jungle, yet this man from Louisiana was the purest primitive she had ever known.

"So do you, huh, Johnny?" she said finally. "You belong in the other group?"

"Not true. I've changed, Neesay. I'm responsible. Sensitive, even."

She patted his stomach the way a horseman might pat the flank of his mount. "You have trimmed down somewhat over the past year. Eating less or exercising more?"

"Both. Which reminds me, have you eaten? I don't suppose there's any point in trying to get into the restaurant."

"I'm not really hungry. I have some food in my room, though, if you are."

He gave her an instant of amused incredulity—as if Rodrigue the Pirate would be in need of such charity. "What I need is a drink. But there's no point in trying for that, either." He cast a doleful eye at the crowded lounge. "Looks like Mardi Gras at Pat O'Brien's."

The lights winked off with a collective *Ohhh!* from the crowd. They came back on, but dimly and stayed on no more than four or five minutes. Neesay tentatively reached out and touched his arm in the darkness. It disturbed him for some reason.

The sudden appearance of huge shadows filling the room told of lights being lighted in the backstage of the hotel. An emergency generator, Rodrigue figured, would be used to keep the refrigerators and essential work areas going. Then the hotel staff fanned out and placed six-volt battle lanterns on shelves and tables, their tight beams stabbing the blackness like sunlight through the portholes of some dank wreck. Strangely, Rodrigue found it to his liking.

Now there was the sound of an angry sea rushing toward them. Rodrigue stiffened in sudden icy panic. The noise was coming from the stairwell, where water was crashing through the marina-level hallway.

"Tidal wave?" asked Neesay. Her dark eyes glittered in a ghostly face.

Even as he shook his head, the sound faded. People thought of the storm surge as a huge wall of water like the tsunami produced by an earthquake. Actually, it was just a superhigh tide. It was the most dangerous part of a major hurricane, but it came on gradually, not roaring inland in one big, towering comber.

The gurgling rush of water came again in a few moments—abated and came again. The tide *was* rising dangerously. Waves had lapped up over the docks, the pool area—were in his office by now, he thought without a tinge of regret. They had broken through the marina-level doors and now were sloshing higher and higher up the stairs to the lobby. The panic he had felt earlier congealed into a haunting memory.

The sound of water surging through the cabin woke him just as the boat broached in the storm, in the night, far from port. The water tore him from the bunk, slammed him against the overhead, stung his eyes and nostrils. He was only five years old, but he knew instinctively what was happening—their boat had turned over and now it was going to sink and they were going to drown.

It was unfair, dying with his father. Things were supposed to be okay when Papa was around. They had already been down the Gulf to the Bay of Campeche and everything had been okay. It was his first trip, where they had spoken French from dawn 'til dusk instead of English the way Mama insisted (the better to raise the family's social standing in these *américain*-influenced times). They had talked about women and drinking and the horse races, things of which Mama certainly wouldn't have approved. But aside from these moral lapses, Papa had taken very good care of him—seeing that he ate everything on his plate, and slept enough, and making him brush his teeth morning, noon, and night. The storm had taken them by surprise when they were well north of Tampico and there was no place to run.

Just as he knew he would have to gulp seawater, a hand like a vise found his leg and pulled him down into the sinking boat. He fought but it was no use. Water still seemed to be rushing downward, and he and the hand were being swept along with it. Another hand came and grabbed his arm, roughly. It hurt. And then he just had to breathe—

It was mostly air he sucked into his burning lungs. His papa shoved him high, and he saw the slope of foam-webbed blackness overtake them—but it lifted them with it. Stinging spray and howling wind assailed their senses.

They all clung to a hatch cover from the shrimp boat, all but the young John Rodrigue figuring that they would drown soon enough. But, praise Mary, the Mother of God, not now. . . .

"We'd better go on up," he told Neesay.

"Up?" She seemed dazed.

"You can stay in my room. We're on the fifth floor."

"We?"

"Leyton's with me. You've met Leyton, haven't you? Sure you have."

"Yes. Yes, of course." A sense of urgency animated her, and she grabbed his hands. "Why don't we go to my room? I—I'm alone."

Rodrigue pulled back and gave her a quizzical cockeyed stare. Was this a come-on? No, he decided, she was just frightened. With good reason.

A battle lantern threw grotesque shadows in the stairwell as people trooped to their rooms. The stairs were narrow, with small landings cluttered with a fire main and valve on each floor. Conversation was spare, just a whispered word here and there. The exertion was too much for nervous chatter.

Rodrigue thought he could feel the building trembling beneath his feet, and he wondered—as undoubtedly did each of them—whether this was really the place to be. As if they had a choice at this point.

When they reached his floor, he paused. "I want to pick up a few things," he said. The door opened with a whoosh of stale refrigerated air.

". . . *motorists who were stranded on Highway Three when floodwaters overtook the slow-moving traffic . . ."*

It was a squelched voice on a portable radio. Most of the doors were open, flickering rectangles of candlelight, some of them. Others flared briefly with flashlight beams, and some stood dark and still in the long, dim hall.

". . . *using airboats were ferrying the motorists to National Guard trucks on the interstate until the winds made that effort too dangerous for the volunteers. No word at this hour on whether . . ."*

Rodrigue let them into his room. The howling of the wind was instantly louder, yet somehow distant. The room was on the lee side of the building.

Leyton wasn't there. Rodrigue moved quickly to find his new Tekna underwater flashlight.

"Fill the tub and sink while I gather some stuff, Neesay, please?"

"Okay. Why?"

"Water supply'll be polluted. We'll need all the safe water we can get."

Rodrigue gathered a small duffel with his shaving kit and a change of clothes. And when Neesay disappeared into the bathroom, he found his .45 pistol on the dresser with the flashlight beam. He grabbed it and stuffed it into the duffel.

He didn't want to alarm her, but he knew what sometimes happened when the lights went out and the phones went dead.

14

Outside, in the darkness, the wind screamed. It screamed from sheer velocity, not needing a building's corner or the taut, bowed electrical wires to produce sound. Even the crashing of the waves could not be heard over it.

On the lake, Weizman's boat pitched violently. Weizman had optimistically hoped to hold it with two anchors placed at a right angle from the bow—or maybe he, like most boatmen, hadn't had time to come up with something better.

The lighter of the two anchors dragged a deep furrow in the gooey mud of the lake bottom. The line to the larger anchor chafed on a hawse pipe until it popped silently. The boat, with Pritchett aboard, drifted wildly northward, dragging the smaller anchor.

The anchor snagged the submerged railing of the low NASA Road 1 bridge near the hotel, but that line, too, quickly parted. Careening on the tips of black waves, the boat flew with ghostly speed toward the unseen treetops in the far back of Armand Bayou.

15

Rodrigue and Neesay lay together on top of the bedspread in the darkness of her room. The air had grown hot and muggy, but still they snuggled together, she with her back to his belly, he with his heavy arm over her. It was unspoken: Neither of them wanted to make love, only to be close.

They hadn't uttered a word for over an hour—maybe way over—but he knew she was awake. Her body was too taut to be sleeping.

The first time the building shook—really shook, beyond the slight trembling they had been feeling all along—Rodrigue became frightened. More than anything else, it was his fear of height. It was as though the hotel were of no more substance than it was of form in the complete blackness, and that they were hovering high above black waves dashing madly against black rocks. Or, no, the huge shards of the concrete foundation, oozing with iron reinforcing rods like severed nerves.

But the wind, the ceaseless screaming of the wind drove the fear away—if only by driving him nearly crazy. After a while, he couldn't hold the sound apart from himself, and then it was being created in his head—and then it *did* drive him crazy—and why in the hell hadn't he thought to bring the fucking rum?—and what in God's name was wrong with him?

Tense. He was tense.

Maybe it was because he was lying here hugging this coil spring.

Her soft firmness and her scent were so appealing and yet so damn unsettling. Goddamn, this was *Neesay*! Yet it was hardly the skinny teenager who used to bash him with dependency theory. Yet that Neesay was still there, too, peeking through the sad grown-up eyes. Or maybe he just wasn't ready for another woman yet.

He knew better than to savor once more the good times with Ann Eller, but goddamn it, he needed her now. Like he needed a drink, only worse.

Flying back to Cozumel from Tegucigalpa that time, Rodrigue had not indulged in his usual ration from the drink cart. He had not wanted to blow it. Because the more he thought about it, the less he could understand what she had ever seen in him.

She was a fragile thing, with thin ivory skin that showed her veins, and golden freckles, and soft, pale eyelashes like a child. And at the same time, she had big firm breasts and long legs and full hips and maddeningly round buttocks, and when he imagined the warm, thick nest of auburn hair she had to have between her legs, he almost started panting.

But it wasn't just lust. She touched something in him with her innocence, her inexperience, something that made him want to cuddle her every bit as much as he wanted to peel her open like a ripe fruit.

Question was, What the hell did *she* want?

They had met on the plane to Cozumel when Rodrigue was in search of some people who had murdered friends of his. The trail had become confused there on the island just long enough for them to become better acquainted—not physically, but there seemed to be that promise—and then he was off to Belize and Honduras in pursuit of a bloody revenge. But they had been together long enough to leach some of the hardness out of his heart. When finally he could've killed them all, all he could think about was Ann.

Sweet, innocent, incredibly sexy Ann.

She was waiting for him at the airport, wearing a rose sundress, holding a big straw hat, her beautiful red hair all coppery from the days in the sun and wild from the ride in the open Volkswagen Safari she had rented. She bounced on her toes and smiled when she spotted him.

He was wearing his eye patch again, even though the injury that had prevented him from wearing his artificial eye earlier had since healed. Maybe it was cowardly—it *was* cowardly—but what if it had been the piratical black patch that attracted her to him? Later, only later, would he let her see the whole him.

And later, of course, he had.

Rodrigue was swept with groggy embarrassment when he realized that he had an erection nestled comfortably in the cleft of Neesay's firm buttocks. He eased away from her, only then realizing that the room was gray with dim light.

It sounded like sand being shoveled against the window—but at least there was a window. He was almost surprised that the hotel had stood up, considering the pounding it had taken.

Neesay was breathing steadily. Rodrigue rose gently from the bed, finding the carpet soaked beneath his bare feet. For an instant, his boatman's instincts told him it was seawater. You put your feet down in water on the cabin sole and you had better save yourself, because it was too late for the boat. But this wasn't a boat—and, God, if the Gulf had risen *this* high, Oklahoma City was in trouble.

He dampened his finger on the carpet and tasted—fresh. Windows had blown open and let in the rain. But theirs, on what had been the sheltered side of the building during the most violent part of the storm, was still intact. He padded over to it and looked out.

"What's it like outside?" Neesay asked without rolling over.

Her voice was small, anxious. She stayed in a fetal position on the bed.

"Wind's coming this way now," he said. "Eye must be pretty well inland. That was a rough son of a bitch."

He tried to see the ground, but all he saw was the purple-gray haze of rain.

"I wonder if they fixed the problem with the shuttle," she

said, rolling over to look at him with the wildness of a cornered animal.

"I missed most of that last night—what's wrong with the shuttle?"

"Something with the computers, they said." Her voice broke.

Rodrigue sat beside her and took her into his arms while she sobbed uncontrollably. Finally, she stopped and went into the bathroom.

He got up and leaned out into the hall, surprised to see people huddled against the walls like sacks of laundry. A man looked up from the floor with red eyes and a haggard face.

"Winda blew plumb out," he said with a tone of wonder in his voice. "Liketa sucked me out with it."

People were awake, but like zombies—stunned by the night of relentless din as much as by the terror. Rodrigue went down the hall, peeking in doors, listening for a portable radio. Finally, he saw one, silent, on a dresser. A man and a woman sat on opposite beds, staring—at him now, but with no more or less interest than they had been staring at each other when he looked in.

"That thing work?" he said, poking his chin toward the radio.

"Yes, it works, but there's nothing on the air," said the man. "Not around here, anyway. I picked up a station out of Nacogdoches or somewhere like that earlier, but they're not getting any news from down here. And I lost them when it turned light."

"What about the space shuttle? Anything about that?"

"Apparently they've lost control of it. I didn't hear anything new about that."

Neesay was still in the bathroom. Rodrigue slipped on a shirt and shoes, and tucked his .45 into his pants where it couldn't be seen.

"I'm going down to see if I can find my boat," he called through the closed bathroom door.

"Will you come back?" she said.

"Yes, if you want."

"Of course, Johnny." Anything else she left unsaid.

Men were gathered at the bottom of the stairwell. Nobody

was speaking. As Rodrigue descended to their level, he could see the first floor of the hotel was flooded.

"You fellows make it all right?" he asked.

Blank faces, red eyes looked back at him.

"Gonna get rougher around here before it gets better," said one man.

Another nodded. "I was down in Corpus during Celia. Sonuvabitches come and took everything people owned. I mean they'd kill you for it. Folks had to band together to protect themselves before the National Guard got down there."

"Same thing happened in Gulfport after Camille," said the first man. "There was a killing or two—of looters, I mean. Not a word about it in the papers, either."

"How deep's that water, anybody know?" asked Rodrigue.

Someone shrugged.

"I'm not getting down in there to find out," one man said. "Probably full of snakes." He shivered.

"Bullshit," said Rodrigue roughly. "There aren't enough snakes around here to fill a washtub."

Rodrigue didn't like snakes any more than the next man, but being reared in the swamps of Louisiana, a certain bravado toward them was built into his character.

"Lemme by here," he said.

He waded down the stairs until it reached his testicles. He started to pull out his pistol, only to save himself the trouble of disassembling and cleaning it later. But a little soaking wouldn't hurt it. A government-issued .45 was designed to take a tremendous amount of abuse and still shoot. He decided it would be best if no one knew he had it, so he left it hidden under his shirt. He waded on in, and when he reached the ground floor, the water had reached his armpits.

The hotel lobby was like a cavern, echoing with the sound of water trickling inside the walls. The front doors were gone and the soft, steady rain covered the gaping entrance like a curtain.

Rodrigue nearly tripped on something—there was all kinds of debris under the water. As he approached the gaping doorway, he bumped into something that moved with a neutral buoyancy that triggered a sickening recognition.

He reached into the oily black water and grasped a human body. It was a woman, fifties or maybe younger; it was hard to tell with the shriveling. He raised her higher and let out an anguished groan—the corpse wore Alice Garcia's dress. He floated her easily to where he remembered the front desk was and shoved her over it. He could tell them where to look.

The rain was very fine now, almost a mist, and it blurred the boundary between water and sky. The top branches of tall oaks, stripped of leaves, were etched in black on a featureless background. Islands of debris were everywhere. Some of the cars were bobbing just beneath the surface like crippled submarines. Rodrigue had to start swimming halfway across the parking lot. He did a lazy sidestroke, not knowing how far he'd have to swim.

He found a foothold again on the spongy grass of the high NASA Road 1 shoulder next to a subdivision of expensive town houses west of the hotel compound. Only two stories of the three-story buildings stood above the black water, and most of those were now only peeking brick fire wall above the second floor. They looked like some kind of ancient icons silhouetted against the dim gray sky. It was like witnessing the last gasp of Atlantis.

The water was getting shallower as he waded westward along the unseen channel the roadway had become. The whole area as far as he could see was like a vast dark lake, here cluttered with ruins, there dotted with debris. The full-grown trees in the parking lot at the Johnson Space Center were just naked bushes, barely breaking the surface.

But true to the word of several long-gone Texas politicians, the buildings at JSC were high and dry, sitting on little plateaus of earth bulldozed up from the prairie.

When he drew near enough to see his boat clearly, Rodrigue laughed out loud. The *Haulover Queen* had floated off her trailer and was bobbing contentedly over the flooded road. The Blazer was squatting in about three feet of water, but the Whaler looked untouched. Even the aluminum mast was unbowed.

The boat had peeled the line from the winch until it reached the end of it. Then it had just sat out there and ridden it out somehow. Rodrigue stood at the trailer and, hand over hand, pulled the *Queen* back up to shallow water. He tied it off to the submerged trailer and climbed in over the transom.

The boat was full of sodden leaves and twigs, but the little cabin was as dry as he'd left it. Both outboards started on the first try. Rodrigue crawled onto the bow, leaned over, and released the winch-line hook from the bow eye. He let it fall into the muddy water. Then he went back into the pilothouse, killed the port engine, and raised it with the power tilt. With the water full of submerged objects, including downed electrical and telephone wires, it was wise to keep one propeller in reserve. He put the starboard outboard in gear, and cautiously threaded his way around the fallen utility poles, flooded cars, and dislodged roofs toward the original basin of the lake.

He steered around what he first thought was an uprooted stump and saw it was another body.

He left it floating.

The Whaler wouldn't be big enough to hold them all.

16

Rodrigue aimed for the Hilton on a course that he knew would keep him over the relatively uncluttered roadway. He veered left at the hotel and then made a wide circle to the right. His Lowrance X-15 chart recorder clearly showed the lake bottom falling away beneath him.

Looking across the water, it was impossible to tell what was supposed to be land and what was supposed to be lake. Within the original boundaries of the lake was a mass of floating debris, including several crumpled wood-frame houses, while the land had its share of boats now. Rodrigue navigated by the surviving landmarks—the Hilton, of course, the South Shore Harbour Hotel across the way, and, down at the far end of the lake, the white tip of the high bridge spanning the submerged creek exit.

The rain had quit and a high gray haze covered the sun. It was like steam. Sweat stung his good eye.

Rodrigue used his chart recorder to pick his way up the creek at this end, where it fed the lake. It was a disturbing experience. In the pungent squiggling of the stylus, he kept imagining he saw dead bodies in grotesque poses. Finally, he told himself he was wasting chart paper and turned off the machine.

The condos along the creek, sheltered from the battering of the waves, had fared better than those on the lake. Although the drainage canal where he had left the pontoon boats had disappeared beneath the floodwaters, Rodrigue could tell where it was by the top floors of the condos lining the right side and the office buildings on the left. There was no sign of the boats. If the wind funneling up the canal hadn't jerked them loose, their own buoyancy probably would've. Rodrigue hadn't allowed enough scope for their anchors. He hadn't counted on this high a storm surge. Nobody had.

Rodrigue had to turn his chart recorder back on to pick his way over the inundated Hilton Marina. The water had receded from the first floor, but the marina level, including his office, was still under. He hooked his anchor over the concrete wall of the east parking lot.

People were emerging from the hotel like inmates from some insane asylum, suddenly free and not sure what to do about it. Some fanned out over the lot, looking at the muddy wrecks of their cars. Others stared dumbly at the flooded landscape.

Rodrigue started sloshing down the *Queen* with buckets of floodwater, washing the leaves into piles at the scuppers aft, where he could scoop them up in his hands. A man detached himself from the group and stood at the rail.

"John Rodrigue?" he said in an accent, Eastern European maybe. He was short and wiry, with white hair that grew tight to a noggin that looked as tough as a coconut. His fresh white dress shirt was rolled neatly past the elbow, English style.

"Aye," said Rodrigue, giving the man the pirate squint. "An' who be you, matey?"

The man was unaffected by the burlesque. "That is not important. I'll pay in hundred-dollar bills."

This got Rodrigue's attention, if not his respect. "Cash money?" he said, his eye darting furtively about for imaginary eavesdroppers. "An' whose throat, matey," he rumbled in his most evil voice, "do I have to slit?"

"This is serious." Now the man was losing patience.

"Well fuck you, then," said Rodrigue. "I've had enough serious to last a week."

What he really wanted was a drink. He'd go salvage some ice from one of the machines before any of these zombies thought about it, get a bottle or two and some limes from his room, and go sit out in the lake and watch Texas rise from the sea.

"Captain Rodrigue—" The man looked for a moment as if he was trying to swallow a small fish tail first. "I'm sorry. I—I have a problem and I need help."

Rodrigue was suddenly ashamed of himself. He had a tendency to look after number one and just fuck everybody else.

"All right," he said. "What is it?"

"I am a homosexual," the man began.

"That is a problem," agreed Rodrigue thoughtfully. He wasn't being a smart ass this time, merely candid.

"A man who was my—lover—was on my boat—" His gaze rose. "Out there."

Rodrigue turned and looked at the calm black sea.

"Big sailboat anchored right out there?" Rodrigue asked.

"Yes." The man's eyes narrowed.

"And your buddy, he have a heart problem and bright yellow shoes?"

He didn't mean to be flippant. Now he had another face to pin on one of the bodies—poor sweet Alice Garcia and now that frantic little man in the yellow shoes. The awful human toll of this killer storm was flooding into his consciousness. His heart was beating faster, suddenly, and his palms were sweating.

"Yes," said the man uncertainly. "Have you seen him?"

"Yeah," said Rodrigue, blinking a tear. "He borrowed a dinghy from me to get out there. God*damn* it, I knew I shouldn't have let that son of a bitch go." He threw the plastic bucket down with a loud clack. It bounced and spun on the fiberglass deck.

The man's thin lips flattened almost imperceptibly. "Nothing we can do about it now. But he had a family. And I—I'm known in the community—for what I am—Do you understand? It would ruin his memory to be found on my boat."

Rodrigue trained his moist eye on the man skeptically now. He smelled a rat—if for no other reason than his poor first impression of this man's charity. But that was good. It made these surreal surroundings somehow much more familiar.

"How much?"

"I beg your pardon?" asked the man, taken aback.

"How much will you pay me to find your boat and remove the body?"

The man smiled. "You are a mercenary sort, aren't you?"

"Yes I am."

"Good, good. This is a task for a cold-blooded man. Five hundred dollars, I will pay you. Two now and three upon satisfactory completion."

Rodrigue laughed. "Forget it."

The man grew angry. "What are you going to do, hold me up?"

"Listen, they shoot to kill looters after something like this. And that's just about what I'll be, won't I?"

"Okay, all right, how much?"

"Fifteen hundred."

The man looked as if he wanted to leap over the wall and whip Rodrigue's ass—and he almost looked as if he could do it. But Rodrigue was no cherry in these negotiations. People almost invariably offered about a third what they were willing to pay.

"Five now," he growled. "A thousand when you bring me one of his shoes."

"Which one?" Rodrigue was only half-joking. As a professional, thoroughness was his hallmark.

"It doesn't matter, does it? It's my proof. I don't want you to touch his wallet or anything in his pockets, you understand? I certainly don't want any suspicion of foul play to arise if and when they do find his body."

"What do you want me to do with it, then?"

"Take it out onto the bay," the man said. "I don't believe his will be the only one they find out there after all of this drains out."

Rodrigue took the man's five hundred-dollar bills. Then he brought his deck bucket into the hotel. There was people noise now—loud talking, even laughing. The survivors seemed to be blowing off steam. Footsteps clattered on the stairs.

He tried the ice machine on the first landing. It was full. Nobody had thought of ice yet. He put a scoopful into his bucket and shut the lid. No point in being greedy. . . . But what the hell—he opened it up again and took two more scoops.

His room was empty—no sign that Leyton had even been there since the storm. Probably shacked up elsewhere. Rodrigue grabbed the duffel that contained his diving mask, wet suit, weights, fins, and a few odds and ends. He also grabbed an unopened half-gallon of rum from the liquor box, a couple of clear plastic half-gallon bottles of club soda, and a bag of limes from the grocery box, and he locked the door on the way out.

Neesay's door was also locked, but she was inside. "Who is it?" she called in a frightened voice.

"John."

She opened the door quickly—shut and locked it as soon as he stepped in. She was wearing blue-jean cutoffs and a T-shirt, and was drenched with sweat.

"What's the matter?" he asked.

"Some guys were talking funny. Probably just pent-up hysteria, but I didn't feel I should take a chance."

"Want to go for a boat ride?" He was in a hurry. He wanted to move the boat before the receding water left it sitting on the walk in front of his office.

"God, yes! Anything to get out of this heat. Where?"

"I've been hired to find a body. I can't find Leyton and I need someone to tend my air hose."

Maybe he should've colored it a little. He could tell by her eyes that she was reconsidering. But finally, she nodded.

"Do I need a raincoat?"

"Not anymore."

Aboard the *Queen*, he poured them each a stiff rum and soda, and then idled on one engine toward the spot where he had seen the sailboat anchored before the storm.

Running a search grid with loran and chart recorder, Rodrigue quickly realized he would be earning his fifteen hundred. There were wrecks everywhere down there, and no way of knowing which was the man's sailboat. He'd have to dive on every one of them.

The one thing Rodrigue would not do was blow off the job. Good commercial divers—and he had been one of the best—were very sensitive to the suspicions that naturally arose about men who did high-paying work out of anyone's sight. Delivered as promised was their credo. Do or die. He couldn't have told you now whether it was pride or the man's thousand dollars that made him determined to recover the body.

He picked a wreck and anchored over it. He was unbinding his lifeline—arranging the big figure eight of hose where Neesay could feed it to him without causing the air-squelching kinks the divers called "assholes"—when he spotted the big white boat sitting keeled over in what looked like a field of stubble about a quarter of a mile to the north.

"So *there* she is," he muttered to himself.

"What? What?" asked Neesay nervously.

"That's the boat we're looking for, Neesay. In all likelihood, the dead man's still on it."

The "stubble" was actually the tops of flooded live oaks, the pliant limbs stripped of leaves. The boat had been washed over the NASA Road 1 bridge, up a wide slough, and into the woods. Beneath the water between here and there was not only the bridge but also what was left of a tangle of electrical and phone wires. The water was draining down fast. Did he have time to get in there and out again before the bridge surfaced and trapped him?

Of course, then it would just be a matter of time before he could get out under the bridge like a proper vessel, but any time at all with a rotting corpse aboard would be an eternity in this heat.

"I'm going to go aboard, wrap him up in a tarp, and bring him back on our boat. Then you and I will take him out and hold a burial at sea. If any of this seriously does not appeal to you, I can run you back to the hotel first. But I gotta tell you, I don't have a lot of time before the water comes down too low for me to get in and out of there."

She didn't balk. She wasn't especially anxious to become involved in whatever Rodrigue was doing for Weizman, but neither did she want to hang around the hotel. The place had the smell of anarchy about it. And Neesay had the ancient Spanish fear of anarchy in her blood.

Rodrigue kept the chart running as he plodded over the submerged roadway. The transducer—the small disklike "antenna" that transmitted and received the sonar signal—was located a good ten feet forward of the engine's lower unit. At that speed, he'd have time to put the one engine in neutral before he ran over anything. As it turned out, the bridge railings were still a foot and a half below the hull—and if he'd been on a plane instead of at displacement speed, he could've added another foot, foot and a half of clearance.

He quickly took a sight bearing so he would know when he was approaching the bridge on the way out—the red tile roof of a flooded pavilion in the park to his right, and to the left, one of the tall NASA buildings untouched and glowing in the sunshine on its own little island. Then he noted the depth on the recorder: about twenty-two and a half feet. Less than, say, twenty feet on the way out and he was trapped.

The boat, a big, expensive Cheoy Lee, was heeled over in the treetops, showing the barnacle-dotted belly of her hull. The other side would be a tangle of ruined mast and rigging, so Rodrigue put the *Queen* just over the sailboat's keel and fed a dock line through a stanchion of the Cheoy Lee's lifeline. He gave the end of the line to Neesay.

"Just keep us alongside here," he said. "If the boat starts to settle suddenly and this line gets real tight, just turn loose."

"Huh, *Johnny!*" Neesay said, breathing sharply. She pointed into the brown water at the stern. A snake with a distinctive triangular head swam unhurriedly, like a whip popping in slow motion, away from the sailboat.

"There goes the last one." He hoped it was so. Water moccasins were not only poisonous; they were mean.

He found the cheap plastic tarp, still in its K Mart package, down in the vee berth. He shucked the wrapper and put it in the trash can in the cabin, then rolled the tarp and tied it over his shoulder like a Confederate soldier, the better for boarding ghost boats. The hull was slippery and Rodrigue had to pull himself up to the rail solely with the strength of his arms—good thing he had dropped a little weight lately. The sailboat's lifeline was sagging like an old wire fence, and he slid through easily.

The deck sloped away at a steep angle and the opposite rail was underwater, but the boat seemed solid enough. The entrance to the cabin gaped, a black rectangle against the bright hazy day. Rodrigue regretted leaving his flashlight in Neesay's room. He squeezed his right eye shut and felt his way down into the cockpit to the entranceway.

The ladder was useless at that angle of heel. Rodrigue eased his foot down until he touched something solid, a galley counter or stovetop, undoubtedly. Still blind, he tried to heighten his sense of feel, of motion. He sure in the hell didn't want this thing sliding under with him.

He couldn't help but think of the water moccasin as he felt warm liquid enveloping his ankle. He opened his eye and instantly saw the body.

It was just barely floating in the flooded cabin. The only parts visible were the curve of his back, where the gases in his body cavity provided the most lift, and the very back of his head. The hair was matted with clotted blood. It looked like a drowned rodent. Rodrigue welled with anger at God, that He thought so little of the human form once the precious fucking soul was gone.

He steeled himself to come face-to-face with the drowned man, and he thought for a moment the buzzing in his ears was nervousness.

But then it became the noise of a small boat, coming fast.

17

Either the heat or the mosquitoes finally woke Special Agent Wilson. He was lying on the carpeted floor of a mezzanine-level conference room in his boxer shorts, and his white flanks were covered with little red welts.

A group of maids, cocktail waitresses, and a teenage busboy who had also taken refuge there were huddled nearby, staring blankly at him. Seidenhaur, who at least had a shirt and trousers on, was sprawled out nearby, still asleep.

The hotel staffers were staring because of the extraordinary pitch and volume of the snoring they had been witnessing only moments earlier, but Wilson didn't know that. He rose indignantly and tore a drape from the glass wall facing the mezzanine rail, and he wrapped it around him like a cloak.

He and Seidenhaur were lucky to be alive. When the storm hit, the side door facing the lake had held back the seas like a dike, so when it finally did go, seawater roared through the first-floor halls and into the back rooms in one foaming wave. Their senses dulled by two weeks of constant surveillance, Wilson had been asleep on the bed, Seidenhaur nodding at the desk. In an instant, they were both awake, thrashing for air. While Seidenhaur had preserved his gun and ID and the clothes on his back, Wilson was down to his skivvies.

"Where's the manager?" Wilson demanded. He would see about getting some clothes first, maybe a waiter's uniform, and then let the other priorities fall into place.

"Dead," said a waitress. She said it without emotion, but her eyes were red and puffy from crying. All their eyes were.

"They're all dead," said the busboy. "All the management, I mean. There were guests caught downstairs and they were trying to save them. They ordered us up—" His voice broke momentarily. "Jesus, it's like we was a sinking ship or something."

Wilson woke Seidenhaur. "You go up and peek in on our two friends," he said, just loudly enough for the other agent to hear. "I'm going down and look for my gun."

The lobby was a misshapen world of dull gray-brown. Corners were rounded with drifts of gumbo mud. The floor was cluttered with unrecognizable shapes. Even a sofa, upright and probably moved very little from its proper place, was at first camouflaged by its new dun color. The mud-caked floor was slick and Wilson plodded carefully in his bare feet.

The first body drifted into Wilson's consciousness like something seen in a cloud. Gradually, the vaguely familiar shape became a short man in work clothing, probably a maintenance man or groundskeeper. There was another body, possibly the manager himself, in the hall outside the offices where Wilson and Seidenhaur had been set up.

It wasn't quite as muddy in the little office, but their effects were nowhere to be seen—not even a suitcase. The wall between their room and the adjacent office was sagging and the roll-away bed was lodged in the enlarged doorway. Otherwise, it looked as if everything but the desk had been literally scoured out. Wilson took a turn around the lobby and found more bodies. There was already a hint of the horrible stench to come.

He trudged dejectedly back to the mezzanine and found Seidenhaur coming down the stairs. Seidenhaur was panting—from exertion, Wilson supposed, although the younger man played tennis—and there was a dazed look in his eyes.

"Cara's door is locked," he said. "I knocked but nobody answered."

"Rodrigue?"

"Gone. His room is full of women."

"That doesn't surprise me."

"I mean every size and shape of female. And babies. I heard babies crying."

"You must've gotten the wrong room."

Seidenhaur shook his head slowly. "It was the right number. But the place is—I don't know, *strange*, Roy. Everybody seems afraid or suspicious or something. Somebody's already put graffiti on the walls. Reminds me of one of those British punk-rocker movies. I was definitely glad to be packing a piece."

"Come on!"

"I'm serious, Roy. It's like we woke up in a whole new world."

"Yeah, well, we are going to have to rearrange our priorities temporarily. Rodrigue and Cara can't get far. Meanwhile, we've got to do something about the bodies downstairs or they'll be a health problem in this heat," said Wilson. "Apparently, there's nobody left in charge of the hotel."

He led the way back into the conference room, where the hotel employees were still huddled.

"We're going to need to set up a temporary morgue," he told the group. "Preferably someplace cool and definitely someplace away from the rooms. Any suggestions?"

"How about Lakeview Manor?" a maid asked the others.

"Where's that?" asked Wilson.

"A renovated mansion on the property," said a waitress. "Used for conferences. It's perfect."

"You know the way?" Wilson asked the busboy.

"Sure."

"Come show us. We'll need your help."

"The rest of you should block this door with a chair and stay quiet until we get back," Seidenhaur warned. "Something strange is going on around here."

Lakeview Manor was a yellow brick ruin with large grottolike rooms. Swarms of mosquitoes buzzed out of the uprooted shrubs to greet them.

Still in his bare feet, Wilson had to hobble gingerly back to the hotel through thick mud that concealed all sorts of painful objects. He let Seidenhaur and the busboy carry the bodies. He stayed in the lobby to search for more. He found a woman behind the check-in desk and dragged her around, just as Seidenhaur and the busboy returned for another corpse.

Suddenly, a woman screamed somewhere above. Seidenhaur started to reach for the revolver hidden under his shirttail, but Wilson stopped him. This was no time to blow their cover. They would have to act as concerned civilians.

The conference room's curtain flapping behind him, Wilson led the charge up the stairs like a mauve Batman with a pair of Robins in tow. On the third-floor landing, a young woman was surrounded by a group of men.

"What's going on here!" yelled Wilson, ready to fight.

"Maan, everyting's under control," said a black man with a bald head and an earring. He looked like a negative of Mr. Clean.

Wilson ignored him. He shouldered into the group and looked at the woman. "What happened?"

Seidenhaur maneuvered to back him up.

"It's okay," she said weakly. "These men came to my rescue."

Wilson looked around and nodded a greeting. So someone had already formed a committee of vigilantes. Good. "What happened?" he repeated.

"Couple of guys, they grabbed me. Just playing, I guess." Her face contorted with silent anguish.

"Seen them before?" Wilson asked.

"It's taken *care* of," said one of the men testily. He was a wiry, weathered little man with a red plaid lumberjack shirt.

"Yeah? You guys police officers?" asked Wilson.

"You might say that," said the man. "Close as there is around here right now, anyway." He conspicuously eyed Wilson's garb.

"Hey," said Mr. Clean. "Mebbe you guys wanna help out?"

The lumberjack led the grumbling.

"Well why not, maan," said Mr. Clean. He was young despite the bald head. "What about it, you guys wanna help out?"

"Of course," said Wilson, eyeing Seidenhaur.

"C'mon, I'll take you up," said Mr. Clean.

"Up?" said Wilson.

"To see the Colonel," said the testy man.

"Yeah? Who's the Colonel?"

"He's some kinda army man, I guess. I don't know; he started telling people what to do, and people listen to him."

"It's because he knows what he's about, maan," said Mr. Clean. "In no time at all, he had organized our security. There is no law here now, maan."

Seidenhaur raised his eyebrows at Wilson.

"Some of you men need to go down, then, and finish picking up the bodies in the lobby," said Wilson. "This kid'll show you where to put them."

"Bodies?" said one of the men.

"Not everybody made it. There's going to be a stink you won't believe if we don't get them away from here."

It was a long climb to the top floor, and Wilson soon understood what Seidenhaur had been talking about. The unlovely stairwell, with its drab walls and exposed fire main, had the air of a public housing project in a ghetto. Doors were open and the sounds drifted to them—men talking boisterously, maybe even drunkenly. A portable radio was giving a statical report of many deaths along the Gulf Freeway. Babies cried. Even laughter now echoed in the tall stairwell—a menacing laughter.

Sullen men leaned in the doorways to some of the floors, obviously guarding their turf. Nods of recognition had passed between them and the young black who led Wilson and Seidenhaur to an entertainment center on the top floor.

The man they called the Colonel was sitting on a stool behind the bar like some kind of judge. He was in his early sixties, it seemed, pale and scrawny but powerful somehow. He looked tough.

He was holding a conference with two other men. Wilson and Seidenhaur waited with their escort in the hall in front of the useless elevators. They could see into the suite through wide French doors, still intact. Sofas were arranged face-to-face for intimate conversations, and there were a couple of poker tables—the kind of place executives like to go to grind out projects. Two large windows open to the air were the only apparent sign of the catastrophe.

The other men left and the young black ushered them in. The Colonel watched them approach with frank appraisal.

"Dese guys, dey want to help out, Colonel," said Mr. Clean reverently.

"Good. Excellent," said the Colonel robustly, with a somewhat pleasing foreign accent. "Mr. Mills, see if you can find this fellow something better to wear."

"Extralarge," said Wilson gratefully. "And any kind of shoes, as long as they're size ten and a half or eleven."

"Now, what are your names, men?" asked the Colonel, opening a notebook.

The two agents exchanged glances. "I'm Roy Wilson and this is Phil Seidenhaur. And you're—?"

"Andres Weizman." He offered a dry, hard hand.

"They call you Colonel?" said Wilson accusingly. A lot of people called themselves Colonel who weren't and never had been.

"Retired. Israeli army."

Wilson and Seidenhaur looked at each other again. This time, Wilson lengthened his jaw appreciably.

He had been wondering about the accent. It was vaguely familiar. In the back of his mind, he had been thinking of some elegant old film actor from the thirties or forties.

"So, where do I put you?" asked Weizman, writing their names in the notebook.

"We were down on the ground floor, picking up the bodies," said Wilson. "Some of your volunteers are still moving them. You might want to spread the word that if anyone has someone missing, the place to look is in that old mansion next door—what'd they call it, Phil?"

"Lakeview Manor."

"Excellent, good work," said the Colonel. "Now, would you men like to assume responsibility for a floor? We still have more than half without security. There're almost enough to put one man per floor, but I believe in two-man teams."

Wilson glanced at the door. Their escort had disappeared. Two other men were standing in the hall outside.

"Show him, Phil," he said to Seidenhaur.

Seidenhaur pulled out his ID wallet and flipped it open.

Weizman's face was stony.

"No farther than right here, okay?" said Wilson, leaning over the bar. "We're on surveillance."

Weizman's thin lips spread into a smile. "Anything I can do, of course, I will."

There for a minute, Weizman had thought he was caught. It had been risky of him to step up and take command at a time like this, but he had been forced into it when the window of his room shattered and drove him into the chaos of the hallway. He couldn't have abandoned his spy equipment, and he couldn't have secured it without taking control of the situation. Besides, it was the little indiscretions that caught spies, not the big ones. Bold strokes were seldom suspect.

"How many men have you signed up?" asked Seidenhaur.

"A dozen. Fourteen with you two—but of course you should be taking over this task. I only thought to—"

"No, no, you're doing great," said Wilson. "We need to remain under cover. Tell me, is there by any chance a John Rodrigue on your list?"

Weizman went through his notes slowly, careful not to show any sign of recognition. "No."

Wilson rubbed his jaw. "No, of course not."

"What's he done, if I may ask? This Rodrigue?"

"I can't get into that, Colonel. You understand, I'm sure."

"Oh, of course. Certainly."

Wilson leaned forward for confidentiality again. "We would very much like to keep tabs on Rodrigue and a woman by the name of Eunice Cara without them knowing it."

This was taking a big chance, but how else to get off dead center? It would be weeks before phone service was restored. Meanwhile, whatever was going to happen would have happened.

"If you have some people you can trust, who can keep their mouths shut, it might be helpful to have them keeping an eye out for them."

Weizman frowned. "These men are good public-minded citizens, but they are not trained policemen. If these people are dangerous—"

Wilson shook his head. "He's just a crooked businessman, that's all. She may or may not be involved."

No point in laying out the whole scenario, Wilson thought.

Weizman smiled. "In that case, I'll discreetly arrange a surveillance. What are their rooms?"

Seidenhaur told him and Weizman wrote it down.

"Now," said Weizman slyly, "do you men want to take a role here in the meantime? It would give you more leeway to ask questions without revealing your identities."

It wasn't a command, exactly, but somehow it had more weight than a mere suggestion. Wilson could see how Weizman had organized the hotel's defenders so quickly—the man was a natural leader. The FBI men agreed to help.

Weizman assigned them to the next floor down, where he said they would be close at hand should his information network turn up any sign of Rodrigue.

One of Weizman's lieutenants, who had been standing out by the elevators, escorted them down a flight of stairs and introduced them to the unofficial "mayor" of the floor and then left with a fading *squish, squish, squish* on the wet carpet.

The "mayor," a fat woman in her fifties wearing a flimsy gown with ostrich feathers on the collar and sleeves, had the nerve to roll her eyes at Wilson's costume. A cigarette bobbled in her lips as she spoke.

"How're you gonna dance and hold on to your cape at the same time, honey?"

Wilson colored. "Maybe you've got something in your wardrobe that would be more appropriate. Leopard-skin pedal pushers, perhaps?"

"The Colonel is finding something for him," said Seidenhaur. "What do you mean, dance?"

She shrugged, and brushed a fallen ash from her bosom. "We're all right here if you can just keep them from coming in from the stairs," she said. The way she said it, punctuated with a sigh, evidenced doubt.

Wilson reached under his cape and scratched his side. "At least the mosquitoes don't seem so bad up here."

"It won't be really bad until it gets dark," said the woman. She glared at Wilson. "And I don't mean mosquitoes, I mean looters. I went through this in Gulfport once. They come in the night. You can hear them sneaking up. . . ."

The woman shuddered and more ash fell on her bosom.

18

After Rodrigue disappeared on the big white sailboat, Neesay felt more alone than she ever had in her life. Obviously it was Weizman's boat, but who was in it? And why?

She had to stop agonizing over everything and trust Weizman. Maybe the problem with the space shuttle was a coincidence. Or if he had caused it, surely it hadn't been intentional. Or if it had, there was a valid purpose behind it.

There was another option. She could confide in Johnny, put it in his hands. It might feel good to have a man take control—not as Weizman controlled her but as her father had controlled her mother. It was yet another choice between the easy thing and the hard thing—and she would choose the hard thing, as usual.

Whatever Weizman was doing might benefit the gaunt, staring faces of the children she visualized when she thought of home—the montage of faces that all looked like poor little Elena of years ago. And even if it was too late to benefit Elena—who was grown if she was still alive, and probably had pitiful, tormented little Elenas of her own—it might somehow avenge her.

She had to remember that for decades, for generations, the North Americans had robbed the resources of the south, had chained the people to one-crop economies that produced bananas or sugar or coffee or cocaine for export but nothing for the growers to eat. They had corrupted the governments and thwarted every popular movement.

With the United States as a model, all the countries of the south had run up huge debts. And then when they were unable to pay them off, the International Monetary Fund had demanded austerity, the cutting of social programs, which, in turn, had led to unrest, like the strike in which Elena's father had been killed. And then the North Americans stood by oblivious—no, *aloof*—to the suffering they had caused.

Neesay looked at the Johnson Space Center, its bright beige buildings floating above the chaos and destruction like a mirage. She imagined men in clean white dress shirts with neckties passing each other in air-conditioned halls on their way to conferences or to the Coke machine.

They, not Weizman, were the enemy.

The noise of a passing boat didn't even enter her consciousness at first, and then it didn't really seem out of the ordinary—after all, the only way you could get around now was by boat. She became curious enough only to turn around and look when the pitch of the outboard motor changed. It was a boxy aluminum boat painted olive drab, the kind duck hunters used, and it was now circling back toward them.

Two men were aboard, and they looked like duck hunters. The one sitting back by the motor, driving, wore a camouflaged shirt with the sleeves ripped off and a headband of the same material. The other one, riding in front, had a black T-shirt and a camouflaged ball cap. He was smiling broadly, that one.

The little boat roared in very close, then slowed abruptly. The wave it produced rocked Rodrigue's boat and made it bang up against the sailboat. Neesay started to call out but thought better of it—nor was it necessary after all that. Surely Rodrigue had felt the arrival.

The men eased forward and brought their boat alongside.

"Hi," said the smiling man in front. "Whacha doin'?"

"Recovering a body," said Neesay loudly—loudly enough, she hoped, for Rodrigue to hear.

"Oh? A friend?" The man was still grinning but it was a mean grin.

"Yes," she said coldly. "A friend."

"Who's with you?" asked the other man, rising. He did not smile. And he dragged a shotgun from the floor of the boat.

Neesay was frozen, throat too constricted to make a sound.

The man trained the shotgun on Neesay and stepped onto a seat and then down into Rodrigue's boat. He grabbed her roughly by the wrist and twisted her arm behind her back.

"I'm gonna like this," he said with a panting snicker.

"You an' me both," replied his grinning friend.

"*Hey!*" yelled the man with the gun. He lifted Neesay's wrist for punctuation, sending blinding pain shooting from her shoulder and elbow.

"Hey, you in the boat!"

The other man had climbed in with them and was looking inside the little cabin. "This beats the shit outta your flatbottom," he muttered.

"It'll be our base. We need the flatbottom to get in shaller. *You!* Y'ont me to blow this little gal's head off? Getcher ass out here where I can see you!"

There was no movement on the sailboat, no noise. Neesay was disappointed in Rodrigue for cowering in there like that—and yet prayed he continued to do so. Surely the man with the gun would shoot the instant he appeared.

He twisted her arm again, and smiled at her. He had little teeth, or they looked little in his puffy blond face. "Ah'm gonna fuck you 'til you split," he said in a confidential tone.

Suddenly his expression changed, distorted—his head actually changed shape and his eyeballs bulged grotesquely. Neesay realized that the shock she felt was part noise. It was as though the man had flown away. Her ears were ringing. She never even heard the second shot, only the sound of the other man smashing into the cabin. She looked in horror at the pool of rich red blood spreading from the misshapen head of the first man, lying on the deck.

Rodrigue was in the water on the other side of the men's aluminum boat, a big black pistol in his hand. He pulled himself around the front of the aluminum boat to the back of his own, where the motors were. He reached over and put the gun in the boat, and then climbed in over the back. His face showed the effort of pulling himself up, and that was all. It was as though he had only gone for a swim.

"Johnny . . ." she said, feeling suddenly weak. The muscles in her thighs quivered.

"Sit down, Neesay," he said roughly. "Before you fall down."

Her head was spinning. She took his advice, sitting back by the motors and staring at the Johnson Space Center, rising castlelike from the flood.

Rodrigue was already back on the sailboat. He threw the tarp that he was going to cover the body with back down into the *Queen*—so much for niceties—then shoved the drowned man's body through the ropes around the edge of the boat. He was a very old man or looked it, his face white, wrinkled, and puffy. She found it hard to believe he had ever been alive.

She rose to help in spite of herself.

"Let him fall, Neesay," said Rodrigue. "I'll get him if he goes in the water."

Curiously, the drowned man was wearing bright yellow shoes.

In the next horrible moment, she recognized Cordell Pritchett. She didn't actually *recognize* him—couldn't see humanity, let alone an individual in that wadded gray mass—but somehow knew—put Weizman's cruel little puzzle together.

And in the moment following, the body bent backward over the edge of the sailboat and groaned, and with it came death's putrid breath. Neesay reeled and heaved vomit into the men's little green boat.

Rodrigue lowered the other motor into the water and started them both. He puzzled over the shotgun for a second, then without warning blasted it down into the men's boat. Neesay saw black water bubbling through a ragged hole the size of a coffee can in the floor, mixing with the vomit. Rodrigue threw the gun into the little boat, and with his foot shoved them away from Weizman's yacht.

She had to hang on as their boat suddenly leapt up and was going fast—so fast. Rodrigue was inside at the wheel. His face frightened her. But she didn't want to be far from him, either. She stood in the cabin and hung on.

He looked around rapidly, side to side, and gritted his teeth. In a moment, he breathed a sigh and slowed the boat. Neesay realized they were back in the lake—or where the lake used to be before the whole world became a lake.

Rodrigue shut off one motor and raised it, and finally stopped the boat.

"We didn't have more than a few inches to spare getting back out of there," he said distractedly. "Water's going down fast."

He arranged the three bodies side by side on the deck as though they were a cargo of mahogany from the jungle. He sloshed them down with a bucket. The blood thinned and then ran off the deck like watercolor. Finally, he covered the bodies with the tarp. Then he started up again.

Other boats were moving about, most of them slowly like they were. One, in a small green boat just like the one Rodrigue sank, was zipping noisily through the remains of an apartment complex.

"Idiot," commented Rodrigue.

To the east, the bay and the lake intermingled between the ruins of buildings and boats. The high bridge was a useless arch—and not nearly so high anymore. Rodrigue switched on a machine that drew a picture of the bottom, and he followed a winding course toward the bridge. There, the water ran like a river, with a sucking noise.

Far out in the bay, with only tiny landmarks dotting the horizon, Rodrigue unceremoniously dumped the bodies of the two looters into the muddy water. But then he covered Pritchett's body back up.

"What are you going to do with him?" asked Neesay. Obviously Weizman had hired him merely to remove the body from his boat—and for obvious reasons.

"I don't know," said Rodrigue. "I can't just dump him like that. He probably doesn't deserve it."

"What are *we* going to do, Johnny?" She felt tears streaming down her cheeks and she was embarrassed. She turned away.

Rodrigue held her briefly, but without the tenderness of the night. "This is just God's way of hosing us down a little," he said.

He mixed them both a rum drink, and set out toward the

south, toward Galveston Island, puttering along on both engines now but slowly, almost leisurely.

They spotted a roof and for a moment it put Rodrigue in a mild state of panic. He pulled out a map and compared it to readings from another of his machines. It was so perfectly level, it looked as though there was a building under it, and Rodrigue feared they had wandered back over flooded land. But it turned out to be just a roof, floating. He nudged the boat alongside and swung his leg over, testing the buoyancy with his foot.

"What are you going to do?" asked Neesay.

"Lay our friend out in state," he said.

Moving gingerly, he spread the tarp out on the roof, pulled Pritchett's body onto it, and, with the hands crossed over the chest, wrapped it securely. He came back to the boat with one of Pritchett's yellow shoes. Whatever Creole ritual *that* was, Neesay decided to ignore it.

"Where are we?" she asked.

He unrolled the map again and pointed to a place where two points of land pinched a body of water—Galveston Bay, she assumed—like the waist of an hourglass. But there were no points of land visible.

"We'd better stay out here tonight. Be safer. I was going to try to get down to the island, but I can see right now there's no point. Can't be much left down there."

There was a new hardness in his face she had never seen before.

"Hungry?" he asked. "I've got some sardines and crackers aboard."

The sardines were packed in mustard and were really quite delicious.

The rum helped, too, although she soon had had enough of it. Rodrigue hadn't, however. They sat on the deck in lawn chairs, with their feet up on the side of the boat, watching the sunset as though they were on vacation.

She finally realized what was so eerie about the scene: no lights. The land was just a black smudge against the purple sky. There weren't even car headlights—nothing.

"It's horrible," she said, suddenly choking back a sob.

"Oh? I thought it would've reminded you of home."

She didn't look at him, but she imagined the evil grin he had when he was teasing.

"Yes, you *yanquis* like the blackness of the jungle," she said bitterly. "We, on the other hand, like lots and lots of lights."

"Yeah," he laughed sadly. "*Pero*, it's like a candle in the wind, eh? Hard, hard, hard to keep lit."

This was the Johnny of old who had so often infuriated her with his *que sera sera* attitude. He could still get to her, even though her own attitude had changed diametrically. As a teenager, she had been a devout Communist. Now, she thought with gritty satisfaction, she could truly be described as a militant capitalist.

"I think it's quite the other way around, Johnny. I think the lights are inevitable."

"Ah, Neesay. You've joined the rat race."

"Yes, and so have you, I see."

"Only to keep from being run over by it," he said angrily. "Can't depend on you fucking Communists to keep things on an even keel anymore."

She shrugged. "Adolescence. Not just me. World adolescence."

"I'd not trash Old Man Marx too soon if I were you, Neesay. There's gotta be something more than just buying and building."

He got up and poured himself another drink.

"Did you go to college, Johnny?" She was beginning to wonder whether she knew him as well as she thought. Surely he hadn't read Marx in the oil fields.

He sat down again, stirring his drink with a finger and smiling. "I went to LSU once. To pick up a date in the girls' dorm. Didn't seem to have clouded my thinking any, though. Guess I wasn't there long enough—five, ten minutes."

"I didn't mean any—"

"Look, Professor, college isn't the only place where it's possible to read history. Did you know that Jean Lafitte gave aid and succor to Karl Marx? You didn't know that, did you?"

"I read somewhere how he supposedly helped Bolívar, but—"

"Piracy has gotten a bad name in this century, and I think

it's probably because of the practices of so-called legitimate businessmen. The old pirate strongholds—like the one right down there on Galveston in the 1820s—they were socialist societies. Did you know that?"

"Well—"

"My ancestors were pirates," he said proudly. "In the Caribbean. They raided the Spanish treasure fleets. The Spanish stole from the Indians, and they stole from the Spanish. From each according to his ability, to each according to his need."

"You're no socialist, Johnny. You know where you would be happiest? In a tribe."

"A tribe! I like it."

"A tribe. Totally egalitarian. Unfortunately, it's just a little outmoded."

"Hey, don't be too sure. I can show you places in Belize and Guatemala where there used to be cities—*big* cities. Lotsa lights. Now there's nothing there but jungle. And a few happy, *supremely* non-fucking-industrious Indians."

Neesay laughed. She had thought he was baiting her, while all along he was just drunk.

19

Over in Building 30, Joe Bain walked into the branch chief's office. He was haggard, red-eyed, and solemn.

"That's it," he said. "Nothing."

The branch chief sat up on a couch where he had been grabbing a nap. "Nothing?" He rubbed his eyes.

Bain was nearly in tears from fatigue. "We went through all three NOMs and every single chip performed according to specs."

"Unbelievable," said the branch chief, blinking. "What on earth is happening?"

"We've lost, is what's happening. We have *got* to switch MCC to Goddard for safety's sake."

The branch chief stood and walked over to an impromptu coffee mess atop a file cabinet, an electric teapot, jar of instant coffee, cup and spoon on a paper towel.

"That might not be possible," he said.

"Why not? Didn't Charlie get through?"

Charlie was a NASA security guard, an affable outdoorsman with a high four-wheel-drive pickup truck and an aluminum johnboat jutting perennially from the tailgate. He had volunteered to carry the new GN&C program across the flooded terrain to Ellington Field, the decommissioned air force base where the JSC aircraft were based.

The planes had all been evacuated to Andrews Air Force Base, which was just down the Beltway from Goddard. But once contact with the outside world was established, it would be a simple matter for Andrews to send one of the supersonic T-38 jet trainers down to pick up the software and fly it back.

Straight overland, Ellington was about five miles from JSC. There was a cluster of homes, condos, and office buildings straddling Bay Area Boulevard, immediately north of the Space Center. The rest of the way was undeveloped land, now either flooded or too boggy for even Charlie's four-wheel drive. God only knew what obstacles lay in the way.

The plan had been for Charlie to drive to a small creek called Horsepen Bayou, which drained the prairie on which Ellington was built, coursed just north of JSC, and emptied into Armand Bayou. Now, of course, Horsepen Bayou was much larger, much nearer. He would launch his small outboard-driven boat and try to follow the course of the bayou onto the old air base. He would abandon his boat and proceed on foot, if need be, to rendezvous with the T-38.

"He got through, all right," said the branch chief wearily. "He's been in radio contact the whole time. Said it was a nightmarish trip—debris blocking the way, bodies everywhere. . . . He was even chased by looters at one point. But he made it. The plane wouldn't."

"What?"

The teapot hissed and the branch chief poured steaming water into his cup. "Coffee?"

"No, I don't want any coffee. Why wouldn't the plane make it?"

He was angry beyond civility now.

"The runway at Ellington has drained off but Charlie said about half of Clear Lake City is strewn across it. I'm talking about *houses*, Joe. Vehicles, billboards, fences, you name it. We've commandeered some National Guardsmen to clean it off, but they were all busy gathering up the bodies along the Gulf Freeway."

"Oh for God's *sake!*" yelled Bain in a rare burst of blasphemy. "Those people are *dead!* Let's worry about the crew!"

"Yes, yes, but you have to understand that you can't just pick up a phone and call the right person to explain that to. Messages had to be radioed and relayed and lines of authority are unclear, to say the least. All that has taken time. Yes, the Guard has been diverted. But they can't get any heavy equipment in there. They're having to dismantle houses and move overturned cars essentially by hand. Charlie said he doesn't see how they'll get it done in a week."

Bain sank to the couch. "Oh my God," he moaned.

The branch chief stirred his coffee. "We've still got a little time, Joe. And if worse comes to worst, the crew can always reset the IMUs with the optical sight. I want you to try to get some sleep. You're no good to me like this."

"Sleep?" Bain looked up, bleary-eyed. "How can I sleep?"

The branch chief opened his desk drawer and pulled out a bottle of pills. "Take one of these. There's something we're overlooking, Joe. I need you to be able to think."

Joe nodded glumly and took the pill. He felt like taking the whole bottle.

20

The quiet shuffle of footsteps in the stairwell woke Seidenhaur as abruptly as if it had been a stampede. It was more ominous—someone—more than one—approaching with stealth.

It was still dark. Seidenhaur had been nodding off, on his feet, leaning against the wall beside the door to the stairway. Wilson was at the other end, clutching a nightstick fashioned out of a broom handle. All the guards had been issued them, including Seidenhaur. He had thought it best to keep his pistol out of sight.

Now he drew it, resisting the urge to thumb back the hammer. Controlled double-action fire was what was called for in combat, especially at close quarters. But this was all academic. He wasn't going to shoot anyone. All he'd have to do is wave the pistol and whoever it was would be gone.

Seidenhaur was not prepared to shoot anyone. He had finished near the top at a good law school and he had his eye on politics. The FBI was like prep school for entry-level Republican candidates. Meanwhile, he had been chasing white-collar criminals. They usually had good lawyers but no weapons.

The footsteps grew louder, just on the other side of the door, which did not lock. Seidenhaur couldn't decide what to do—try to hold the door closed, or just stand there calmly and poke the revolver into the face of the first man coming in? But it was such a small revolver, really. A Smith & Wesson Chief's Special .38, a five-shot snub-nose revolver. It wasn't as if he were Dirty Harry.

By the time he made up his mind, it was too late. The door opened against him, and feeling resistance, the intruders immediately shoved it open, knocking Seidenhaur on his butt. They swarmed in, looming black silhouettes, panting and smelling of beer. One kicked him painfully on the inner thigh—not kicked, stomped. They were raising their feet and stomping down on him.

The muzzle blast blinded him for an instant, and the explosion rang in his ear. "Jesus God!" he heard the man say, almost a gurgle. Now the footsteps sounded like bat wings, fading down the stairwell, curses echoing up.

Wilson was kneeling by his side. He was wearing a too-tight pair of coveralls, the kind old men buy at Sears.

"You hurt?" he demanded, huffing. It almost sounded like an accusation. Then the hall was full of people, some waving flashlights.

Seidenhaur sat up. His legs were on fire where the intruders had stomped him. "I'm all right," he said. "Check on him."

"Deader than hell," said someone nearby.

"Good!" said someone else. "Maybe it'll put a stop to this kinda shit."

"You!" barked Wilson, singling out the man who had just spoken. "Run up and tell the Colonel what happened. Tell him to pass the word down to be on the lookout."

The man nodded curtly and worked his way past the crowd.

"A couple of you men watch that other door. The rest of you get back in your rooms. They might be back and they're probably armed."

The crowd began to disperse rapidly.

"Hey, you with the flashlight," called Wilson in a low voice. "Come hold it on this guy a minute."

In the wavering beam of the flashlight, Wilson and Seidenhaur checked out the dead man. He was not armed. He was white, young—maybe just a teenager—and he wore expensive casual clothing, the kind a kid might wear to a mall. Wilson went through his pockets, examining, then handing the items one by one to Seidenhaur.

According to the driver's license, he was twenty-two years old, a resident of Bellaire, a suburb of Houston, and he was supposed to wear glasses when he drove. Either he had lost them or he was wearing contact lenses.

Any damage to his corneas that might result if he was still wearing contacts no longer mattered.

The young man's pockets also yielded some jewelry—an expensive wristwatch, three diamond rings, an ugly brooch with huge stones the FBI men couldn't identify—and quite a lot of soggy cash. Apparently the gang had been on a robbery binge.

In the wallet was a University of Houston student ID card.

"College kids on a lark?" Seidenhaur said incredulously.

"Things like this turn people into animals," said Wilson. "Let's get him down to the morgue, then start circulating his driver's license—hell, just in case he was a guest."

They paused on one of the lower floors to rest and listen to a radio report in the hallway. Martial law had been declared and National Guard units from Louisiana and Mississippi had been deployed by helicopter to keep order. More were on the way with equipment to start the cleanup.

The water had receded completely from the lobby, leaving drifts of sticky gumbo mud and debris. The sweet putrid air in Lakeview Manor made them gag. Buzzing flies made their fresh crawl. They dumped the body on the muddy floor and retreated.

"Jeez, we're gonna have to get some lime or something somewhere," said Seidenhaur, wiping his eyes.

He felt like a criminal himself. Had he absolutely *needed* to kill that boy? It was clearly self-defense, but the kid was unarmed. The feet of a half a dozen college kids don't carry the weight of one pistol, or even a length of pipe. He wondered how it would look on his record.

Three men approached from the lobby, all smiles. "Way to go," said one of them. He playfully socked Seidenhaur on the arm.

"We got the rest of 'em," said another man, nodding smugly.

"Got them? Where?" demanded Wilson.

"The Colonel's interrogating them now," said the first man. "Got their boat, too."

"Boat?" said Wilson, a grin spreading across his red puffy face. He snapped his fingers. "Sure, a *boat!* Rodrigue has gone in a boat!" said Wilson. "Probably Eunice Cara, too. I'd bet money on it. That's why they're not turning up anywhere."

"Where'd Rodrigue get a boat?"

"Where'd *that* guy get a boat?" Wilson cocked his head back down the hall toward the temporary resting place of the young looter.

"But where would he go?"

"Hell, I don't know—let's go see."

Wilson's grin looked almost demented to Seidenhaur. He was worried about his partner's apparent obsession with this Rodrigue character. They had already made an illegal wiretap, and now here they were with nothing but a Jewish thug between them and anarchy. Was Wilson losing it?

"What are you thinking?" Seidenhaur asked.

Wilson looked at the other man. "Where's this boat you're talking about?"

The man seemed uncertain. "I dunno. I gotta check this out with the Colonel."

"Fuck the Colonel!" barked Wilson.

Simultaneously, Seidenhaur whipped out his ID holder and flipped it open in the men's faces.

The three vigilantes looked at each other and shrugged.

"Okay," said one.

Two of them led the FBI agents through the lobby and out to the east parking lot, while the third slipped away, undoubtedly to inform the Colonel.

The sun had risen like a heat lamp. It smelled like rotten cabbage outside. At the bottom of the cement steps that led down to the devastated marina, a black speedboat with a hull like a dagger and the chrome engine bristling with exhaust pipes basked in the admiration of another group of men.

"You had better move this pretty soon or it's going to be sitting on mud," one of the onlookers called up.

"Yeah, we're going to move it right now," said Wilson. "Any of you men from around here?"

"Born and raised," said the man who had just spoken. He was a well-fed fifty or so, wearing yachting whites and an expensive chronograph on his wrist.

"Good. You want to come along with us? We're federal agents in pursuit of a fugitive. I can't force you, of course, but—"

"Be happy to," said the man. "I'm Dr. Perkins. George Perkins." He offered his hand. "Just need to run up and tell the wife. Be right back." He hurried up the muddy stairs, nearly slipping once.

"Now hold on a minute," said one man, squaring himself up to Wilson. He was wearing an outdoorsman's red plaid shirt. Seidenhaur remembered him from the confrontation over the woman.

"This here boat rightly belongs to the hotel defenses, not to some wild-goose chase."

The others murmured in sympathy.

"What's your name?" demanded Wilson. That was how you dealt with a mob, by focusing on the key individuals.

"What difference does that make?" His face was coloring and he was doing a nervous little dance on the steps. "Point is, first things ought to be taken care of first!"

Another man moved in behind him, then another. He was a little guy but a roughneck, Seidenhaur could tell, the kind who smoked unfiltered Camels and had a snake or a dagger tattooed on his scrawny bicep. The way he was dancing around, it looked as if he was about to take a poke at Wilson, just on principle. Seidenhaur steeled himself to jump in.

"Okay, okay," said Wilson, both hands up. He eyed the boat quickly—it was a hot-rod speedboat with four padded deep seats. "We'll need help in case there's trouble. You look pretty handy—you up to it?"

"You fuckin-A," said the red-shirted man with angry satisfaction. He hopped into the boat and started doping out the controls.

When the doctor arrived, the four of them pulled away, the angry little man at the wheel.

"He might've gone to South Shore Harbour," the doctor yelled over the rumbling of the souped-up V-8 inboard.

"They're bound to be in better shape than we are, being over on that weather shore."

Riding left front, Wilson, with a patronizing flourish of his hand, invited the helmsman to head for the other hotel. The little man, missing the sarcasm, replied with a fighter pilot's upraised thumb.

But a small fireboat was standing in the narrow entrance to the other marina, blocking their way. The two men aboard wore shorts and T-shirts and police-style pistol belts.

"The harbor's closed," one of them said through an electronic bullhorn.

"FBI!" yelled Seidenhaur.

"I don't care if you're the fucking Texas Rangers," said the bullhorn. "The harbor's closed."

Seidenhaur started to argue, but Wilson stopped him.

"He's worn out," the older agent whispered. "Tired people don't always think straight. Let's not push him."

Wilson turned to the driver. "Ease forward."

"Stand off!" said the bullhorn. One of the men on the fireboat trained the water nozzle at them as though it were a machine gun.

"We're chasing a fugitive," yelled Wilson. "Has anyone come in here since the storm?"

"Not since the water's gone down." Some commiseration, finally, in the voice. "We've had our share of looters. Killed two of 'em."

The last remark seemed more self-congratulatory than a warning.

Meanwhile, the boats drifted close enough for normal conversation.

"We're looking for a big one-eyed fellow named John Rodrigue," said Wilson.

"Rodrigue? What the fuck's Rod done?" The two men were suddenly hostile again.

"Nothing! Nothing!" Wilson threw his hands down disgustedly. "He's just a material witness, that's all! Now, have you seen him?"

The men on the fireboat shook their heads and shrugged at each other.

"Well, tell him to check in with the nearest office of the FBI when you see him," said Wilson sarcastically. "Go, driver!"

Sitting in the back, Seidenhaur laughed until tears flowed. And then he had an embarrassing time stopping the tears.

21

"Uh, *Columbia*," said CAPCOM, bored as always.

"Standing by," responded Alicia the same way.

"Uh, we're go on the COAS shots."

"Thank you, Houston."

Marsha was relieved. She was tired of Houston screwing around with the computers. Well, now they had decided they weren't going to fix it that way, and they had given the crew the go-ahead to reset the IMUs using the optical-alignment sight. It was just a little matter of them getting home alive.

They were all relieved, but nobody dared show it. Without comment, Pilot Betty Kim flew back to where the telescopelike COAS was mounted in the overhead observation window of the aft flight deck.

Marsha handed her the star chart, then shrank back to give the pilot room to scan the spangled darkness through the window. Betty found the star she was looking for, and using the aft controls, she rolled the orbiter's broad back toward it. Squinting through the sight, she fine-tuned the spacecraft's attitude with brief hissing squirts through the vernier thrusters.

When the star was centered in the sight's cross hairs, Betty would hit a button labeled ATT REF—attitude reference—and the position of all three IMUs relative to the location of the star, already programmed in the software, would be electronically logged. She could, and probably would, try again until she was certain she had gotten a dead-solid fix on the star, and then she would enter the fix into the computer program.

A second known star between 60 and 120 degrees from the first would be selected and the process repeated. It was basic celestial navigation, the way the ancients found their way around the globe before computers and radio beams and even compasses.

Marsha found herself smiling as Betty stroked the verniers, neck craned, squinting upward through the sight. This was so easy, so practiced, so *human*.

Finally, Betty pressed the ATT REF button, and sent the fix straight through to the computer. She was that sure.

"Un-uh," said Alicia from the commander's seat, studying the array of instruments before her. Simultaneously, the error light flickered on the aft control panel.

"Damn," muttered Betty. "That was a good one."

"Try again," said Alicia.

"That *was* a good one."

"Try again."

"We're showing a reject down here, *Columbia*," said CAPCOM. MCC's capacity to read the orbiter's telemetry had not been impaired.

"Roger, Houston," droned Alicia.

Betty shot the star again—more hesitantly this time, logging three fixes before sending the final one into the computer. Again the computer rejected the information.

"Uh, stand by, *Columbia*. We're going to look at it on this end." CAPCOM's voice was flat and calm.

It infuriated Marsha. What *was* this shit? her mind screamed. If we don't get a fix, we're going to die, and everybody's goddamn *bored* with the situation!

Betty gazed at the stars almost dreamily. Alicia stared at the flight-deck instruments. The other two astronauts looked up from the middeck with arched eyebrows, only mildly interested.

But what was she herself doing? Marsha thought. Hovering next to Betty, with a face just as blank as the rest. They were all frightened—too frightened to show it.

CAPCOM's voice was startling: "*Columbia,* we need you to move the COAS to the commander's station for de-orbit."

"We're aborting the IMU reset?"

"That's affirmative."

Alicia was silent for a long while.

"That's a roger, Houston," she said finally.

Whatever was wrong with the computers was preventing them from resetting the IMUs. The only cure was to upload new GN&C software, which only JSC had but only Goddard could do. Some effort was under way to physically transport the software up to Goddard, the astronauts learned, but all of southeastern Texas was a disaster area.

The orbiter would have to be turned around and flying tail-first for the de-orbit burn, then rolled nose-forward as it plummeted a hundred miles. Somebody at JSC was busy trying to come up with the star that would offer Alicia the proper bearing for a survivable descent.

She was going to have to fly it by the seat of her pants, like some World War II pilot nursing a riddled B-17 back to England—except instead of clearing the hedges at the end of the runway, they had to worry about entering the atmosphere at 16,000 miles an hour. Too much pitch would create too much friction and the shuttle would burn up. Too little pitch and the shuttle would retain too much speed. And burn up.

22

"Like to open this baby up," said the man with the red lumberjack shirt.

The doctor leaned forward hurriedly. "Don't recommend it. Too much garbage in the water. Mess up your prop."

The rakish black speedboat was puttering slowly across the lake. Wilson, riding in front next to the red-shirted driver, was astounded by the devastation he saw. One pile of debris included something that looked like a body, but he ignored it. He quit examining flotsam so closely after that. Even things like sofas and chairs where people used to sit were disconcerting to see. Better that it remain all featureless crap.

"Want to take a look out in the bay?" suggested the doctor. "If he's running away, there's a good chance he's floating around out there with a crippled propeller by now. What kind of boat's he in?"

Wilson turned and looked at the doctor. "It's a big white outboard, looks a little like a shrimp boat with the cabin. How do we get out there?"

"Very carefully," said the doctor.

The angry little helmsman didn't like being told how to drive, but after he nearly nosed the boat into a row of barely submerged pilings, the remnants of somebody's boat house, he started taking the doctor's advice. In the channel, a vicious current grabbed them and flushed them into a swirling raft of stinking flotsam that spread out slowly on the broad expanse of liquid mud. They had to put the engine in neutral and clear a path using a board they picked up as a paddle.

Behind them, black skeletons of trees and buildings rose from the gray earth. There were no leaves on the trees and all the grass was covered with mud. Flecks of color had no shape and no dominance, just as you'd expect if the pieces from a thousand jigsaw puzzles were scattered over a plowed field.

Ahead was a vast sea of water the color of coffee with milk, dotted with darker clumps of odd shapes. No land could be seen on the horizon.

"There!" said Seidenhaur, pointing.

Something glinted in the hazy sunshine, flashing white, tinged with blue. It was a boat, all right—ambling their way, it seemed.

"Pick up the pace a little," Wilson ordered.

"Not too much," the doctor cautioned from the backseat.

Two men were in the other boat. It was long and low like their own but with a huge outboard engine on the back. Breaking the sleek silhouette front and back were what looked like stadium seats on thin pedestals. Wilson recognized it immediately—it was a bass boat, designed for high-powered fishing on large inland lakes. The thing on the nose that looked like a torpedo tube was an electric auxiliary motor in the stored position. The anglers sat on the high seats and used the electric motor to position the boat while they fished.

The outboard engine was probably two hundred horsepower or more, Wilson knew. It would be fast, if they decided to run for it—but not fast enough.

But the boat didn't run. It edged closer to them. When it was near enough for Wilson to see the two men plainly—a couple of rednecks with big belt buckles and plastic-mesh ball caps—it finally stopped. The men in the blue boat talked it over. Their boat glittered like tinsel in the veiled sunlight. Then they began to move in again, all smiles.

"Don't wait for them," Wilson warned Seidenhaur out the side of his mouth. He grinned back.

"Hi there!" he called.

"Wachoo boys doin' out here?" said one of the men. He stepped forward, moving sideways like a crab, and sat on the pedestal seat. His eyes swept the commandeered speedboat appreciatively.

The other man remained at the wheel, hunkered behind a low console.

"FBI!" yelled Seidenhaur, whipping out his revolver. "Get your hands up! Get your hands up!"

"Move in! Move in!" Wilson was urgently whispering to the little man in the red shirt.

The two men were frozen in indecision, jaws slack.

"Get 'em up or you're a dead man," Seidenhaur said, looking at the hunkered driver. The man quickly complied, followed almost instantly by the man on the bow.

"Good move," said Wilson. "You, up front—turn around!"

"I got my hands up, man!" the man said.

"Yeah, yeah, *move!*"

In his pants at the back was a huge blued pistol with the distinctive wild West curve to the handle. The boats bumped together and Wilson stepped uneasily onto the high carpeted deck of the other. He jerked the pistol out of the man's pants, cocked it, and pointed it at the man at the wheel.

"Back by the motor. Do *not* lower your hands."

The man stumbled and a short rifle fell at his feet. It was a western-style lever-action gun. The man kept his eyes on Wilson as he stepped onto the casting deck aft, beside the other pedestal seat.

"Looks like we've got a thirty-thirty carbine down there," Wilson called back to Seidenhaur. "This one's a damn forty-four magnum!" It felt good to be armed again, even if it was a cumbersome hog-leg right out of Tombstone Territory.

With Seidenhaur covering them, Wilson tied the men's hands behind them with some rope he found in the bass boat. He made them both kneel on the back deck, facing the outboard, while he searched their boat. The doctor leaned over the side, holding the boats together.

In a long compartment intended for storing fishing rods, Wilson found a damp grocery bag with objects in it. He lifted it to the deck, careful to keep from tearing it. He reached in and gathered several wallets. Next, he pulled out a watch, then another. He peeked in to see whether there were any more wallets—which would aid in identifying victims—and saw the unmistakable form of a human finger.

At first, he thought it was just rubber, a gag finger—he *hoped* that's what it was, but he knew better. With nausea spreading from his gut and tightening his jaw, he picked it up and examined it. An engagement ring with a decent rock was the reason it was in the bag. The cut was clean just below the ring, but the bone, having been popped loose at the knuckle, protruded nastily. The nail was polished, manicured, while the finger itself was shriveled and white. Wilson set it on the deck beside the wallets and hurled himself at the stern. He slammed the two looters' heads together and began pummeling them, viciously punching the tops of their heads.

"Roy! Quit that! Roy! Roy!" Seidenhaur scrambled to get into the other boat.

Wilson's mind said quit but his fist kept pounding. Finally, Seidenhaur pulled him away. The two looters were sobbing and cursing.

"What the hell got into you!" demanded Seidenhaur.

The doctor and the red-shirted man looked on unbelievingly.

Wilson showed Seidenhaur the finger. Seidenhaur looked at it for a long minute and then lurched to the side of the boat to vomit.

In the bag were more wallets and more jewelry—and something that looked like a kid's computer game in a plastic bag. Wilson puzzled over it a second and then tossed it down.

After he had rinsed his face in muddy bay water, Seidenhaur turned around and looked at the objects coming out of the grocery bag. He picked up the large object in the plastic bag curiously.

"Shit!" he said. "You know what this is?"

"Tell me," said Wilson, in no mood for guessing games.

"It's an electronic key used to scramble and unscramble computer data."

"You sure? Looks like a kid's game to me."

"No, no. Look, it has a serial number on it. For security purposes. Hell, they use them at NASA to access DOD telemetry. Probably standard procedure on all flights, for that matter."

"Where'd you get that?" Wilson demanded of one of the looters. He jerked him around by the hair.

"Found it," said the looter, grimacing. "Body."

"Way down yonder," said the other. "Laying up on a roof, all wrapped up in a tarp. Had on one yaller shoe."

"On a roof? Was he shot or something?"

"Nah, he was drowned."

"But he'd been bonked on the back of the head," interjected the other man, anxious to be helpful. "Remember, Billy? Back of his head was all fucked up."

"Been in the water, though. You could tell that," said the first looter. "Hey! He had a NASA badge in his pocket. Yeah, that was the one."

"Where is it? The badge!"

"Shit, what was we gonna do with that? I figured that other thing was a Nintendo game or something my kids could play with."

"Which one is his wallet?"

"Fuck'f *I* know!"

"You shitheads are new at robbing the dead, aren't you?" Wilson said disgustedly.

Seidenhaur carefully peeled the soggy wallets apart and excised the stiff plastic-coated driver's licenses.

"Here he is: Cordell M. Pritchett."

"Pritchett, Pritchett . . ."

"He's on her list."

It was a long list of NASA employees interviewed in depth by Eunice Cara over the past year and a half.

"Oh, and financial problems, too, right?" remembered Wilson. "The one with the bicycle shop?"

"That's the one."

"Wonder what the hell he was doing with—"

"*My God!*" Seidenhaur looked as if he'd been shot.

"What?" demanded Wilson.

"Roy, this could be the key to the shuttle problem!"

"What are you talking about?"

The doctor and the red-shirted man darted puzzled looks at each other.

"Shit! Don't you see? They were *sabotaging* the shuttle! That's their game. It's a *computer* problem they've got.

Whoever she's working for, for whatever reason God only knows—but that has to be it!"

"God*damn!*" said Wilson, considering it. What the hell would a NASA computer expert be doing on a rooftop halfway to Galveston? Head bashed in. Rodrigue on the loose.

Sure! They had sucked Pritchett in the way they always do, probably with a little harmless industrial espionage. He was vulnerable; he needed money. Then they had him by the nuts, could blackmail him into bigger and bigger crimes. But when he realized what the game really was, he balked, and he had to be taken care of. So they called in Rodrigue.

But why hadn't Rodrigue taken the key? And why had he wrapped the body in a tarp? Why not just dump it in the water with all the others? Strip it of ID at the very least.

There was no second-guessing Rodrigue. God only knew what kind of motives and superstitions drove a man like that—goddamned voodoo, maybe. He came from that kind of people. Son of a bitch was a savage.

"We've got to get this key back to NASA, Roy!" said Seidenhaur. "Maybe it'll tell them where the problem is."

Wilson looked at the mean-faced little man in the lumberjack shirt. "If I tie these shitheads up where they can't get free, would you be afraid to drive this boat back to the hotel?" His phrasing was guaranteed to get rid of the nasty little fart.

The red-shirted man snorted derisively. "Be their problem, they get loose," he said.

Wilson believed it. With the man's help, he sat the two looters on the forward deck and tied their hands to the seat pedestal. Then he took the weapons and crossed back over to the speedboat.

"All right, then, you turn them over to Colonel Weizman, okay?"

The red-shirted man flashed the thumbs-up sign again and bumped the throttle forward, gingerly pulling away in the commandeered bass boat. He bumped it up a little more and roared off a hundred rpm shy of planing speed, the bow wagging in the sky and the tied-up looters looking very uncomfortable.

"Not so fast!" yelled the doctor.

It was doubtful the red-shirted man had heard him, but he soon pulled the speed back, if for no other reason than to see over the bow.

"You take over here, Doc," said Wilson. "Take us as close as you can get to the Johnson Space Center."

"Hell, that's probably going to be the Hilton."

"Fast as you can without tearing something up. The lives of those astronauts may be in our hands."

"Don't look now," said the doctor, "but here comes another boat."

Wilson and Seidenhaur squinted in the direction he was pointing.

"Got a cabin," said the doctor. "Looks like—"

"That's Rodrigue's boat," said Wilson. He felt his stomach shifting, a sensation almost like nausea except that it was pleasurable somehow.

"Aw, how can you tell?" asked Seidenhaur skeptically.

"It's a Boston Whaler Frontier," said the doctor, still squinting at the boxy white shape slowly approaching from the east. "Kind of a workboat designed for up in Alaska. Don't see many down here."

"That's right!" said Wilson happily. "We had him under surveillance for a week—it was the only boat like that in Galveston. Let's get him!"

"Wait! What about NASA?"

"What about it?" Wilson's choice was made. Now the rationalization was setting in—but the choice was made first.

"Look," he said. "He's probably got Cara with him. She can tell them what the hell they've done to sabotage the shuttle and why. That's a hell of a lot more valuable than just this electronic key, wouldn't you say?" Sarcasm had crept into his voice.

Seidenhaur sighed. "Let's do it," he said.

"Ease toward him, Doc," said Wilson, taking the front passenger seat. He slid the little rifle forward, muzzle under the foredeck where it wouldn't be seen.

Seidenhaur took the big .44, a better long-range shooter than the short-barreled .38.

The white boat abruptly turned around and headed back the way it had come, but not in any big hurry.

"Full speed!" ordered Wilson.

"That's crazy!" protested the doctor.

"Full *speed!*"

The doctor angrily slammed the throttle down and the speedboat nearly jerked out from under them. It literally flew over the water, the tenuous connection of the prop and rudder and a ridiculously short length of skeg made it feel as though they were balanced on a peak of Jell-O. The wind pulled their faces tight and made tears stream from their slitted eyes. And the white boat was already much closer.

Wilson knew it was crazy. He was making some bad decisions—or at least making them for bad reasons. He consoled himself with the silent promise not to fire until fired upon.

But he wasn't sure he could keep it.

23

Rodrigue was crouched in the stern of the *Haulover Queen*, pistol in hand. The raised starboard engine afforded him a little cover. He watched the rapidly approaching speedboat with disbelief.

"Johnny—!" Neesay squealed. She was in the tiny pilothouse at the wheel, anxiously watching the boat approach through the rear door.

"Stay down, Neesay. Just keep 'er pointed straight and try not to hit anything."

When the boat got close enough, he'd put a shot across her bow—right across her bow and into the black heart of the helmsman if he could. This was war.

Rodrigue was feeling totally alienated. Having to kill again had hardened him—maybe this time for good. It was eerily like Vietnam—the boat, the brown water, the blood. . . .

There had been a time in Nam when he had come dangerously close to enjoying the killing. He hadn't understood the war and had felt trapped between a vicious enemy and callous and sometimes stupid officers. He would've liked to think it was the action, the pure physical exertion, that vented his steam. But, no, there was satisfaction in the killing. Maybe not enjoyment, exactly, but undeniably satisfaction.

The boat was closing rapidly and would soon overtake them. The helmsman chose the *Queen*'s starboard, and

Rodrigue turned to be ready. He spread his knees for stability and let his waist compensate for the slight loping motion of the boat. The passenger up front—a beefy blond who seemed vaguely familiar—was yelling something. Rodrigue took a two-handed grip on the .45 and aimed.

Then the speedboat stopped, suddenly, burying its bow in the flat surface of the bay.

The beefy blond did not stop suddenly, nor did the man in the passenger seat aft. Both flew over the bow with their arms and legs spread, eyes wide, mouths forming O's like a pair of caroling cherubs. Bound to have gotten a good drink, both of them, Rodrigue thought nastily.

He was still chuckling when he went back into the pilothouse—but the blond man troubled him. Where had he seen that man before?

"Did you shoot?" Neesay asked. "I didn't hear anything."

"Nah, they ran over something that killed their engine. Don't know what took 'em so long, actually."

He took the wheel again and circled to the north. They would make another try at getting back to the hotel. Rodrigue was a little worried about Leyton.

24

Weizman sat behind the bar in the top-floor suite, glaring at the two looters. They had been brought in by the sour-faced man in the red plaid shirt now standing behind them, serving as a bailiff.

And Weizman was the judge, his authority unquestioned. For all their vaunted independence, these Americans—even these backward Texans from the surrounding lowlands—they all hungered for order.

It was because there were women here. When the windows first started breaking out in the darkness, and the couples and the families spilled out of the howling rooms, dazed and drenched, the panic arced through the hall like lightning. Men—just men—would've laughed it off, even enjoyed it. But men with women had to protect them, and the panic came from all the way back through humanity, from the first hominid who bared his fangs to protect his mate.

Weizman had stepped into the chaos, speaking calmly to the men, grouping them, promising order. He had had to do it or risk having his spy equipment plundered, maybe even discovered for what it was.

After he had succeeded in organizing the fourteenth floor—and commandeering the entertainment suite for himself, even enlisting men to carry the cased receiver and computers—he would've preferred to blend back into the wall of frightened faces. But by then it was too late. Frightened people on other floors came to him for help. And truth be known, it felt good to take command. Now maybe it would be useful. . . .

"Where was the dead man when you found him?" Weizman demanded.

"He was on a roof way out in the bay," said one of the looters. "He was laid out on his back, with his arms crossed over his chest and everything, just like he was in a coffin."

"One shoe was gone," chirped in the other looter. "Weird shoes. Real bright yaller."

"Yeah, and the back of his head was all boogered up. We seen it when we rolled him over to get at his wallet."

"He was a NASA guy," said the man in the red shirt from the door. "That's what those FBI agents said. They figured he must've found out something about someone sabotaging the space shuttle, and that must've been why he was killed."

"Did they find anything on him? Shall we say important papers or anything?"

"Yeah! Yeah! Something looked like a computer game."

"Actually *we* found it. Billy thought it *was* a computer game. Remember, Billy?"

"But I swear to you that we never killed that man and we don't know nothing about *no* sabotage," said Billy with moist-eyed sincerity.

Weizman only half heard him. He was trying to decide what to do. This was an extremely dangerous situation.

It was starting to make sense now, NASA not being able to fix the problem with the shuttle—it had to have been caused by the intercept device Pritchett had installed in the Mission Control Center!

Perhaps he had wired it incorrectly. Or perhaps the tiny transmitter that relayed the pirated data to his own receiver was causing interference within NASA's equipment.

Like everybody else, Weizman had been getting scraps of the story over the radio news broadcasts they could pick up at night, from stations in Dallas and San Antonio: The shuttle was doomed, spinning out of control. It should appear as a brilliant flicker in the sky over Puerto Rico tomorrow night.

It had been just a freak accident, really, but when those idiot FBI men came roaring back to JSC with Pritchett's crypto-key, sabotage might appear to be an attractive alternative—especially if a convenient scapegoat could be found.

Too bad he couldn't toss them Cara. She had already evoked their suspicion. But all she would do would be to turn and point at him.

Damn Rodrigue, anyway! Why hadn't he dumped Pritchett where the crabs would eat him?

For a moment, Weizman considered going to JSC himself and confessing everything. Immediately—in time to save the astronauts. They would go much easier on him then.

His spy equipment and Pritchett's personal computer were tucked in the bar at his feet. The DAT cassettes were in his pocket. As long as he had those, he could prove he was merely committing industrial espionage, not sabotage. Surely the U.S. State Department would be interested in a Chinese plot to short-circuit the world computer market.

No! Weizman stopped himself, his heart pounding like a man on the ledge of a skyscraper. In prison, even one of the famous American "country clubs," he would never be safe from the Brazilians. The arms peddlers of Brazil were as crafty and ruthless as any Colombian drug lord. They would have to kill him as a matter of honor.

This was no time to panic. Cara was the only one who knew about him, and she didn't know about the intercept device in Building 30. Even if she guessed, she wouldn't say anything. She was just as guilty of spying as he was, having knowingly furnished him with information on NASA employees. Besides, she hated the Americans.

But wait! He almost forgot the telephone repairman who had installed the second device, the one on the utility pole outside Building 30. But that man didn't know his name and probably wouldn't make the connection between bugging a pay phone and the shuttle losing its computers. Weizman had said he was a detective hired by a suspicious wife. It was a quick exchange of cash, a few winks, and no more questions asked. Besides, the man probably had his own troubles about now. Certainly the utility pole wouldn't still be standing after all this.

So the only real problem was the presence of the first device *inside* Building 30, the one that Weizman felt with growing certainty was causing the trouble aboard the shuttle. It was the only thing that could throw suspicion on him.

Those miniature transmitters were of Israeli origin and so, obviously, was he. He hadn't felt he could risk coming here on a phony passport—especially when, if he was checked on, the Government of Israel would identify him only as a retired army officer, with no mention of his brief service in the Mossad.

However, under the present circumstances, that would be enough to throw the spotlight on him. He had to retrieve that device.

But how? With Pritchett dead, who would know where to look? If he could find Cara before the FBI did—he would tell his men to alert him if she came back to the hotel—then perhaps she could thumb through her notebook and come up with another NASA employee to sneak in and—

"Colonel?" the man in the red plaid shirt had apparently been trying to get his attention for some time.

"Yes, yes," said Weizman, momentarily flustered. "What is it?"

"What do you want me to do with 'em?"

"Tie them up with the others," said Weizman with a sudden burst of confidence. Things were not as bleak as they had seemed. In fact, there might even be enough data on the DAT tape to satisfy the Chinese.

"Is that their boat over there?" Weizman asked after the looters were consigned to the group of vigilantes in the hallway. He motioned for the red-shirted man to join him, and together they leaned out the open window, craning to see into the ruined marina. Ahead, the abutting communities of Nassau Bay and Clear Lake were emerging from the flood. It was an ugly sight—wreckage strewn everywhere. And cutting through the middle was the bronze-colored canal that had been NASA Road 1.

"Did you notice how much fuel was left?" Weizman asked.

"Tell you the truth, I didn't," said the red-shirted man. "I can go check."

"Please do. And while you're doing that, you might also make sure it's moored over deep water. There are bound to be a lot of obstacles both in the breakwater and beyond. We don't want the boat becoming grounded on anything when the tide falls, do we?"

Weizman spread his thin lips. "You are our navy now, after all."

The red-shirted man grimaced and rubbed the stubble on his face in embarrassment, or perhaps just false modesty. He turned and left.

Weizman returned to his bar stool. Now, at least, he had a means of searching for Cara if she didn't return to the hotel. Now to plan . . .

Assuming Cara did know another Pritchett, how could she contact him with all the telephones dead? And how to secure the loyalty of yet another NASA engineer? Even Pritchett, who had been so ripe, had required considerable cultivating. Now there was so little time.

Certainly there were others who were also ripe for the picking. Rare was a man in his forties who hadn't seriously compromised himself in one way or another. With her far-ranging interviews and prolonged contact with her subjects, Cara had discovered many chinks in the space agency's security armor.

Such chinks were normally probed very delicately, in the manner of an expert acupuncturist. Now, however, what was needed was the combination of cunning, bravado, and viciousness of a matador's sword thrust. Weizman couldn't expose himself in that manner, and Cara wouldn't be taken seriously. Who . . . ?

Weizman paused to take a deep breath, to calm himself. Now he smiled the thin-lipped smile. Maybe the answer would turn up in the shadow of Eunice Cara, a man who seemed uniquely suited for subterranean tasks in times of chaos.

This man Rodrigue . . .

25

The railroad trestle beneath the Seabrook-Kemah bridge had strained debris from the floodwater pouring out of Clear Lake into the bay. The ancient wooden latticework, still submerged, was obviously clogged with all matter of debris that had been swept down the crooked channel—boards and snapped utility poles and sunken boats and great slabs of asphalt-shingled roofing and all types of signs and probably a fair share of drowned bodies, too, Rodrigue figured. The gumbo-colored water rolled steadily over it like a big Gulf comber. Instead of a surflike roar, though, the noise it made was a loud, eerie sucking.

The old swing bridge was in the open position, leaving a gap in the trestle through which the channel coursed. The gap had attracted its share of debris, but here the water rushed more freely, pouring over the wreckage like a river rapid.

If he could just remove a little of that garbage, Rodrigue thought, he could open the channel—but only temporarily. As the water level fell, more debris would be exposed, until there would be an effective barrier across the exit. Once in, he would be locked in.

Rodrigue was fearful of giving up his mobility—but what, really, was he giving up? True, Galveston Bay opened to the Gulf, which opened to the Atlantic, and so forth and so on. Theoretically he could go to China from here by boat. Rockport would be good enough. . . .

If they could only get some more fuel someplace, they could go down the coast to Rockport, or better yet, Corpus Christi, and get a room with air conditioning and room service. Or they could go up the coast into Louisiana, but that was on the dirty side of the storm. Rodrigue didn't know how far that way the destruction extended.

He was thinking of his father, who ran a supply store for shrimpers in Delcambre, right on the low, marshy Louisiana coast at Vermilion Bay. He wished he could call and check on him, but that, too, would be impossible for quite a while.

But he didn't have any fuel, or hopes of finding any. And everything he owned in the world was back at the Hilton.

So was Leyton—who was probably shacked up with three or four rich sisters whose daddy would send a helicopter to airlift them and their new boyfriend to Palm fucking Springs. Yet the lad seemed almost helpless in some ways and Rodrigue felt responsible for him.

The Blazer was obviously totaled, but the trailer would be all right—maybe require rewiring for the lights and penetrating oil for the winch. As soon as he could get out of here, he'd get a ride to Delcambre, pick up a truck of some kind, and come right back for the boat and his belongings.

Then what?

That was getting too far into the dim future to worry about. The thing to do now was to get back to the hotel. Rodrigue nosed the *Queen* into the muddy bank in the midst of the sunken Vietnamese shrimp boats where the honey barge had been tied. He gave his .45 to Neesay.

"Anybody tries to come aboard, you shoot them right here." He indicated the center of his chest. "Keep shooting until the gun quits, okay?"

He showed her how to take the old navy-issue weapon off safety, and then he climbed ashore.

Highway 146 into Seabrook was washed away in great gaps that Rodrigue had to ford. Down by the intersection with NASA Road 1, dark figures stalked back and forth. As he got closer, he saw the familiar profiles of M-16s propped on their hips. An old two-ton army truck with a canvas canopy was parked off to the side. Diesel, unfortunately.

The guardsmen watched with increased interest as he

approached. He spotted a noncom and walked up to him, eyeing the truck conspiciously the last fifteen yards of the way.

"That thing got a winch on it?"

"Huh?" He was a big, soft-looking man in his thirties, likely a good ol' boy from a small town where the National Guard served as a social fraternity.

"Truck have a winch?" Rodrigue demanded. "We've got to get the channel cleared for the sheriff's boats to start gathering up the bodies."

"Who are you?"

"John Rodrigue. I'm a commercial diver. I'm here to clear the channel but I don't have heavy-enough lifting gear."

"Where'd you come from?" asked the noncom, squinting back down the road as if a parade might appear next.

"My boat's down there in the creek. Where the channel goes through the railroad bridge, it's clogged up with some pretty heavy debris. I can hook onto the bigger pieces for you if you can winch them up—or, hell, just drag 'em up with that truck. Got any kind of wire rope?"

"I'm not supposed to be clearing debris," said the noncom. "We're guarding against looters."

"*Looters?* What the fuck's there to loot around here except mud and wet mattresses? Let's restore goddamn navigation!"

"Ahh, gwan, Sarge," said another Guardsman. "We'll keep the traffic flowing."

The other men guffawed. There wasn't another soul in sight.

"Ain't got no winch," complained the sergeant to his comrades.

"Look, get two of your boys. We'll wind us up some of this cable," said Rodrigue, pointing to the high-tension wires snaking harmlessly across the muddy, cluttered highway. "You drive to the top of the bridge and tie it on the truck. Drop it over; I tie it on a log. You drive off and up she comes, *comprends?*"

From the sergeant's point of view, it must've seemed about that easy. For Rodrigue, it was almost as dangerous as it would've been crossing the trestle during the storm. The level of the water had gone down considerably in the time it had taken him to fetch the Guardsmen and get them set up on the bridge, but it was rushing seaward a lot faster than it had washed inland. It ripped at Rodrigue's legs and tried mightily to drag him down into the logjam as he waded along the submerged trestle out to the channel. If this had been a commercial job, he'd have been in a brass hat and canvas suit, with a team of tenders and a diesel winch to pull him free. Rodrigue did it in his Levi's with a hangover.

One big creosoted utility pole was the key to the puzzle, but there was too much pressure on it and the cable snapped. Rodrigue hung on for dear life and fumed while the Guardsmen made their way back off the bridge for another length of the high-tension wiring.

This time, Rodrigue wasn't so greedy. He made a quick rolling hitch around the leg of a wooden roadside sign and up it went, according to plan. The Guardsmen hauled it over the bridge railing and lowered the cable again. Next came a small section of redwood fence, and then tattered bimini top that had been wrenched from a boat frame and all. The utility pole still wouldn't come up, but it moved enough to dislodge a mass of wreckage that gurgled and sank unceremoniously as it resumed its trip to the bay.

The channel was clear, but Rodrigue knew it wouldn't stay that way long. He let the current rip him from the trestle and swam toward the *Haulover Queen* with all his might. He missed the *Queen*, quivering against the bank, but he snagged a shrimp boat mast not far below it. From there, he was able to work his way ashore and back around to the boat in a fraction of the time it would've taken him to wade to shore on the trestle.

He had to lower both engines for power and control against the flow. He was now risking both props on the garbage still coming down the channel. He trimmed the engines up until his ears told him he could trim no more lest the intakes be deprived of cooling water, then he gritted his teeth and plowed ahead. Debris was hitting the hull with solid thunks he could feel though his feet. The Lowrance X-15 chart recorder was going nuts trying to draw the mess streaking below.

Back on the bridge, the Guardsmen watched them go, small figures with their hands on their hips.

Rodrigue still needed both engines to combat the current in the twisting creek, but he put one in reserve as soon as they emerged onto the lake.

Much of the surrounding land was visible again, scarred, drab, and lifeless. Many large yachts that had been sunk were now exposed, the slick fiberglass shedding the mud and gleaming in the diffused sunlight—a graveyard for dreams, Rodrigue thought.

He picked his way through the mess and tied up outside the hotel breakwater, where he would be sure to have plenty of depth as the water level continued to fall. Also tied there was a blue bass-fishing boat. Rodrigue recognized the type right away—low, with carpeted decks fore and aft almost reaching the gunwales, and gaudy sparkles of metal flake in the gel coat. The outboard on the stern was bigger than one of the *Queen*'s. He didn't remember seeing it here before.

The breakwater was now an obstacle, a tall wooden wall to be scaled. Rodrigue lifted Neesay, then pulled himself up. The walkway on the other side was gone in places, and they had to walk the top of the breakwater itself as if it were a tightrope.

Rodrigue sighed. "Guess I ought to check my messages."

Neesay wearily put her forehead on his shoulder. She seemed to be trying to laugh, but it wasn't coming.

Of all the junk that was in his office, only the filing cabinet was his. His desk was either gone or battered to unrecognizable pieces. New were half of a rowing shell, a Kenmore drier, and a wind turbine from somebody's roof, among the things he could identify. The mud was piled in a drift against the back wall and more objects protruded from it.

"I'm tired, Johnny," said Neesay. "I'd love to lie down in an air-conditioned room."

"You can forget that for a while. I imagine you can even forget a shower. It'll be weeks before utilities are restored."

"Let's go lie down, anyway. I didn't sleep a wink last night."

"Aw, hell, Neesay, I can't leave my boat unattended. Somebody would steal the damn thing. I'll see you safely inside. Swing by my room and check for Leyton, okay? Send him down if you see him."

As they approached the marina-level entrance, a group of men appeared and fanned out in the gloom of the overhanging building. They all held sawed-off broomsticks, and they were slapping them nervously in their palms. "It's the woman," one of them said.

Rodrigue reached for his .45, but then he remembered giving it to Neesay. She had set it down in the boat someplace.

The sensible thing, of course, would've been to surrender peacefully. But he had Neesay to think of. Hurricanes—danger in general—gave some men a double shot of hormones. With law and order temporarily suspended, who knew what their appetites would demand. He was probably in for a hell of a beating, but if he played it right, maybe Neesay could get up the outside stairs and into the hotel where someone else could protect her.

He flicked a glance toward her; she seemed frozen with fear.

"When I act," he said in Spanish, "you run to those other stairs back there. To the hotel. And no looking back."

Rodrigue sucked in a big breath, then kicked off his shoes in two quick motions and crouched in a lethal-looking combat stance. It wasn't karate. It was a bluff he had developed on the tough Louisiana waterfront at a time when people looked at all Vietnam vets as either baby killers or Green Berets with flashbacks. Rodrigue discovered that a one-eyed drunk could hold off a whole barroom full of irate husbands just by kicking off his shoes.

It worked again. The men with the clubs backpedaled cautiously.

"Now just hold on," said one of them. "No reason for anyone to get hurt here. We're not looters or anything."

"Yeah, and you're not out hunting muskrats, either."

"No, no, no. Look, we're on the defense committee. We've been organized to protect the folks here against—"

"*Va!*" barked Rodrigue. Go! it meant in Spanish—and he prayed she would.

Neesay did not disappoint him. She flicked away like a startled deer, dashing up the cement steps.

"*Hey!*" yelled one of the men with the broomsticks.

"Let her go," said another. "She can't go anywhere." He turned his attention back to Rodrigue. "Look, all we wanted to do is take her up to see the Colonel. He just has some questions for her, is all. C'mon up and he'll tell you that himself."

"Who's the Colonel?"

"Retired army man. A trained leader, you know? So he just naturally took charge until we get us some real law in here. We're just good citizens helping to maintain order. Honest."

Rodrigue uncoiled. "Okay," he said.

What was the harm? They were legitimate—*he* was legitimate. . . .

Why did he feel like ripping out their throats?

26

J oe Bain was summoned by the branch chief. It was urgent, the note said. What did that mean? How could anything be more urgent than five brave, intelligent women about to meet instant death?

Or maybe not *instant* death. The horrible lesson of *Challenger* was that human beings were a lot more resilient to an in-flight catastrophe than anyone had suspected—just not resilient enough. There had been serious talk about providing astronauts with a means to end it quickly to avoid suffering, but it had been quietly stamped out as soon as it reached the first political stratum.

Now the five women had nothing to do but wait to die. All five of their cold, information-processing companions on the journey had absolutely refused to help. Without a valid GN&C program, the GPCs simply would not accept realignment data for the IMUs. It was not a problem Bain and his colleagues had considered. Who could've forseen losing all five GPCs in a whack?

The hall outside the branch chief's office was crowded, soldiers in muddy boots mixing with shirt-sleeved NASA workers. On a stretcher on the floor was a man in muddy civilian clothes, his arm in a sling. Bain stopped short when he realized it was one of the FBI agents he had met a few months before. His clothes were tattered and the exposed portions of his skin were covered with bruises and abrasions.

"You men will have to excuse my appearance," the young agent said to no one in particular. "We were thrown from a boat in pursuit of suspects. Then the boat took forever to get back to land—something was wrong with the engine. And now you can't get under the bridge because of the debris. We had to land on the bayfront and hike halfway here before the National Guard picked us up. It has been a hell of a morning."

The agent's voice had a peculiar singsong quality to it. A uniformed soldier, apparently a medic, knelt beside the stretcher and murmured, "Yes, sir. Yes, sir."

In the office, another haggard civilian stood in front of the desk. He turned around as Bain entered—it was the other agent, the big blond named Wilson. However, he didn't show a flicker of recognition. Bain, too, tried to keep his face blank. It wasn't hard—he was starting to feel numb all over.

The branch chief held up a crypto-key, threatened Bain with it as though it were a knife.

"You know whose this is?" he asked angrily.

"Give me the serial number and I can soon find out."

"It's Cory Pritchett's, and he's dead."

"Cory?" Now Bain's mind went numb.

"It looks like he was a saboteur," said Wilson. "There may be more people involved."

"Saboteur?" Now Bain's mind was reeling.

"The FBI has been investigating a damned *spy* ring operating here at JSC," said the branch chief. His tone said that he had just found out—and that he was taking it all very personally.

So was Bain—he had every right to. So Neesay had been using him, after all. Or rather was probably setting him up to be used, since she had never actually asked him to do anything illicit except make love to her over lunch.

So she *was* a spy. But, my God, sabotage . . .

"Sabotage?" said Bain, still incredulous. He knew Pritchett was disgruntled, but he couldn't imagine him killing the astronauts. Astronauts were not considered management—especially not Marsha Janke.

"Is it possible?" the branch chief asked. "Sabotage, I

mean." He gave Bain his look that meant to dispense with protocol and speak the unvarnished truth—as though Bain would be the least bit interested in protocol at a time like this.

"Possible? Yes, of course. Likely, no," said Bain acidly. "I mean, *why?* This isn't a DOD mission. And what would Cory Pritchett have to do with the NOM? He was involved with the downlink, not the uplink."

"Understand that this is not to leave this room," said Wilson solemnly. "We've been investigating the activities of a Venezuelan national who is a known agent of the INPE, the space program of Brazil."

Wilson met Bain's eye for a flicker. Apparently he intended to continue keeping Bain's affair with Neesay confidential—for the time being, at any rate.

"While operating openly as an anthropologist, she has had surreptitious contact with an individual we believe to be a foreign agent," the agent continued. "What country, what their agenda is, we have no idea."

Everybody paused to give the notion an instant's thought. Bain could imagine only one thing: Some computer company was afraid of MurTech's impending breakthrough and sought to prevent it. But was the computer industry so competitive nowadays that businessmen were willing to kill national heroes?

"*Could* the problem in the NOM have been a result of sabotage?" the branch chief asked Bain.

"I suspected a faulty chip, a glitch," Bain said, reviewing it in his own mind. "But we changed out all the circuit boards and still had the problem. Then we tried to isolate the faulty chip, thinking the whole batch—the original and each replacement—was flawed. If we could've found the right one, we could've maybe wired around it. . . ."

He was still wrestling with the idea of sabotage. Bain's analytic powers would carry him only so far and then he was treading in mystery.

"I guess if you were going to sabotage the NOM," Bain said, "you'd want faulty replacement chips, as well. . . ." The thought trailed off.

"But they weren't faulty," said the branch chief.

"Well, they met specs in a simulated prog—" Suddenly he knew what the problem could be—*had* to be.

A radio frequency. A stray radio frequency could affect a specific chip in a specific way. What was a computer chip, anyway, but a crystal? And when they had been tested, they had been taken into a different area, well away from the NOM, so they were no longer near the source of the interference.

Nobody had thought about radio interference because Building 30 was heavily shielded. But if it was sabotage, someone—Pritchett?—could have smuggled a transmitter into the MCC. It had to be someone—like Pritchett—with enough access to the NOM circuitry to find the right frequency that would have the desired effect. . . .

Bain's eyeballs vibrated with excitement.

But how could anyone *program* a glitch to have a specific effect on the orbiter's GPCs? It apparently had jumped from the one GPC doing payload duty to the IMUs—the IMU warning impulse had been the first sign that anything was wrong—and then back into the guidance, navigation, and control program in all the GPCs. It would've taken a genius, and Cory Pritchett was a talented technician, not a genius.

As aerospace technology grew in complexity, the ugly word *glitch* had more use, if less acceptance. Accidents could still happen. But what on earth would've created an accidental source of radio waves? There was nothing in the NOM that hadn't been there during the last twenty-five or so missions—unless Pritchett had placed it there.

Maybe there was a genius out there somewhere who, supplied with schematics and specs for the NOM, could figure a way to reprogram the circuitry—or at least scramble it—via an RF frequency. And maybe Pritchett's only job had been to install it in the cabinet somewhere.

And Neesay's job was to recruit Pritchett. Maybe she didn't even know what she was getting into. . . .

"Do you have a device to scan for electronic signals?" Bain asked Wilson abruptly.

"What, like radio signals?" asked Wilson.

"Precisely. A small radio transmitter."

"Like a bug?" said Wilson. "No, the bureau has people in

Washington who do that. We would use contract people locally."

"Why?" demanded the branch chief.

Bain bit his tongue. He was so confused. He had thought he was through with her, but now his instinct was to protect her. After all, she was only a suspect now. If he could find and eliminate the source of the interference—if that was what it was to begin with—then the problem would be solved and there would be no proof.

Wait! This would make him an accomplice. She hadn't asked *him* to do anything, but this would make it look as though she had—if he got caught. . . .

But all he would be doing is trying to stop the interference. . . .

In secret?

But what could the others do? The branch chief pawing through the NOM would be like a bear doing brain surgery. It had to be done systematically, by someone who knew the NOM—and that, at this point, with NASA's manpower literally scattered to the wind, was nobody but him.

"Do you think Pritchett *bugged* the NOMs?" demanded the branch chief.

"No," said Bain. "I still think it has to be a glitch. It would be tough enough to program a hard chip to do what has happened aboard *Columbia*, but to do it with a radio frequency would be impossible. I merely wanted to see if one of the UARTs was throwing off a stray frequency. I just wanted to try *something*, that's all."

It was amazing how well an honest man could lie when it became necessary. Suddenly he slapped both hands loudly on the branch chief's desk. "We've got to switch to Goddard! It may not be too late!"

The branch chief sneaked a conspiratorial glance at Wilson. The FBI agent was stony.

"The runway at Ellington is still a mess," the branch chief said.

"I've got to get back to work," said Bain crisply. He hurried out of the office.

So that was that. They had given up hope.

Still, maybe he could find it—the odd electronic component

in a bewildering mass of circuitry like the NOM. On paper, it would stand out to him immediately, but in the dark recesses of the steel cabinet . . . ?

Still, he had to try.

27

No one was in sight in the top-floor suite. Rodrigue's two escorts waited patiently just inside the entrance for several long minutes. Finally, one of the men called, "Colonel?"

No answer.

"Colonel?" called the other.

The two men shrugged at each other in the silence. One of them ventured a peek behind the bar—in the event the Colonel had passed out, perhaps. His search carried him into the adjoining bathroom. He came back shaking his head mutely.

"What do we do?" asked the other.

"I don't know, put him in with the rest of them, I suppose."

"If you assholes are talking about me, you'd better go get some help," said Rodrigue hotly. "I'm not about to be 'put' anywhere!"

"Now, look—" said one of the men, taking a martial stance.

Now they were both straddle-legged, slapping their broomsticks in their palms like the shore patrol in Saigon. They were both younger than Rodrigue—middle thirties, he guessed—and had the trim look of joggers or tennis players. But it didn't matter.

"*You* look," growled Rodrigue. "Wave that fucking stick at me again and the next person to see it is going to be a proctologist. I mean it, I'm pissed! Get outta here!"

He made a start toward the two men and they shrank back,

but they didn't run. Instead, they separated and tried to flank him.

Uh-oh, he thought.

The man on the right attacked suddenly, swinging the makeshift nightstick at Rodrigue's head with a long, straight-over-the-shoulder arc. Rodrigue was too quick for him. He caught the man's forearm and then pulled it in the direction it was already going, at the same time lifting his left thigh. The attacker's momentum was checked when his groin met Rodrigue's knee.

Meanwhile, the other man came from Rodrigue's blind side and got in a swack across Rodrigue's left shoulder and head. It made his ear ring and deepened his rage. He let the first man crumple to the floor, and he whirled to face the new attacker. This was basic street fighting, one-on-one now, and never mind the little fairy wand the son of a bitch was waving. Rodrigue was amazed to discover that he was enjoying himself.

He had done his share of drunken brawling in his youth—all right, *more* than his share—but he had never liked it. He was big, and big men attracted trouble in the kinds of bars where sailors and soldiers, or weather-hardened shrimpers, or tough oil-field workers gathered. Plus, he was hotheaded and always something of a smart aleck. As he grew older, though, Rodrigue learned to finesse his way around a fight. He became what he had always been in his heart, anyway—a lover, not a fighter.

Until now.

The man couldn't make up his mind to attack, so Rodrigue did. Instead of fending him off with a jab in the solar plexus with the nightstick, the way the shore patrol would've done, the man tried to club him over the head. Rodrigue blocked the swing and grabbed the man by the neck, lifting him off his feet. He dragged him over to the open window and shoved him through it—wondering all the while what in the hell he was doing.

"Motherfucker!" he said through gritted teeth. "Would you like a goddamn motherfucking flying lesson before I turn you loose?"

The man was squirming weakly in Rodrigue's grip, his back

arched over the bare masonry sill. His eyes jerked side to side and he knew the ground was far, far below. His voice was rasping something unintelligible in raw panic, and the unmistakable smell of urine tainted the hot, damp air.

Why in the hell am I doing this? Rodrigue thought.

He realized that he hadn't been bluffing at all, that he had intended to drop the man thirteen stories through the arched skylights in the ground-floor lobby. By the time he heard other voices and felt strong hands pulling him and the other man back, he was weak and limp.

It was Leyton and the first attacker. Leyton was standing over him, glistening with sweat, face contorted by shock.

"What in the *world* were you doing?" he asked in perfect English.

Rodrigue could manage only to shake his head.

"Maan, you gonna have to come relax in de room. You gattin' way too intense."

"You know this man?" demanded the man Rodrigue had kneed.

"Yes, maan. He has a business dounstair. In de marina. I work for him. Any of de hotel staff can tell you dat."

"Oh, well, I guess you're free to go." With Leyton to reinforce him, the vigilante had regained his officiousness.

"You son of a bitch!" said Rodrigue, scrambling to his feet.

Leyton jumped him, wrapping his arms around Rodrigue's thick torso. Both the Colonel's men fled, not looking back. For just an instant, Rodrigue and Leyton tested each other, but then they collapsed in laughter against the bar. They could still hear one of the men wheezing as he ran down the hall toward the stairs.

"How're you doing?" Rodrigue asked as he searched the cabinets in the bar for booze.

Leyton shrugged. "Been workin' my butt off."

Rodrigue found a collection of empty and near-empty bottles. The only rum was a Bacardi with one good drink left in it—two in a pinch.

"So," he said. "You working with these goons?"

There were a couple of empty plastic glasses behind the bar and Rodrigue sniffed them for noxious residue.

"I was helpin' dem keep order until my domestic duties overwhelm me," said Leyton.

He accepted Rodrigue's offer of a drink.

"You gonna see," he added cryptically.

Rodrigue ignored the comment. He tossed the drink back and smacked his mouth appreciatively.

"I need another drink. Do me a favor, will you, Leyton? Go down and pull the ignition keys out of the *Queen* for me, will you? I want whoever steals her to work for it."

He wasn't that worried. If someone did steal the boat, he couldn't get out of the lake with it.

"I'm going to check on Neesay, then I'm going to the room and crack a bottle. Hold my calls."

"Okay, sure, maan. But fust I better come wit you. Introduce you to our houseguests."

"Houseguests?" asked Rodrigue irritably.

"Mos' o' de windahs on de eas' side was blown out, maan. Mek it mos' uncomfortable for women wit' chi'ren."

"Chi—*children?*"

Rodrigue didn't have anything against children, but for some unfathomable reason, Leyton might as well have told him the room was full of poisonous snakes.

He snatched Leyton's unfinished drink and downed it.

28

The smell of rotting flesh hit Neesay's nose when they walked down from the pool area to the lawn of the old yellow mansion being used to house the dead.

"Must we go in there?" she asked.

"Yes," said Weizman distractedly. He was watching a man in a red plaid shirt coming from Johnny's boat. The man was frowning darkly as he approached them.

"Is the key in it?" Weizman demanded quietly when the man joined them. The three of them kept walking toward the mansion, toward the horrible stench.

"There's two of them," said the man in the red shirt. "One for each motor." He was clearly not happy about something.

"But they're in there?"

"Yeah, they're there, all right. And there's gas, but—"

"And the equipment? Did you store it aboard?"

"Yeah, yeah, but what *about* that? What's that all about?"

He stopped angrily in front of them, halting their progress. Neesay could hear the buzzing of the flies now.

"Are you going to steal that boat?" said the man in the red shirt. "And what is all that stuff? Looks like a radio and stuff. I got about a half a mind to find that FBI man and tell him about all that stuff."

Neesay squeezed her eyes shut. The stupid little man had just cut his own throat.

"The FBI man knows about me," said Weizman calmly.

"We're working together. Have you ever heard of the Mossad? Israeli intelligence. We have reason to believe the saboteurs are Arab terrorists."

Instantly, the man's anger was turned to awe. Weizman was powerful in that way. He knew how to elicit trust. Hadn't she just now sought his protection in spite of everything? But then what choice did she have? Johnny might be able to protect her from looters, but he couldn't save her from the FBI. Only Weizman could do that.

"Tell me," said Weizman as he placed his hand on the little man's shoulder. "Can you operate a firearm?"

"*Hell*, yes!" said the man, grinning nastily. "I'm from deep east Texas. We still live by the gun over there."

The two men were actually about the same height, but Weizman, by sheer force of personality, seemed to tower over the other.

"I don't mean a squirrel rifle. I mean a semiautomatic pistol."

"I can handle a pistol."

"Good," said Weizman. "Come with me."

"I—I'll wait here," said Neesay.

"No," said Weizman in the quiet steady voice that implied threat. "You come also."

As soon as they entered the temporary morgue, Weizman whirled and jabbed a knife into the red-shirted man with an upward motion. The blade must have found the heart. The man registered surprise, tried with jerky movements to look down at his stomach, and then folded to the muddy floor. The buzzing of the flies welled louder at the prospect of fresh meat.

Neesay turned and rested her hands on her knees while she vomited. It wasn't the killing. She had seen killing. Venezuela had gone through some very violent periods during her childhood. It was the smell.

"Sorry you had to see that, my dear," said Weizman. His voice actually seemed amused.

"No you're not." Neesay kept her back to him while she wiped vomitus from her chin. "You brought me in here to see it."

She whirled angrily to face him. "So I would understand the stakes, eh? Now may we leave? This is not pleasant."

"You'll grow accustomed to the smell quite rapidly, and I really do not choose to draw attention to ourselves by standing outside. Let's put the body in with the others before anyone comes. We can say we're looking for a missing friend."

They were in the mansion's entrance foyer. The bodies were in a large room with a wide doorway. The first ones, those by the farthest wall, had been laid in neat rows. The nearer ones were piled helter-skelter, limbs askew, in all stages of dress, with their awful wrinkled faces staring.

Neesay and Weizman added the red-shirted man to the pile and retreated from the cloud of flies to the doorway of the mansion. A breeze off the lake would've been a godsend, but there was none.

"Of course you needn't know the details," said Weizman. "But I have a small radio transmitter hidden in the Mission Control Center that we must retrieve. *We* cannot do it, obviously, so we must find someone who can. I don't know where it is, exactly, but I know what it looks like and what its function is, which should be clues enough for the right technician, wouldn't you agree?"

He didn't give her a chance to answer. "Now, we will use your friend Rodrigue to coerce this individual into helping us. We will borrow Rodrigue's boat and we will pretend I am holding you hostage aboard it. What do you think of my plan so far?"

Again, he didn't give Neesay time to reply.

"Tell me," he said. "Whom shall we get for this job? One of our photo stars, certainly. We need instant loyalty."

Neesay shut her eyes again. Was it too late to stop this? It was so dirty—so dirty. But even if she did get away from Weizman, there was still the secret transmitter he had just told her about. She could either go along with Weizman and put her hopes on Johnny or she could run away and confess the whole thing to NASA. If she did it in time to save the astronauts, surely they would go easy on her.

But it was ridiculous to be thinking like this! It wasn't a matter of take this action or take that action—it was a choice between cultures. If she went to NASA, she *belonged* to NASA, would have given her future to North America. With Weizman, cruel and treacherous as he was, she was still with her own kind, with Latin America. Weizman might try to cut her throat if she became a burden—but he wouldn't do it lightly. She had value at INPE. And besides, a Latin American was nothing if not fatalistic.

She had a choice, all right. Another inevitable choice. Maybe she wasn't avenging poor little Elena, after all. Maybe she was trying to absolve herself of the guilt—the humiliation, almost—of staying clean and fed as her friend became tattered and hungry. It hadn't been fair. . . .

"Joseph Bain," she said finally.

This was truly not pleasant. Bain was really a nice little man. But he was the only one of that group—the ones she had had to seduce—who worked in MCC. He was a key man in the operations involving telemetry and would probably be on the ride-out team.

Bain was among the clean ones, the ones with no skeletons in the closet, no grudges, nothing for a spy to use as leverage against them—except that they were men, thus could be leveraged with sex.

Weizman had supervised the installation of the trap—a hidden video camera focused on her kitchen table. The subject, rather than being lured into her boudoir—her "lair," as it were—was made to feel the sex was totally spontaneous. The camera operated automatically and was triggered by a radio switch hidden under the table. Weizman had produced still photos from the tape to be used when it became time to demand services from one of the subjects.

Neesay had hated it; she hated most of all the emotional power it gave Weizman over her. It had made her feel she was just a thing to be used, like the camera and the kitchen table and Weizman's bloody knife. But she deserved degradation, didn't she? Having been spared it when she was young, she should suffer it now—and maybe for her having suffered it, other children in Latin America would be spared. It was a simple matter of economics. Everything was a simple matter of economics.

"Bain will be there?" Weizman asked.

"He will be there."

"How will Rodrigue get to him?"

"Johnny will think of something. He's very resourceful."

"Yes, but *will* he? After seeing the photo? Won't he feel you have betrayed him?"

"By spying? Johnny is no Boy Scout."

"No, I mean by having sex with this other man."

"He doesn't think of me in that way. He's like an uncle. He won't let anything happen to me."

She smiled suddenly.

"He will be very mad at you for stealing his boat," she said. "You can't go anywhere in it, you know. The passage to the bay is blocked with wreckage from the storm."

Weizman smiled back. "Let me worry about Rodrigue; I've handled as tough as him and tougher."

He thought for a minute.

"I may have given him a bad first impression, however. Wait here."

He opened his long-bladed knife and went into the room with the bodies. The flies seemed to scream at the intrusion. Slowly, drawn by curiosity, Neesay moved to where she could see what he was doing. She shrieked and ran from the mansion, well out into the yard, where the air was better and she couldn't hear the angry buzzing of the flies.

But she couldn't shake the image of Weizman crouched over the red-shirted man's body, methodically sawing on the neck.

29

On Rodrigue's bed, a young blonde sat nursing an infant, her swollen blue-veined breast undraped. She looked up, smiled a weak Mona Lisa smile, then turned adoring eyes back on her child.

An older woman turned from the window with a smirk and one of Rodrigue's plastic tumblers. She was square-shouldered and narrow-hipped—or at least her hips were more narrow than her shoulders, which looked as if they belonged on an offensive lineman. She had three bracelets on one arm and two on another, and it was impossible to tell how many necklaces made up the gaudy tangle on her mountainous bosom. It also seemed as if there was a ring on every finger.

From the alcove beside the bathroom, a thin Oriental teenager in a microbikini stepped out to look curiously, followed by a towheaded girl of about twelve wearing makeup like a Bourbon Street stripper. She still had a lipstick in her hand.

"Ladies, dis is de maan I tol' you about," said Leyton with devilish glee.

Greetings of varying degrees of enthusiasm followed, with the bejeweled woman at the top of the scale.

"I look like a looter, don't I?" she said in a hoarse whiskey voice. "Sons of bitches are gonna have to strip it off me."

Rodrigue smiled wanly.

"Which one's yours?" he whispered to Leyton.

"Oh, she's wit her husband now."

Leyton tipped his hand toward the young mother. "Dis is Mary and son Sean. Dis"—he indicated the bejeweled woman—"is Mary's mother, Miz Kilpatrick."

An inhuman shriek came from the bathroom.

"An' dat'll be little Oliver," said Leyton without breaking stride. "He ate somethin' dat didn't agree wit him. His mother, Miz Picard, is wit him. An' dat one wit de cloun face is also her daughter. Joy." He tousled her silky hair and she pouted.

The Oriental girl detached herself from the child's play and stepped forward to be presented, a hip provocatively thrust sideways. Maybe, Rodrigue considered, she was older than he had thought.

"Dis young lady is Barbara Li. She's traveling wit her father, who is on de Colonel's defense committee."

"Nice to meet you," said the girl in that West Coast drone all teenagers seemed to have nowadays.

"Charmed," said Rodrigue flatly.

The bathroom door opened and out backed a thirtyish woman, shapely butt first.

"Leyton, that you?" she called in an irritated voice. Then she looked up and said, "Oh!"

She scowled at Rodrigue. She was pretty, with delicate features, but her too-blond hair and the remnants of too much mascara and eye shadow made her look gaunt, almost skeletal, as though motherhood was sucking the life out of her.

"Miz Picard, John Rodrigue," said Leyton nervously.

The little boy in the bathroom continued to scream.

Mrs. Picard ignored Rodrigue. She proffered a handful of damp gray bathtowels flecked with bits of half-digested food.

"Can you wash these out someplace, maybe? Or better yet, steal us some more. This is it."

Leyton took the towels with ill-masked disgust. "Maybe . . . maybe Neesay will have some extras. I'll go see."

He turned and exited. Rodrigue could hear him running in the hall.

Mrs. Picard disappeared back into the bathroom.

"Join me in a drink?" said Mrs. Kilpatrick, bracelets

jangling. "We beefed up your stock a little. You were out of gin. Leyton found some still downstairs in the bar. Can you imagine that?"

"Don't minds if I do," growled Rodrigue, doing Long John Silver out of habit.

"Are you really a deep-sea diver?" asked Barbara Li.

"No longer, missy. I'm retired."

Rodrigue settled in the corner with a drink—rum and rum, since the club soda was gone and ice long gone—and tried to let it all waft over him. It wasn't easy. Mary discovered mosquito bites on young Sean and became hysterical. Mrs. Picard, who was still ignoring him, complained about the heat and then fussed at her kids for complaining. Mrs. Kilpatrick started on her late husband, and Barbara Li kept mopping the sweat from her lithe body, watching him watch her do it.

"John," said Mrs. Picard, suddenly acknowledging his presence. "That *is* your name, isn't it? John?"

"Yes, ma'am," Rodrigue found himself saying.

"John, do you think we could find a way to open that window where it would close up again? Be so nice if we could get some air in here, but then the mosquitoes were so bad last night—"

"Do you have a glass cutter in your tools?" offered Mrs. Kilpatrick. "You could tape the window where it wouldn't fall out, then cut it with a glass cutter."

"I'm a diver, Mrs. Kilpatrick, not a burglar. I've got a cutting torch up here but no oxygen bottle. Why don't I just knock it out and then we can duct-tape a blanket over it tonight?"

Mrs. Picard vetoed that idea. "We tried a blanket in our room and of course it doesn't work."

Of course, Rodrigue thought, admonishing himself mockingly. Shut up and have another drink, you idiot.

"The mosquitoes get in somehow," she continued.

"They're probably breeding in the hall by now." He got up and fixed himself another drink.

"Why aren't you on the defense committee?" asked Barbara Li. "You look big and tough. Certainly a lot tougher than *my* dad."

"Disabled vet," said Rodrigue.

He went over and eyed the window to see what could be done about it. He couldn't see anything, so he sat down again, hoping they would quit trying so hard to entertain him.

The topic of the need for more fresh water came up, and then the heat again, but then they seemed to wind down. The heat was working for him, he decided. He drank his tepid rum and brooded.

He couldn't remember chapter and verse. It was Genesis something:something. Nor could he quote it—what Catholic could quote Scripture?—but well he remembered the gist of it because it dovetailed so neatly into his worldview:

The woman took the fruit from the Tree of Knowledge and she bade the man to eat of it so that he could figure out how to open the motherfucking window.

That was and is the crux of the situation, the hallmark of the human condition. It is not a man's world and hasn't been since Eve joined Adam in the garden. They let men pretend to be lords of the skyscrapers, but if it wasn't for the eternal discomfort of women, there wouldn't even be fucking *houses*.

He remembered how sweet it had been when Ann Eller began to boss him around. It was while they were still on vacation in Cozumel, and he had known she was only doing it because she needed to maintain some semblance of control. He was the first man she had opened herself to, literally and figuratively, and she was feeling very vulnerable. So she laughingly stopped him at three drinks during dinner one evening. And she very lovingly steered him into a shop to find some more conservative replacements for his loud Hawaiian shirts. She was like a plucky Fay Wray in the palm of the beast—and he, the big gorilla, would've died before rearranging a hair of that beautiful red head.

He felt like a dog the first time they made love. She had not particularly enjoyed it—not the actual coitus, anyway. The next time, she loosened up and may even have had a climax, a brief and tense one like a stifled sneeze. The third time, she seemed so urgent, so active and vocal, that he instantly tumbled after her, lost in the hot pleasure of his own release. He vowed not to let that happen the next time.

The afternoon rain was falling and the curtains were drawn tight, making her room dark. She took the precaution of turning off the bathroom light before she opened the door. The shower smells floated with her like perfumed steam.

It was his turn to shower, but in the dim light he saw the unmistakable signs of her nakedness—the delicious silhouette of a bare breast against the white plaster wall, and the dark shadow at the apex of her long, slender legs. A major step for her—before, she had only let him undress her under the covers. Rodrigue the Pirate nearly swooned.

As she neared him, modesty quickened her step. She dived into bed and welcomed him, still in his damp bathing suit, under the covers.

The depth of her kiss was greater than the heat of her skin and the excitement of her scent. Rodrigue the Pirate was in love.

He kissed her neck and shoulders, and snuggled her breasts. Her hands brushed back his hair as he very gently sucked her protruding nipples. She softly bemoaned her loss of control as his head dipped lower and his lips brushed the tender flesh of her belly. Her thighs spread even as her arms tugged ineffectually at him.

"No, John," she said in a small voice.

He ignored her—and this time she let herself go. Feeling gushed from her like a huge storm wave rolling shoreward, gathering and peaking and finally exploding, subsiding so slowly.

And Rodrigue, still aching in his groin, felt like the king of the universe.

Leyton came back with the towels and a sealed envelope with Rodrigue's name on it in Neesay's hand.

"Where'd you get this?" asked Rodrigue groggily.

"One o' de men below. What is it?"

Rodrigue opened the envelope. The note read:

Johnny,

I am sorry. This man has asked a favor. Please meet us in the middle of the lake at midnight. Take the blue boat. The key is in the back compartment, under the water. I am fine.

Neesay

The words screamed at him. It wasn't her usual flippant style. Neesay was in danger.

Rodrigue ran downstairs and outside, to the marina. The blue bass boat was still tied to the breakwater, but the *Haulover Queen* was gone.

30

Beads of perspiration ran unimpeded from Joe Bain's smooth crown past fine pale eyebrows and into his earnest blue eyes. He wiped them against his upper arm without breaking his concentration. He had good reason to sweat.

He was cross-legged behind the NOM racks, their innards exposed, and he was methodically comparing the mosaic of circuitry inside with a schematic, unrolled in his lap like a mariner's chart.

No one bothered him—no one dared interrupt him. Everyone assumed they knew what he was doing: continuing to search for the glitch. One or two might have the inside knowledge to figure he was looking for a transmitter. If Cory Pritchett could be a spy, anyone here could.

Assumption was always a dangerous luxury to a scientist, but this was a new arena for Bain—espionage. Somehow the word didn't sound dirty enough. You could thank Hollywood for that, he supposed.

This was real. Like the car wreck with the body still behind the wheel and the policemen just standing there beside the road, waiting for an ambulance, and you on the way to Astroworld with the kids. Have a nice day.

Here we had hundreds, maybe thousands of people dead from this terrible storm, including maybe friends, maybe neighbors. And five talented, almost too-perfect women very likely about to die horribly—and some of these people busying themselves around MCC might be responsible. Purposely.

Now, go have a nice life, Joe Bain.

Ah, if that was all there was to it, he *could* live with it. He could do what he could do, and if it worked, it worked. And if it didn't, well, he had tried his best.

But there was more to it than that: There was Neesay.

Maybe she was innocent. . . . No. She was not innocent. But maybe her intention, her aim, her motive was not to kill—or if it was, there were reasons. . . .

None of that mattered, Bain knew. In a way, it felt good to surrender his meager principles. He didn't care whether she was evil—that was not a judgment for him to make, anyway. She was wonderful, that was all that counted. Her smile, her eyes, her body, her voice—her laugh, especially that. She was *wonderful*.

Bain loved his wife and was permanently bound to her, but he would always somehow belong to Neesay, too, down in some secret part in what the poets called the heart. It was too deep to be even mental, had to be a soul thing.

He would never see her again, but the least he could do was save her. All he had to do was find the device and then get rid of it. Without that piece of evidence, how could they prove anything against her?

It all played behind his conscious thoughts, the machinelike register of first a component and then its symbolic equivalent on the schematic, as Bain doggedly inched his way up through the NOM, left to right, level by level. . . .

31

It was as black outside as midnight in Neesay's Amazonia. Rodrigue had to feel his way carefully along the damaged portion of the breakwater. With no light reflecting from its sparkles, the blue boat looked velvety, insubstantial.

Rodrigue lowered himself gingerly to the carpeted deck. He bumped against the front pedestal seat and felt his way down into the cockpit past the low console to the wide aft deck.

Under his lumbering weight, the little boat felt more solid than it looked. But it had to be. Bass fishing was a boat race nowadays. Refineries, construction companies, even big law offices had employee tournaments. The object was to put twice as many boats on a lake as there were places to fish and then let them race for it. The huge gasoline outboard engine on the transom would probably propel the sleek nineteen-foot hull over sixty miles an hour.

Rodrigue felt around on the aft deck for the recessed lifting rings that were common to most small boats. Instead, he found loops of nylon strap. He pulled one up and opened a large hatch. But it was dry storage. What he was looking for, he knew from Neesay's description, was a bait well—a watertight compartment plumbed to circulate water from outside the hull and keep fish alive.

He could see a little better now. He found another loop and pulled.

A nauseating smell escaped. It wasn't fishy, but something

was rotting. He reached in and felt a large, hard object with a soft, rubbery covering. Something brushed against his fingers like a spiderweb, strands of something. He grabbed them and lifted the thing out and came face-to-face with a man with grizzled whiskers and pinched, sort of ratlike features. The eyes were staring, mouth slack. With a startled yelp, Rodrigue flung it into the night.

He had thought for one heart-freezing sliver of an instant that it was Neesay's head. But he probably still wouldn't have been able to hold on to it.

He made himself put his hand back in the well and feel around. The ignition key, by itself on a small split-ring, was there in a corner. Disgustedly, he rinsed his hand and the key off in the muddy water of the lake.

The outboard started surely. A plunger switch illuminated the instrument panel. The fuel gauge said one-quarter. Rodrigue tapped it. Fuel gauges were notorious liars. What the hell—he was going two miles at the most. Four, going and coming. He left the running lights off, and put the engine in gear.

The hotel was a lighter shade of black, a giant ghostly domino looming over him. He used it as a reference to aim for the center of the lake. He took it slowly, mindful that he had only one propeller now.

Even idling along, the boat throbbed with power. It made Rodrigue want to rev it up and use it as a projectile—skip it right into the cockpit of the *Queen* and kill the son of a bitch, whoever he was.

Oh, he could kill the son of a bitch, all right. He could do that. But where would that leave Neesay? When you had someone else's life in your hands, the choices weren't that easy.

He had to calm down, he knew that much. He knew he would, too. He always did, once he was committed.

And now he was committed: The pale boxy profile of the Boston Whaler appeared, hovering in black space.

Rodrigue stopped the engine and stood up. And his blood would've cooled ice.

32

For a man who had just discovered a severed human head, Rodrigue was unnervingly cool, thought Weizman. The insolent bastard was standing in the blue boat, hands on his hips, as though he was on holiday. If he had needed a moment to recognize Weizman from their meeting after the hurricane, he didn't show it.

"I guess you found the yellow shoe in the pilothouse, there, so where's my thousand dollars?" he said easily.

"And since *you* found the key," said Weizman, "you know I'm not a man to play games. It would perhaps be best if you remain silent and listen."

"A man's gotta have some fun in his life, Colonel. Is that you? Are you the Colonel?"

The man's tone was upsetting to Weizman. Could he be drunk? Cara had said he drank too much.

"Gave your lover a nice send-off, I think," Rodrigue added casually. "Nothing elaborate. Brand-new tarp for a shroud, though. I should add that to your bill."

Weizman bristled. "He was not my lover. I am what you would call an industrial spy. That man was helping me steal secrets from a company that had purchased payload space on the shuttle *Columbia*. We may have inadvertently endangered the shuttle and its lovely astronauts. Now it's up to you to save them. And Miss Cara."

"Where is she?" His attitude wasn't so jocular now, Weizman noticed.

"I will not say to you that she is safe, because she is not. She will die unless you do exactly as I instruct you."

Actually, it probably hadn't been necessary to tie her up. At this point, she clearly thought her interests lay with him. She would cooperate, however distasteful it was. But the bonds were a small precaution that bought a great deal of reassurance.

"I'm listening," said Rodrigue roughly.

"The man whose body you retrieved from my boat had placed an electronic intercept device, which you might know as a bug, in the Mission Control Center. Apparently, its radio frequency is somehow scrambling signals to the shuttle. So we must remove it from Building Thirty—*you* must remove it. Bring it to me, and Miss Cara goes free. It's as simple as that."

"Auh! Right!" said Rodrigue disgustedly. "You're telling *me* to be serious? I wouldn't know an electronic bug if it bit me on the ass, and I'm gonna find one in a three-story building chock-full of electronic shit? Get real, man! I couldn't even get in the gate over there."

"There is a man there named Joseph Bain. He is supposed to have been working during the storm, so presumably he is there now. Bain—Joseph Bain, remember that. He is in charge of the apparatus that enables the Mission Control computers to talk to the shuttle's on-board computers. Find him and tell him the device looks very much like a remote wand for a television, with several wires connected at one end and an antenna about two inches long at the other. He'll find it for you."

Rodrigue groaned. "Look, even if I can get to him and he can find this bug, what's to keep him from just turning it over to his security people? It and me with it."

"Show him this."

Weizman handed Rodrigue the photograph. It was a slightly fuzzy black and white taken from a television screen, but it very plainly showed Joseph Bain and Eunice Cara in the act of copulating. Cara was bent over a small kitchen table, grasping the forward edge, her lovely breasts dangling

175

enticingly a fraction of an inch above the tablecloth. The distorted expression on her face, mouth gaping, eyes squeezed shut, could've been pain or passion. Bain, standing behind her, had his eyes wide open. He was looking at her and at the same time almost into the hidden camera. He was quite evidently enjoying himself.

"The tape from which this was taken offers better detail," said Weizman nastily.

Rodrigue's face was disturbingly unreadable as he studied the photograph. This could be the decisive moment. Now he would guess that she, too, was a spy—would be culpable in the astronauts' deaths. Would it be an added incentive for him to retrieve the intercept device? Or would he leave her to her fate, judging that she had earned it? Rodrigue was certainly no prude, but would he feel betrayed?

"Neesay's working with you, then," he said finally.

"She was working *for* me," said Weizman. "But that won't keep me from killing her if you don't produce the device."

Nothing, in fact, would keep him from killing them both when the time was right. Weizman had made up his mind to claw his way to the top of this mess, no matter what. He had almost panicked and surrendered to the mercy of the American government. But now he was determined to stay free. He might lose his standing with the INPE, might even have to change his identity. But nobody was going to lock him up.

"Here, now, we have a rather sticky wicket," said Rodrigue. "Let's say I come up with this bug of yours. You have Neesay. How and where do we make the trade?"

"Out here. Between these boats, just as we are speaking."

"*Un*-uh. Rocket scientists and spies aren't the only people who can see past their noses, Colonel. I come out here alone like this, what's to keep you from shooting me once I give you the bug? And besides, fond as I am of little Neesay, she's just one of your bargaining chips. You still owe me a grand, remember? And that's just a matter of principle. I've got nearly forty thousand tied up in this boat you're lounging around on. It's *your* ass in the crack—yours and Neesay's but not mine. So think again."

"What are you suggesting?" Weizman asked.

"Let's come eye-to-eye here, first of all. You want your little gizmo, you want outta here, and you want all the witnesses dead—preferably drowned so it'll look like an accident. I want Neesay healthy and happy as a matter of principle. I also want my boat back and I want all your money. Obviously, some of our wants are mutually exclusive. But, hey, there's still a lot of room for negotiation here. Lot more than if you were dealing with the feds."

Rodrigue put one foot on the big boat's gunwale and glared threateningly at Weizman.

"The first thing you need to do is stop thinking of me as some kind of victim whose fucking throat you've got your foot on and start thinking of me as a businessman."

Was he bluffing? The safer assumption was that he meant it, Weizman decided. It gave him an idea.

"I'm afraid I'm going to have to insist on borrowing your boat for the time being. Also it appears I'm light on fuel. So here is my offer: You bring me the device—deal with this man Bain as you see fit—and one hundred gallons of gasoline. Do these outboards require oil in the fuel?"

"There're two cases in the vee berths."

"Very well, then. You bring me the gasoline and I'll pay you the thousand dollars. Eunice and one thousand dollars for the gasoline and the device. And the use of your boat. I'll leave your boat in a safe place and drop word to you where to find it."

Rodrigue squinted one eye and looked at him skeptically with the other. "I just hate it when a business partner's deceitful, but I ought to be used to it by now. You're not going to tell me where to find my boat—in fact, you're probably gonna try to sink the son of a bitch so it *won't* be found."

He leaned over and thumped the hull of his boat. "This boat won't sink, and fires and explosions attract too much attention. Just pull it up at a boat ramp or fuel dock someplace and leave it. I'll find it eventually."

Rodrigue glanced along the gunwale of the boat rather lovingly, Weizman thought. Maybe the boat was the real hostage, after all.

"Another thing," said Rodrigue. "There's no way I'm coming out here with everything you want in this little blue motherfucker. I want to meet on land, where you'll have to work at shooting me."

"That is not possible. It would be too easy then for you to shoot *me*."

"Well, then we don't have anything to talk about." Rodrigue kicked away from the big boat and started the other boat's engine.

"Wait," said Weizman. "Where do you have in mind?"

Rodrigue killed the engine again. "The county park back there. Big pavilion with a tile roof."

Weizman shook his head. "Too public. Listen, suppose, then, we do it in stages," said Weizman. "First we exchange Eunice and the device. Then, with Eunice safely on the shore, you bring me the gasoline. And I give you your money, of course."

Rodrigue thought it over.

"Without the gasoline, I cannot go far. I'm helpless," said Weizman. "And I'm certainly not going to shoot you, with Eunice free on the shore to raise the alarm. It is as you said—we have narrowed our wants down to those we can both live with. Quite literally."

"The gas is going to cost you—let's say fifty dollars a gallon. I'll try to scrounge up a hundred gallons but I don't know—"

"My God!" said Weizman, sincerely outraged. "That's five thousand dollars!"

"Yeah, but don't forget, I'm letting you use my boat rent-free."

Rodrigue smiled a cold, toothy smile. It reminded Weizman of a shark.

"Agreed, then," said Weizman coolly. "Tomorrow night. Same place, same time."

"Now if you'll just give me my money, I'll be on my way," said Rodrigue.

"*In advance?*" Weizman could not believe the impudence of this man.

"Do you think me a pirate?" said Rodrigue, feining a scandalized look, one hand flat on his chest. Weizman felt Rodrigue was mocking his accent, too.

"I was talking about the thousand you already owe me. I

think we should square accounts before we enter into this new phase in our relationship."

Weizman grudgingly paid him, and Rodrigue disappeared into the night.

Stopping the motors frequently to listen for other boats, Weizman went down the lake to the cove he had selected and dropped anchor. Then he went below and untied Cara.

Gingerly, she pulled the tape off her mouth.

"Well?" she demanded angrily.

"You were right. I'm certain he'll get the job done."

Rodrigue had also been right, Weizman thought. It was much better to deal with a businessman—especially a dishonest businessman who knew full well that the way out of the lake was blocked with debris.

So he planned to make five thousand dollars, probably on contaminated gasoline from cars that had been inundated, and get his boat and his new little girlfriend back in the bargain.

"Sorry to have bound you like that, my dear," Weizman said sweetly.

She rubbed her wrists and glared at him.

"But of course I'm going to have to do it again before I go to sleep," he said. "You understand."

She was understandably addled, having witnessed the execution of that nasty little man who had been in charge of the blue boat. But she was a smart girl. Eventually, she would realize that the only route to safety was to go inland, on foot if necessary, and somehow be at Houston Intercontinental when planes resumed flying again. She would realize he could move much more quickly—and, more important, much more unobtrusively—alone. He couldn't take her and he certainly couldn't leave her. She was, after all, the prime suspect, was she not?

It was just a matter of time before she—unlike that pig Rodrigue, who was too busy counting his money—realized that he would simply have to kill them both.

33

Rodrigue stopped the outboard engine and went to the bow to lower the electric trolling motor. He had never operated one, but he knew how they were supposed to work.

He sat tentatively on the high seat and found it solid. Then he put his foot on the hinged pedal fastened to the foredeck. A button on the pedal engaged the motor and the boat lurched silently to starboard, into a tight circle. Trying to keep his balance, Rodrigue inadvertently tilted the pedal back and the boat instantly changed directions. He rocked his foot slightly; the boat settled into a straight course. He smiled in the darkness.

He glided silently into a mass of wreckage that had once been a boat dealership and marina. It was here he had bought several new outboards for the pontoon boats. He knew where things were—or had been before the storm.

The big storage shed was a crumpled mass of corrugated iron, rigid but odd-shaped, like a huge tent with a couple of poles missing. One whole wall—or was it the roof?—was gone and the boat came to a sluggish halt on the concrete floor inside. Rodrigue got out and felt his way around. Large boxes of soggy cardboard were bobbing against his thighs. They felt right. He ripped one open and found, as he had suspected, a brand-new portable gas tank.

The shed, he remembered, had been stacked high with the boxes. Portable six-gallon tanks were standard on most small boats. They would serve his purpose very well. He found and stripped the cardboard from eleven of the tanks, stacking them neatly in the bass boat. There were more, but he ran out of room.

There was a coil of water hose beneath his feet. He picked it up, cut a couple of four-foot lengths and stowed them in the boat.

He idled carefully across the still lake. A few faint camp fires flickered on the north shore—National Guardsmen fighting the darkness and the mosquitoes. The only other light came from dim stars penetrating the thick Gulf night.

As he pulled up to the hotel breakwater, he thought of the severed head that might be floating nearby. . . . No, it would have sunk, maybe never to be seen again. Feeding the crabs, probably. Rodrigue shivered.

The water had gone down some more and he had to stretch to reach the top of the breakwater. By now, the railroad trestle would look like a Mississippi logjam in May. No way the *Haulover Queen* was going anywhere for a good while.

He carried two of the gasoline cans and the two sections of water hose to the hotel and stashed them in the wreckage against the building. It was past bedtime for looters and vigilantes alike. On the way up, he heard something like the distant bleat of a goat—a very young baby crying—but there wasn't a soul on the long flight of stairs.

He found Leyton asleep out in the hall, still clamping a pillow around his head for earmuffs. Little Sean, too, must've carried on some, Rodrigue figured. Leyton sat up in a daze when Rodrigue shook him.

"Come on," he whispered. "We've got a little work to do."

"You're kidding." Leyton rubbed his eyes and looked at his watch. "Hey, maan, it's jus' after t'ree."

"Come on, we don't have a minute to spare," said Rodrigue. He had already turned and was headed for the exit.

"Hey," said Leyton, catching up. "What happened to your friend Neesay?" Leyton asked. "She with the Colonel?"

"They're spies," Rodrigue said. "Sort of commercial spies, you might say. But they fucked up and planted a little radio transmitter in the Mission Control Center that's causing the shuttle to go haywire."

"What? Neesay and the Colonel causin' the problem with the shuttle? Hey! If it's the Colonel, we've got to let NASA know! Maybe they can stop him!"

"Shhh. If we just come out and warn NASA, the Colonel will kill Neesay. He's holding her hostage. Don't worry, I've got it under control. Come on, I'll explain when we get outside."

Downstairs, Rodrigue reached into the debris and handed one of the hoses to Leyton.

"Here, remember how to use this?"

"We're gonna steal gasoline?" said Leyton, incredulous.

"Part of the bargain I had to strike to get Neesay back. Come on, we don't have much time."

He led the way into the hotel parking lot, littered with the muddy hulks that had been the guests' cars.

"Here, fill this can and take it down to the marina. Put it in that little blue boat outside the breakwater and grab another one."

"Dis gas ain't gonna be no good, maan."

"Yeah, but I gave him a good price on it."

Rodrigue took off with his own can and section of hose.

It was getting light by the time they stowed the last can aboard the sleek little bass boat. Rodrigue covered the load with a scrap of sail.

He turned and put his hand on Leyton's shoulder. "Leyton, I've given you a lot of leeway, haven't I?"

"Whut you mean, leeway?"

"Have I pried into your business?"

"No, maan."

"No, because your business is your business. But now your business is my business. What I want you to do is cut the island bullshit and give me some good English. Let me hear you talk like an electronics engineer or a computer expert."

Leyton hesitated.

"I'm not asking for any kind of explanation," said Rodrigue. "Just give me a computer expert."

"Is this what you are talking about?" asked Leyton in precise syllables.

"I knew you could do it," said Rodrigue. "You're an educated man, aren't you, Leyton?"

"Some."

"Been listening to the radio?"

"Up and down the hall, sure, of course."

Leyton answered these questions with growing testiness, not sure where they were going.

"So what have you picked up about the shuttle trouble?" Rodrigue asked.

"Faulty computer chips, they think."

"What do you know about computer chips?"

"Silicon. Small. Semiconducting. Just a mishmash. The salient question is how much do I understand what I know."

"Well, you're into role-playing. You can fake it."

"Fake what?"

"We're going to have to blackmail a man at the Space Center into finding the bug for us. Getting rid of the bug will supposedly take care of the problem with the shuttle. Then we trade the bug for Neesay and everybody's happy."

"Blackmail? That's kind of illegal, isn't it?"

Rodrigue waved the objection aside as if it were a pesky mosquito. "Let me handle that. All you have to do is get to the man and get him away from there so I can talk to him. I don't know enough about computers or aerospace technology to pull it off."

"Am I supposed to pose as a computer repairman or something?"

"Yeah, something. Something that'll make him want to talk to you."

Leyton thought a moment.

"If I could get him on the phone somehow, I could probably convince him I work for McGill-White, the company that makes the chips that are malfunctioning. The CEO was interviewed on the radio a half a dozen times already that I've heard, and he's been very defensive. So if I tell this NASA guy I know how to solve the problem but I have to be guaranteed anonymity, he'll almost have to agree."

"Good idea," Rodrigue said.

It was a *great* idea. He suddenly had a chilling thought: What if Leyton was another goddamned Russian spy or whatever the hell the Colonel was—or worse, a fucking fed! Was he being set up for something here?

Well, it was too late to think of something else. He'd just have to take that chance.

"Where are we going to find a phone?"

"Well," said Leyton, thinking. "Let's find the National Guard. Surely they have some way of communicating with the Space Center."

They hiked in the pale golden dawn up the wide muddy trail that had been NASA Road 1. The morning swarms of mosquitoes were vicious. From somewhere far away came the angry sound of a chain saw biting off more than it could easily chew. The only other sign of human activity was a pair of Humvees parked at the main entrance to the Johnson Space Center, way down the road.

What had been a vast tree-lined parking lot at the Space Center now looked like the landing zone for a small fishing village. There were the remains of cars, boats—lots of boats—homes, warehouses, fences, uprooted trees, and thousands of nondescript smaller items scattered across the muddy pavement. One house in particular had landed almost intact in the road that led past Rocket Park. The windows and front door were gaping, and the remains of a front porch sagged, but the roof was untouched and the house stood upright the way a house is supposed to. It was Rodrigue's turn to have a great idea.

He pointed it out to Leyton as they walked.

"We're going to tell those Guardsmen that that's my Aunt Dorothy's house and we want to go up and see if Aunt Dorothy is still in it."

Leyton smiled broadly. "Better make it Aunt Betsy."

"You," Rodrigue continued, "are going to tell 'em you have a cousin at the Space Center, one Joseph Bain, and if they'll let you contact him, he'll secure permission for us to go up and look inside the house. Then I'll try to decoy them so you can talk privately—and then you'll just have to talk your ass off."

"Is Bain black?"

"Black Irish maybe. Hell, they won't know that."

"But what if they just let us go ahead without contacting Bain? Or worse, volunteer to take us in themselves?"

Rodrigue smiled. "Never been in the military, have you?"

"No, but—"

"You don't assume responsibility, and you don't volunteer for anything, and most of all, you don't stir yourself unnecessarily."

Of course, these were really civilians in uniform, most of them. . . . Well, if it didn't go right, he'd just have to think of something else. Maybe they could bonk one of the motherfuckers on the head and steal his radiophone.

The Guardsmen were burning damp wood to ward off mosquitoes. The morning shift had just awakened, apparently, and were still standing sluggishly in the smoke, nursing cups of coffee. Rodrigue selected an E-5, a tall, pink-faced blond, and gave him his spiel.

"We got orders not to let anyone past here," he said. The tone of his voice said he would not be swayed by compassion.

"Can you call the Space Center on your radio?" Rodrigue asked.

"Don't need to. I know what my orders are."

Rodrigue was moved close to violence.

"This guy here's cousin works there. He's a big shot. He can get us permission to go over there and look—hell, it's just right over *there!* You can see the goddamned thing! Man, I don't want that old woman to be lying in there rotting! Come on, let us call him."

"Lieutenant!" called the noncom without taking his eyes off Rodrigue.

A figure moved behind a Humvee draped with mosquito netting. A young black woman in fatigues stepped out, still brushing her teeth. She spat out the foam and wiped her mouth on a khaki towel, frowning at the two civilians.

Leyton laid a hand on Rodrigue's arm and went forward to speak to her.

She glanced over at Rodrigue several times during the one-sided conversation. She looked annoyed. Finally, she walked over to the Humvee, pulled the mosquito-net curtain aside, and picked up a radiophone.

Things were either about to go right or very wrong.

34

"Bain here," came a weary voice.

Leyton nodded at Rodrigue, who was diverting the Guardsmen with hurricane stories.

"Mr. Bain"—he sounded as earnest as he knew how—"I can show you how to save the shuttle, but you have to meet with me privately, alone. And tell no one where you're going. If you tell anyone else about this conversation, I'll deny it."

"Who *is* this?" asked Bain as though he had just heard the world's most offensive joke.

"Who I am doesn't matter. I work for McGill-White. That ought to be enough. If anyone finds out I spoke with you, I won't be working for anyone. Not in aerospace, anyway."

"What are you saying? Is this being done on purpose?"

"No. It's a glitch that's being covered up at all costs."

"A glitch," said Bain—almost wistfully, Leyton thought.

"We have to meet, Mr. Bain. Outside. Now. But tell no one. Can you do that?"

"Where?" said Bain without hesitation.

"There's a house sitting astraddle the road from the main entrance off NASA One. I'll be in that house. Only thing is, you've got to convince the National Guard lieutenant out here at the gate to let me through. Can you sound officious enough for that?"

"Let me speak to him."

"Her."

The lieutenant took the phone. Leyton stood nearby, but he couldn't hear what Bain had to say. Finally, she replaced the handset and glared at him.

"In and out," she said. "It'll take you ten minutes, max, to walk over there. I want you both back here in thirty minutes."

"Thank you, Lieutenant," said Leyton.

"Don't thank *me*. And don't make me come after you."

Leyton nodded to Rodrigue and they started jogging up the road toward the house.

"Very good," said Rodrigue when they had gotten far enough away from the Guardsmen. "You should be in the CIA." He was being nastily sarcastic for some reason.

"I don't know whether he bought it or not. He snapped it up awfully quick."

"We will soon find out."

They jogged for the house, a frame one or two bedroom that once had stood on low concrete piers. Now the wooden floor was on an asphalt slab.

Rodrigue hesitated at the low threshold.

"God, I hope Aunt Dorothy *isn't* here," he said, mostly to himself. "I'm getting damn tired of dead bodies."

The house was empty, no furniture, nothing on the walls, none of the sad treasures that made up much of the debris now littering the countryside. Either it had been vacant to begin with or everything was sucked out by the odd force that had carried it from God knows where and deposited it intact here.

"Hope he doesn't take too damn long," said Leyton, peeking out at the small figures of the Guardsmen milling around their Humvees.

They heard footsteps on the muddy asphalt. Rodrigue ducked into the gloom. A short white man appeared at the door. Leyton held his breath. The man stepped uncertainly inside, apparently alone. His face looked tormented.

"I'm Bain," the man said.

"Mr. Bain, this is an incredible story, and I'm not the man to tell it."

"Really." He didn't seem surprised. "Who is the man?"

"I am," said Rodrigue, stepping out of the shadows.

"What's this about? You people are not from McGill-White

and it's no glitch—we've tested every single chip in all three NOMs. So what do you want?"

Rodrigue pulled a photograph out of his hip pocket and gave it to Bain. Leyton couldn't see what was on it. Bain's face reddened, but his expression didn't change.

"She's a spy," said Rodrigue. "She's also my friend and she's in some very deep shit. Her boss has turned against her, and he'll kill her in an instant."

"Who are you guys?"

"My name is John Rodrigue. I'm a commercial diver and I'm an old friend of Neesay's family. This is my partner, Leyton Mills. We got involved when Neesay's boss needed someone to recover a body, probably one of your coworkers, if I have it right."

"Cory Pritchett," said Bain.

"We didn't know what was going on until Weizman—that's the spy—took Neesay hostage and forced us to come here and talk to you. That is God's absolute truth."

"You'll be saving the astronauts, too," injected Leyton.

"I'm afraid it's too late to save the astronauts," said Bain bitterly. "They're as good as dead."

Leyton felt the words like a blow to the stomach.

Rodrigue spoke calmly: "Okay. But we can still save Neesay. Will you?"

"How?" asked Bain. He seemed very tired.

"Somehow the man she works for planted a bug in the Mission Control Center to steal some kind of inform—"

"A bug?" Bain demanded. "They were only stealing data? Sure—if Cory was involved, it was the downlink they were interested in! The gallium-arsenide thin-film experiment!"

"I know this is going to be hard to believe, but the man wants his bug back," said Rodrigue. "He said it looks like a remote-control gizmo for a TV, but with wires coming out of it. If you can find the damn thing without telling anyone, I can swap it for Neesay."

Bain looked at the photo again—a picture of the two of them, Leyton guessed.

"I was looking in the wrong place!" he said excitedly. "I assumed that since the uplink was affected and sabotage was suspected, the device would be in the NOM. But something to tap information in the downlink would have to be in the PDIS. The racks are ten or fifteen feet apart—close enough for the signal to affect whichever chip or chips in the NOM that were sensitive to it. I—I've got to tell them!"

He whirled to leave, but Rodrigue grabbed him. "Wait a minute! Why do you have to tell anyone?"

"The PDIS is Cory's territory—was. No way I can go in there and start taking it apart without attracting a lot of attention. No way I can get it and smuggle it back out here to you."

Bain started crying, silently, his face fighting the contortion as the tears streamed down his cheeks in ribbons that shined in the oblique light from the open doorway.

"She's going to have to go to prison, isn't she?" he asked.

Beyond him, Leyton could see a Guardsman climbing into one of the Humvees out on the road.

"Jesus! Leyton, here comes the National Guard," said Rodrigue. "Go on out and meet them. I'll be right behind you."

Leyton hurried to head off the approaching Humvee. The squat vehicle jerked to a stop. The lieutenant was being driven by another woman, a private.

"Where's the other man?" demanded the lieutenant.

"He was—"

Her eyes lifted over his shoulder, and Leyton turned and saw Rodrigue and Bain emerging from the house together and walking toward them.

"Get in the back!" said the lieutenant. Leyton climbed in and the driver gunned the Humvee over to Rodrigue and Bain. Bain showed the lieutenant his badge.

"Ma'am, this man has some gasoline we need for a portable pump we're using to get the water out of a storage area. Would you mind driving him back to his boat, and then bringing him back here with it?" He was still red-eyed from crying, but he merely looked tired.

The lieutenant looked at the badge suspiciously. "This is your cousin?" she said to Leyton.

"He's adopted," said Leyton quickly.

Bain snapped to the ruse immediately. "Not by blood. Mixed marriage. This is a crazy world. We really need to get the water out of that area. Do you have any objections to carrying gasoline?"

"No, not at all." She looked at Rodrigue. "Hop in."

The two women soldiers stayed with the Humvee in the parking lot at the Hilton, besieged with questions from the guests about fresh water, protection, transportation out.

"What in the hell is going on?" Leyton demanded when they were out of earshot.

"We're going to create a diversion."

"With gasoline?"

"Bain's going to start a fire."

Leyton stopped in his tracks. "What?"

Rodrigue grabbed him and pulled him along. "He figures there'll be enough pandemonium for him to get into the gear where the bug is."

"Damn! What if he's caught?"

Rodrigue shrugged. "Well, what *else* could go wrong then?"

35

The five *Columbia* astronauts prepared for entry by taking the three mission-specialist seats out of storage and installing them into the recessed receptacles in the floors. The seats locked in with quick-release latches built into the legs. No tools were required.

Several configurations were possible, with places for up to eleven astronauts. Eight was the largest crew any shuttle would lift off with, but there was a contingency for rescue missions on which an orbiter would return with extra live bodies.

Other contingencies that would've made a rescue mission possible—such as another orbiter processed and mated to its vehicular system and ready for rollout at Kennedy—were not routinely done, however. The fact was that rescue was *not* a viable option in most cases, and certainly not in this case. The problem had popped up too late. And even if they had had more warning, the weather at the Cape would've kept them from launching another vehicle.

As they had on lift-off, Roberta Anderson and Amy Simmons were seated in the middeck, in the center forward of the air lock. Marsha was on the flight deck aft, directly behind and between Alicia and Betty, whose seats on the flight deck were permanently installed. They took their seats and fastened their shoulder harnesses and lap belts. There wasn't anything else to do at this point.

There was some of the usual chatter over the intercom—terse one- and two-word sentences that would be stored in the orbiter's version of an airliner's black box but would not leave the spacecraft. Marsha remained silent. She was still thinking of all that might have been.

The bad part was knowing. If one minute you were blissfully unaware anything was wrong and the next you were a cinder, a piece of space dust that would probably ride the high winds for years, that would be fine. The revelation that the *Challenger* crew had survived the explosion and lived through that horrible plunge into the Atlantic had had a chilling effect on the whole astronaut corps. Thank God NASA wouldn't release the black-box tape.

Marsha thought about poor Vladimir Komarov in *Soyuz 1* back in the sixties, when the Soviets couldn't slow the capsule on entry. Komarov had over an hour to think about it—even spoke with his wife on a video link. For most of the time he had bucked up admirably, solemnly instructing his wife on the upbringing of their children, stoically listening to Kosygin gushing about what a hero he was. But the wait was too long, and in the end, the ground controllers had had to endure him pleading in panic, and then his final scream.

That communication hadn't been officially released, either, naturally, but U.S. intercept operators had recorded it, and over the years the transcript had leaked out.

Back when astronauts were all ex–test pilots in the Chuck Yeager mold, there was almost a genetic safeguard against any embarrassing outbreaks. John Glenn rode *Friendship 7* into the atmosphere thinking his heat shield was loose and he was going to burn up, and he sounded almost bored. So it could be done.

"Tell you what we're gonna do, gang," said Alicia unexpectedly. "We're gonna find out where Marsha's island is, and we're gonna have a reunion there."

"Excellent idea," came Amy's voice in Marsha's headset.

"I don't think Marsha's going to tell," teased Roberta. "I think she's afraid we'll discover there's a race of bronze savages there with big—"

"Hey!" Pilot Betty Kim broke in. "This is all being taped, remember."

"Tell you what," said Alicia again. "We'll take the photo and show it around that marina where Marsha bought it."

"What marina?" injected Marsha. "I doubt it's there anymore."

That brought the chatter to a halt, and Marsha wished she'd kept her mouth shut.

After what seemed like an eternity of silence, Amy's little voice piped up from below: "There have to be a lot of islands like that in the Caribbean, don't you imagine, Alicia?"

"Oh, yeah," said Alicia.

"You must accept no substitutes," said Marsha. "You must find *that* island."

"Savages with these huge war clubs," Roberta finally got in.

"Not *too* big," protested Marsha.

"Tell you what—find the island and I'll get us there," said Alicia. "Even if I have to hijack some T-thirty-eights."

"This is going on tape," said Betty.

Commander Alicia Burton's laugh was a sudden snort. "Nobody's gonna listen to that," she said.

36

The sun was going down by the time the lieutenant drove Rodrigue back to the Hilton. There were people around now, picking through the wreckage. Clouds of new mosquitoes rose from the soggy ground to greet them.

"They've opened the freeway," the lieutenant explained. "Only to residents, of course."

She was friendlier this time. She seemed disappointed Leyton hadn't come with him.

Incredibly, sounds of music and laughter greeted them as they rounded the bend in front of the hotel.

"Clearly I need to investigate," said the lieutenant with a wry smile. She climbed out of the Humvee after Rodrigue.

A party had begun in the pool area. Jimmy Buffet was crooning one of his old drinking songs through a tinny sound system, and mosquito-repelling dimethyl-meta-toluamide perfumed the heavy subtropical air.

"What's going on?" Rodrigue asked a man at the fringe.

"Hotel's getting cranked up again," said the man. He happily held up a plastic glass with a salted rim and frosty sides. A waiter in a white waistcoat pardoned himself as he stepped between them with a tray of identical drinks.

"They hauled in some supplies and some big generators on a flatbed," said the man. "Bunch of plastic sheets to patch up the windows. They said we'll have air conditioning tonight! Hell, have a margarita."

Rodrigue declined, much as he wanted something.

"I see your friend," said the lieutenant, pointing into the crowd. Rodrigue edged nearer and sighted along her arm. Leyton was gabbing merrily with a thirtyish woman with a slightly rippling midriff, wearing a straining white tank top and tight jeans.

"Come on," he said, pulling the lieutenant into the crowd.

A confusing range of expressions played on Leyton's face when he spotted them, from pleased to annoyed back to pleased again.

"This an official visit, Lieutenant?" he asked.

"I'm on duty," she said with good-natured suspicion.

"Shoud'a been here, maan," Leyton said to Rodrigue. "Dey done tuk aal the bodies, including one wit no head! The Coast Guard came and tuk down everybody's name. Nobody's s'pos to leave."

"The *Coast* Guard?" said the lieutenant, obviously puzzled at Leyton's sudden change of accent.

"I mean you. The National Guard." He was swacked.

"What's going on with NASA?" asked the woman in the tank top.

Rodrigue shot an angry glance at Leyton. Leyton claimed innocence with a finger to his lips.

"Did the shuttle crash?" she was asking.

"I've been hearing the same as you," the lieutenant said. "Same thing on the radio over and over. Shuttle's in trouble; NASA's working on it."

The lady in the tank top was no bimbo. She picked up on Rodrigue's battered psyche and tried to soothe it.

"I don't know," she said, her pretty brow furrowed. "We seem to get stronger after these things. It's just so hard to focus on the big picture, sort of, with all these people lost, lives shattered."

Leyton and the lieutenant were deep in their own conversation.

"I don't mean to be corny," said the woman. "But it's like you have to have winter before you can have spring, you know? Yin and yang. Death and birth. God, I *am* being corny." She laughed with embarrassment.

"Well, when you get right down to it, life is pretty damn

corny," said Rodrigue, who had spent most of his adult life running from winter.

This disaster, at least, was officially over. In many ways, the area would never be the same—certainly there were many families who would be grieving for a long while. But the chaos, the halted progress, that couldn't go on indefinitely.

Rodrigue was deeply depressed. It was the loss of the astronauts. It was all the faceless dead. But it was also just what the woman said: Things would grow back stronger—"things" being not just the leaves on the trees but the hotels and the houses and the roads and the drainage canals and the bulkheads, the whole patchwork of civilization that had blotched this lush coastal prairie.

Well brought up by his mother, he continued to be a dogged Catholic, ritually observing Sundays and holy days of obligation. But Catholic dogma hadn't made a dent in him. The Church taught that the Tree of Knowledge stood for loss of innocence, knowledge of the difference between right and wrong, as if God's perfect world existed only in the mind of a very young child.

High symbolism. Nothing to do with the real world—about which, in these rich parishes far from the liberation theologians of Neesay's world, the recurring message seemed to be go along to get along.

Rodrigue wasn't buying it. The signs were too obvious. God *had* created a perfect world. Where He fucked up was in creating such a wiseass animal to put on it. In the name of comfort and convenience, in the name of progress—and at the behest of women from Eve right down to Mrs. Picard—we had fouled our nest.

No wonder he drank so much. He would have loved a drink right now, but he needed to be quick and careful tonight. Especially careful. The need to take care of Neesay was pulling him through it.

Leyton and the lieutenant had disappeared—an easy feat in this crowd. The tender, nicely aging beauty in the tank top seemed willing to hang in there with him. And there had been a time, not that long ago, when he would've taken her up on it. But he excused himself politely, saying he had a family to look after.

The margaritas were being dispensed from huge plastic jugs, of which there seemed no end. Rodrigue took two glasses in each hand and climbed up the stairs to his floor. Halfway down the hall, the lights winked on, grew brighter, then dimmer—but stayed on weakly. A sustained cheer seemed to rock the building.

Mary was nursing again, this time lying languidly on her side with her arm stretched out and young Sean beside her, chewing contentedly on her big tan nipple.

The sight stirred Rodrigue in an unfamiliar way. Certainly there was a sexual aspect to it—Mary was a pretty young thing—but a totally different, totally new urge crept into his gut. Whatever it was, it started to produce a familiar reaction. He decided to move on before the condition became noticeable.

Mrs. Kilpatrick was seated at the foot of the bed, and Mrs. Picard was playing cards with her children on the other bed. Barbara Li was missing—probably partying down by the pool, he thought.

"Refreshments, ladies," he said cheerfully. "Rumor is we'll have air conditioning tonight. And they'll be sealing the windows against the mosquitoes."

"Oh," said Mrs. Picard, self-consciously straightening her clothing. "I guess we can move back to our rooms, then." She accepted two of the frosted drinks with an expression of regret.

"Hey, what about you?" asked Mrs. Kilpatrick.

"Not me, I'm driving," said Rodrigue, fending off the return of a margarita.

"Y'all are welcome to stay here," he said. "I think Leyton and I will both be busy tonight."

"You've been a doll," said Mrs. Kilpatrick, rising to give him a wet smack on the cheek. "You can tell the same to that charming partner of yours."

"Yes," said Mrs. Picard. "I'm sorry to have put you out this way, but—"

"Think nothing of it. Please. We were glad to have you. If neither of us comes back before you all leave, just lock up and leave the key with the desk. By the way, they may be serving food downstairs later. I'll try to send Leyton up with some."

Thus acquitted, Rodrigue took his leave. He had no place to go for several hours, no place he wanted to be. He wandered down to the party to look for Leyton, but he couldn't find him. He strolled down the muddy brick walk to his former office, but he didn't feel as if it had ever been a part of his life.

Kelly and the other students, even Leyton—they all seemed like faces from a party he shouldn't have gone to. . . .

Neesay, too. People he shouldn't have liked.

Finally, he walked out on the breakwater, away from the glaring dome of light, and climbed down into the bass boat. He idled out onto the lake to get away from the mosquitoes. The weight of the remaining gasoline made the boat a little more sluggish.

The hotel lights spread a yellow path across the inky water. That could be a problem, Rodrigue thought. For not the first time in his life, darkness was his ally.

He was early. He cut the engine and drifted. He dozed off.

The faint lapping of water against a hard surface woke him with a start. The *Haulover Queen* was slipping up on him, glowing ghostly in the hotel lights. Rodrigue got up quickly and lowered the electric motor. He wanted to make damn sure he could stay between the Hilton and the *Queen*. That way, the Colonel would have lights in his eyes the whole time.

The *Queen* bumped alongside and the Colonel left the wheel. He emerged from the pilothouse, pointing an automatic pistol at Rodrigue.

"I hope you don't mind this precaution," he said. "This is standard procedure in my line of work."

"I don't mind you pointing it at me as long as you don't shoot me with it," said Rodrigue mildly. He thought of all that gasoline and hoped to God there wouldn't be any shooting.

"Certainly not," said Weizman. "It's intended to keep you from shooting me. You have the device?"

"I do indeed. And you have Miss Cara?"

"Eunice, you may come out now."

Holding firmly on to the *Queen*, Rodrigue stepped on the switch in the bow of the bass boat. The electric motor tugged both boats gently, putting the hotel's lights in Weizman's face. It made a low hum.

"What was that?" demanded the Colonel.

"Your little boat here has an electric outboard. I'm using it to keep us from drifting apart." Never mind that he had a death grip on the *Queen*'s gunwale. Rodrigue swiveled his foot slightly and kept the two boats moving, now straight toward the north shore at a creeping pace.

Weizman was suspicious. His eyes narrowed. "Let me see the device," he demanded.

Neesay appeared in the pilothouse door. Her hands were tied behind her back and her mouth was taped with duct tape he had kept on board. Her eyes said she was frightened.

Suddenly, she turned a brilliant, dazzling white. Weizman was a shadow that loomed and then also became luminescent as he fell back, startled, from the gunwale and stared aft. Rodrigue turned toward his blind side and his good eye was instantly stung by white pain. It was a strong spotlight barely fifty yards away.

"Drop it!" ordered an amplified voice. "Federal agents! Drop the gun!"

The feds' boat shot nearer with a burst from well-muffled engines. In the light, Neesay and the Colonel looked like overexposed photos.

The Colonel complied, his face now as calm as a death mask. Neesay was shaking.

Men with the letters FBI and DEA on their backs appeared in the *Queen*'s cockpit. One spun the Colonel around roughly as he slapped on handcuffs. Another bent over and picked up the gun. A bulbous silhouette on the bow of the third boat crawled carefully onto the *Queen*. In the glaring beam of the spotlight, Rodrigue recognized Special Agent Roy Wilson.

"Miranda the hell out of them," Wilson instructed. He stepped heavily up on the gunwale.

"I'll take care of Rodrigue," he said with a satisfied smile.

37

"Good job," said Wilson grudgingly. "That trick with the electric motor got us just close enough just quick enough."

Rodrigue glared. He didn't appear to be enjoying this as much as Wilson.

"Of course, we had a sniper with a starlight scope on Weizman the whole time," the FBI agent continued. "But I'm damned glad to get him alive. Now maybe we'll find out what's at the bottom of this."

Over in the cockpit of Rodrigue's boat, Eunice Cara started mumbling. Someone peeled the tape from her mouth.

"You—you—" she stammered. "You were working for them all along!"

"Shut up, Neesay!" barked Rodrigue. "I'm gonna get you a lawyer. In the meantime, you shut up."

Earlier, when Bain and Rodrigue had come to him with Rodrigue's proposal, Wilson had solemnly pledged that she would not be prosecuted. It was a promise he couldn't keep, of course, but this was no time for brutal honesty.

Rodrigue didn't have any room to bargain, and they both knew it. If he had come out here alone, with or without the bugging device, Weizman would've killed him *and* the girl. His only chance to save her was to turn her over to the law. But cooperating with the law ran against Rodrigue's grain.

Just to make it easier on him, Wilson promised that Cara would merely be deported.

Rodrigue hadn't believed him from the start. Rodrigue was a distrustful, alienated son of a bitch.

Now the big one-eyed Cajun crumpled weakly to the driver's seat in the little blue boat. "What happened to the shuttle?" he asked glumly, expecting the worst.

"It landed fine."

"Landed fine?" said Rodrigue, looking up incredulously.

Wilson grinned. "I've got a little confession to make. The shuttle problem has been under control since about the middle of the afternoon."

"*What?*"

"Goddard Space Flight Center has been acting as Mission Control since about four-thirty or five yesterday."

For a moment, Rodrigue was unable to speak. Then his face took on a pained expression. "Well, what in the hell was all the pissing and moaning about? You mean Joe Bain—"

"Bain didn't know. There were only about a dozen people at the Space Center who did. Anybody who wasn't absolutely necessary was steered away from Mission Control under the pretext that the astronauts had the right to some privacy in their final moments."

"You mean to tell me that this whole thing with the shuttle was just a put-on?"

"Hell, no! *Columbia* was in trouble, all right—especially after the astronauts couldn't get a fix with the stars. But then someone from JSC got on an army helicopter to Bergstrom, and then a jet up to Andrews, and then another helicopter to Goddard, where he turned over a computer program that set everything right again."

Wilson had cause to believe they waited a little longer than they should have—cut it a little too close in the name of turf guarding—but he would keep that to himself.

"We let people at the Space Center believe the astronauts were still in trouble to see if any of Weizman's people would start to crack as the shuttle got closer to burning up. I still thought it was sabotage, remember. And I had no idea you were going to turn around and dump him in my lap."

"Jesus!" said Rodrigue, dropping his head. He had a case of

the shivers that was perfectly normal after having a gun pointed at him.

It had been closer than he knew. The DEA interdiction boat, a flat-black hot-rod Donzi dubbed the *Midnight Special,* had been hard to start. It had ridden out the storm in a warehouse not five blocks from the Houston Ship Channel. They were lucky it even floated.

Now the DEA crewmen were preparing a towline for Rodrigue's boat.

"Hey!" yelled Rodrigue, jumping to his feet. "You don't have to take that boat in tow—take *this* one. That one's mine."

He turned back, mumbling, "Yeah, that's right, search it first, asshole."

"They're looking for more of Weizman's spy toys," said Wilson.

"Well, the forty-five auto in there isn't one of them. Make sure it stays with the boat, will you? I've carried it since Nam."

Wilson was thinking the weapon's serial numbers might still be on a list of misappropriated government property somewhere, but the statue of limitations would have long since run out.

"I'll make sure," he said.

Wilson and Rodrigue looked at each other for a long minute. Resignation was on Rodrigue's face. Wilson wondered what was on his own.

"So was Leyton one of them?" Rodrigue asked finally.

He was trying to make it sound like an afterthought, but Wilson knew better. Men who operate outside the law, outside society, live and die by personal loyalties.

Rodrigue had grown suspicious of his partner, and rather than take a chance on him alerting Weizman, he concocted a wild ruse in which Bain was supposed to set fire to the Mission Control Center. It gave Wilson a chance to run a check on him via the National Guard's radio network.

"Leyton Mills is clean," Wilson said. "He might be a little eccentric, but that's just the way some of these rich kids are."

"Rich kids?"

"Very rich. Family's from New Hampshire. Dropped out of

Dartmouth College last spring and spent a little time in the Caymans, where he hired on as a boat hand on a yacht from Alabama. He bounced around the Gulf on two other private yachts and finally wound up in Galveston working for you."

"Huh" was all Rodrigue said.

The National Guard cleared the runway at Ellington Field for a lumbering air force transport out of San Antonio. Wilson, Andres Weizman, Eunice Cara, and a handful of NASA officials flew up to Washington for a long series of interviews with both Justice and State. Weizman was able to cut a pretty good deal and get into the witness relocation program. He was very forthcoming about the involvement of the governments of both Brazil and the People's Republic of China. Later, the State Department held a press conference in which part of the plot was detailed and Brazil threatened with economic sanctions in the absence of a formal apology.

Not a word was breathed about China, however. Wilson was reminded by a superior that foreign affairs were seldom conducted on a level field.

MurTech Engineering's stock dipped when the first sketchy reports came out. Soon afterward, it soared.

Weizman's candor left Eunice Cara twisting in the wind. Her cooperation wasn't needed and, because of her affiliation with the Brazilian government, there was a strong sentiment to make her a scapegoat.

Wilson tried to work with her, anyway. He didn't owe Rodrigue a damn thing—the son of a bitch had gotten him on a Justice Department shit list that was still crippling him now. But he did it, anyway—what little he could do. He saw to it that she got a few luxuries, woman things. He tried to convince her to act at least contrite and pretend to cooperate.

A lawyer showed up from New Orleans, a real sleaze in a sharkskin suit. Rodrigue had sent him, and he turned out to have all the right moves behind the oily schmooze of the Big Easy. But even he couldn't help her.

Eunice Cara apparently saw herself as a prisoner of war in a vicious struggle between the Americas. Wilson saw her as a cornered animal, frightened, and driven to hopeless ferocity by her fear. She behaved herself all right, but there were sparks of hate in her dark stormy eyes. It was a damn shame.

38

Leyton sat next to David Rodrigue in a huge auction barn in Baton Rouge, Louisiana.

The auctioneer was selling a half-ton pickup with dual exhausts and town-and-country trim. David—John Rodrigue's father—sat quietly, his thick-veined mahogany hands resting quietly on his knees.

A four-wheel-drive Chevrolet Suburban was coming up. It was, David assured Leyton, just what his son Johnny needed. It had been a company vehicle for an ailing oil-field service firm. It was painted dull gray, but it had all the bells and whistles, including a towing package.

The Blazer was garbage, but the boat trailer was none the worse for wear. Leyton was to pick up Rodrigue and the boat and trailer in Clear Lake and they would drive on down to Belize, in Central America. He couldn't wait. Leyton yearned for the real fringes of civilization, like something out of Conrad or early Michener.

His quest had actually begun in the Caribbean, strangely enough. He had gone to Grand Cayman on spring break. But the horror of higher education followed him like some vicious animal with its nose to his spoor. It wasn't really academic burnout. He had maintained a respectable average without any real strain on his social life. His father would've preferred better, of course, but then his father had never had a social life as far as Leyton knew, unless standing around in a tuxedo measuring every word and timing every sip was one.

The horror was the sudden revelation that education was merely a dirty trick the old played upon the young, to make them shoulder the burden for yet another generation. Deceit was the real product of the university.

Oh, to be sure, the faculty was seeded with Marxists. But their argument was like a fairy tale compared to the gritty reality being served up all around. Their logic was too appealing and far too uncomplicated—a critique, really, not an agenda. Eventually, you were to come around and see that one's inescapable duty was to profit.

The Caymans were certainly no escape. The climate and the scenery were wonderful, but the conversation among his fellow vacationers always swung to politics and money. He tried moving among the islanders themselves, but most of them were monied and were worse, actually, than the tourists. The few poor islanders were suspicious and stony.

Then a marvelous thing happened: A visiting yachtsman, a nouveau riche Alabamian, mistook him for a local and hired him to clean his boat one evening. There was something uplifting about the work. It was dependable, for one thing—use enough soap and apply enough pressure and the salt crust and diesel soot were sure to come off.

The Alabamian stood on the pier afterward, beaming at the boat. The Alabamian's wife beamed at Leyton. The next morning, they found him strolling past the marina again and offered him a ride to the United States, a green card, and a steady job.

He had eased into the British-Caribbean accent quite naturally—it actually seemed to flow from his tongue more smoothly than the precise nasal staccato of his New Hampshire upbringing. He grew the beard, and he dispensed with socks and underwear—a decision that, if she had known about it, would've sent his mother to bed.

And not for the first time, Leyton encountered the fascination certain white women had with the biological fact that while a black man's penis was not necessarily larger than a white man's in a like state of excitement, it certainly wasn't as small the rest of the time. It was gluttony without pain, he supposed.

His employer, rather than subject himself to the pity and scorn of his fellow nouveau riche white men in Orange Beach, had merely let him go—with a good recommendation on top of it, rather like laundering dirty money. Leyton landed a job on another yacht and was on his way to this new career.

Rodrigue had enough money in a bank in Belize to tide them over until the FDIC started reimbursing Galveston depositors. And while Rodrigue apparently considered the money for the Suburban a loan, the old man confided in Leyton that it was really a dividend. Rodrigue had bankrolled his father in what was now a successful business on the coast.

What *their* new business would be in Belize was not plain. Rodrigue seemed to be tired of business.

39

After Hurricane Jeanette, Rodrigue lost faith in nature's power of rejuvenation. The Clear Lake area was claimed not by jungle but by Friendswood Development Corporation, a subsidiary of Exxon.

Emergency legislation cleared the way for en masse deals with scattered landowners and heirless estates. Residents were given priority in hiring for the massive job of creating the world's biggest start-from-scratch planned community. Someday soon, everybody in southeastern Harris County would be living in one of about five versions of sixteenth-century English country houses with tall gables and dark-beamed Tudor facades. Meanwhile, temporary villages of identical double-wides sprang up, paved with pine bark and surrounded with redwood fences to shut out the noise of round-the-clock bulldozing and jackhammering and the vicious packs of homeless dogs.

The local space industry was blossoming like a well-pruned rosebush. All the majors, such as Ford Aerospace, Rockwell, and MurTech, were eagerly trading their shattered glass boxes for rambling office parks that blended into the planned community. Congressmen were tripping over each other to pledge support for JSC, centerpiece of the new Lyme Bay.

Rodrigue was going back to Belize to lie low for a while. He had sent Leyton to Louisiana to pick up a truck. Meanwhile, he was a guest of the government, and he had to admit he was thoroughly enjoying it. Rodrigue the Pirate was a big hero for a change.

Joe Bain, too, had captured the public's imagination—the quiet little man with the steamy secret life who, in the end, had done the right thing. The press called them the Super Mario Brothers. They had found the key and saved the princesses—all five of them.

The fact that it was really Goddard Space Flight Center that had saved the astronauts didn't jibe with the big Houston comeback story. And Special Agent Wilson, who of course had actually captured the Brazilian spy, was dismissed as merely having done his job.

In contrast to NASA's usual shirt-sleeve style—and maybe in defiance of the mounds of rubble that still stretched for miles in all directions—the big celebration banquet was a black-tie affair. Someone found Rodrigue a tuxedo that made him look like James Bond. He had never felt so good-looking.

He and Bain and Bain's wife were seated with the astronauts and their dates, which was uncomfortable for Rodrigue at first. He had quickly grown accustomed to being *aahed* and *ooed* over, but these space people were not impressed. Two of the female astronauts were either married to or going with male astronauts, and Rodrigue found even their chitchat too technical to follow.

The flight commander, Alicia Burton, was perfectly matched with a bookish type, undersized spectacles and a wispy mustache sticking straight out under his nose. After the celebration finally became a party, she sat with one arm draped across the back of his chair and talked with a cigarette dangling from her lips, while he was careful to laugh in all the right places.

And Mrs. Bain's favorite mode of communication was a quick nudge of the elbow into Joe's ribs.

The pretty blonde, Marsha Janke, was unescorted, so she wound up seated next to Rodrigue—much to her obvious dismay. Her smiles were so forced, they turned into sighs. After a while, he gave up trying to regale her and she gave up trying to patronize him, and they fell silent and listened to the other astronauts. Thank God, Rodrigue thought, for alcohol.

The Bains left and others pulled chairs up as the pecking

order broke down. There was an air of expectation, people standing around with knowing grins, and it became evident even to Rodrigue, numb as he was from drinking, that a plot was hatching. Sure enough, someone paraded in with five large framed photographs, which were met with squeals and groans from the female astronauts.

Marsha seemed to be the butt of some good-natured joke. She let him see her photo—it was a stippled print, mostly greens, of a small sand cay in a shallow lagoon. It looked like any one of a dozen similar cays he knew of inside the barrier reef of Belize.

The jolly pretense was that they were all going to stagger out, hop into their jet trainers, and fly off to wherever the mystery island was. There, they would all go naked and mate with bronze natives with huge uncut phalluses.

"I have no idea where it is," said Marsha. "All I know is, it had 'Drowned Man's' written on the back."

Rodrigue took a closer look. There were some islands called the Drowned Cays near Belize City, but they were mangrove islands, gnarled clumps of swamp uninhabitable except by birds and fish. Suddenly, he felt a strange compulsion.

"Aw, hell! I know that island!" he announced. It was a lie, of course.

"Where is it?" demanded Alicia.

"About forty miles south of Belize City, in Central America. I recognize the trees." He leaned over Marsha. "See how they seem to form the letters *W I X X*?"

Rodrigue was amazed at himself, and a little ashamed, too. How low would he stoop to reclaim some of the limelight?

Everyone was staring at the photos. There were a *lot* of *W*'s and *X*'s.

"I'm sorry to report there aren't any bronze natives with big phalluses, however," he said. "Not a soul within twenty or thirty miles, in fact."

"Have you been there?" asked Marsha, her bright blue eyes lingering on him for the first time. His second thoughts about launching this fairy tale suddenly evaporated like 151-proof rum.

"Oh, sure. I used to run dive tours out to a fabulous wall on the reef near there, and Drowned Man's is a great place to picnic, obviously." (All this was true enough—about another little island, anyway!)

"I generally called it something else, though."

"Why *do* they call it Drowned Man's?"

"Goes back a long way—1890s." Rodrigue leaned back and ruthlessly mixed history and myth. "A British naval officer apparently looted a Mayan pyramid on the mainland and disappeared. Those places are protected by the spirits of Mayan priests, you know. So the locals assumed the priests got him. Then about twenty years later, his body turned up on this very sand cay after a storm. Thing was, he was still wearing his naval uniform and he didn't look a day older than the night he disappeared. Nobody could figure out what had killed him, either, so they just said he drowned."

The table fell silent for a moment while supremely organized minds tried to process this garbage.

"Well, hell, let's go!" said one of the male astronauts finally—which was exactly what Rodrigue was hoping someone would say, since he was headed that way himself. And then the conversation went spinning back into the fantasy trip—now a treasure hunt for Mayan jade, now a scuba safari with barbecued lobster every night.

Marsha was talking to him now. She wanted to know more about the place. And then she wanted to know more about him. They almost became friends and then the party ended—or was ended by slightly embarrassed NASA officials who seemed to think the augustness of the occasion was in jeopardy.

A T-38 doesn't land on the same long glide path as a big airliner. Rodrigue was certain Marsha was about to fly the little jet into Lake Pontchartrain just north of New Orleans. Normally, he would've been paralyzed with fear, but with such a hangover, he had mixed emotions about dying.

They were the only ones who hadn't chickened out. Alicia was diving in right behind them, but only to transport a NASA pilot who would ferry Marsha's plane back to Ellington.

From a pay phone in the airport, Rodrigue called his father's house and told Leyton to pick up the boat and meet him in Belize City. Anyone who had been to Dartmouth ought to be able to find Belize City by himself.

Then he made a call to Belize City, to one Nicky Fuentes.

And he and Marsha still had time to hop a cab into Metairie and do some shopping before the flight. Rodrigue had neglected to tell the FBI about Weizman's fifteen hundred, so he had a little traveling money.

Four hours later, they stepped from the Boeing 737 into what could've been Hollywood's idea of the Third World. Tall palms and impenetrable underbrush lined the runway. Patroling the terminal were black men in camouflage, with automatic weapons slung casually. In the background beneath camouflage netting lurked the technological might and bored young men of the Royal Air Force, protecting the former colony out of habit.

The horde of dive tourists disembarking made it seem all the more like a tour of Paramount—until they came to a crashing halt in the terminal. The Customs and Immigration officials were moving with typical Third World languor, and the hurried North Americans were instantly impatient. Even Marsha, who had seemed to enjoy the flight as though it were a soak in a hot tub, now made a flat mouth and snorted delicately through perfectly formed nostrils.

Rodrigue drew himself up and snapped his fingers. A pair of officials rushed over to usher Marsha and him around the crowd. He sneaked them a wink. Nicky Fuentes had already slipped them something else—money, probably, but who knew.

Finally, Marsha was impressed. Now they were on Rodrigue's turf.

Nicky was waiting out front, standing beside his nine-year-old Crown Victoria. He was a San Pedrano of Mayan descent, a genuine bronze native of such ill repute with the Creole women of the city that Rodrigue shuddered to imagine the state of his phallus.

Rodrigue maneuvered Marsha to his right, so she wouldn't be on his blind side. While she was fascinated with the splendid squalor of the roadside, the corrugated-iron shanties and barefooted urchins amid rich emerald foliage, he took the opportunity to look her over carefully: She wasn't just pretty, she was perfect—real sun-lightened blond hair and healthy peachy skin and face like a movie star. Her nose was cute and her chin had just the right amount of baby fat beneath it. The oversized T-shirt could not conceal magnificent breasts, and peeking from the slit in her wraparound khaki skirt was the most well-formed calf he had ever seen. Her flowery scent shouldered aside the decaying vegetation along the nearby river, the direct exhaust from cars and diesel trucks, the tang of old grease from open kitchens, even the strong fumes from the sunbaked vinyl covering the Ford's seats.

Rodrigue caught his breath. What the hell was he doing? He had no business falling for a woman like Marsha—not her or any woman.

There hadn't been room in his heart for poor little Neesay, had there? Oh, he would do everything he could to get her out and send her home, but he couldn't have fallen in love with her. Hell, she was just a kid. . . .

Just about Marsha's age.

But that was different—he had *known* her as a kid, while this marvelous creature had dropped full-grown into his life. . . .

Still, he had no business falling for her. Not with good-bye bound to follow so close behind.

He feared good-byes. He had never used to, but he was getting older, softer. And the last one had hit him like a sap against the ear. . . .

The cruelest cut had been that Ann Eller pitied him. Otherwise, she would've just made her announcement and left. But she sat on the deck of his house with him while he reeled from it.

He should've known something was wrong when she came down to his beach house without an overnight bag. She'd had less and less time lately, and this was to have been their first weekend together in over two months.

She was in love with someone else, she said. Someone at work. He wasn't as exciting or as experienced or any of that, she said. But he was solid, sensible, steady—he couldn't remember everything she had said before, but he got the drift of it. Education. A future.

"So what the fuck am I?" he said when he could speak. "The Hell's Angels?"

A little voice down inside of him yelled, *Shut up! Shut up!* but he ignored it.

"No, John, you're a wonderful man—you've been wonderful for me. You—you rescued me from myself."

The way she looked at him with that fragile face, that intelligent mouth, the rich red halo . . . He felt an embarrassing catch in his throat.

"Obviously I need more security than most people," she said. "You know, John, you just sort of cast your fate to the wind. I mean, deep-sea divers are like baseball players—they have to consider what they're going to do when they grow up, you know?"

He looked at her, dumbfounded. He still hadn't figured out what his work had to do with anything.

"But I've got plenty of money," he said finally. His tone was awfully close to pleading.

"Oh, it's not about money!" She jumped up angrily. She had seen the jugular and she went for it. "It's about *responsibility*, John."

Her tone was cold then, and he knew it was really over. . . .

Nicky already had the boat provisioned. There were two hammocks, plenty of fresh fruit, snorkeling gear and a spear gun, and a case of Caribbean rum. There were also more mundane supplies: Alka-Selzer, mosquito repellent, some can goods and condiments, several large jugs of water, toilet paper, a tarp for privacy, and a broad machete that would double as a latrine shovel.

No coconuts. Naturally, since the little sand cay had coconut palms on it, Nicky hadn't thought coconuts were necessary. But it was a long boat ride out to the reef, and Rodrigue had a troubled soul. He escorted Marsha into the open produce market beside Haulover Creek, and they picked out a dozen.

Rodrigue showed off by taking the machete and lopping the tops off a couple without spilling the milk. He poured in rum and squeezed in sweet Jamaica lime. He didn't bother to watch her reaction as she sipped; he busied himself with the dock lines.

Nicky opened a cold Belikin from his store in back, and steered the long open boat down the dirty creek to the sparkling lagoon.

They had several more of Rodrigue's piña coladas before they reached the island. In the glow of the rum and the golden afternoon light, it was more enticing than he had remembered. The tangy trade wind rustled the palm fronds overhead. The lagoon lapped gently on the coral sand while the reef growled harmlessly from a distance.

Marsha slipped off her sandals and curled her toes in the warm sand.

"I don't believe it," she said. If she suspected it wasn't the real Drowned Man's Cay, she didn't let on.

She seemed dazed—but who wouldn't be, going drink for drink with Rodrigue.

Nicky winked and shoved the boat out. "Ah cum bek ta midday tomorra, okey? You mek liss one-one anyting be lack." He jerk-started the outboard and zoomed off without a backward glance.

They snacked on fruit and talked. Rodrigue had the feeling she was telling him things she had told no one else, things about how she had felt as a little girl, and about the jarring discordance between the cold blue planet and God's green earth.

Then, when the sea was turning pink, she peeled down to the scant emerald bikini she had bought in Metairie—and Rodrigue felt his heart race.

He gathered mask and fins and the spear gun and dove for supper, while she tagged along, following just behind and lasting every bit as long. He managed a nice mess of conchs for ceviche, but the good ledge where the lobster were proved too deep for him. He'd get Nicky—who was fifteen years younger—to dive for some when he came back out.

By a sweet driftwood fire, he showed her where to crack a tiny hole on the back of the shell to release the meat. She watched his face as he worked, not his hands.

"I really took a chance coming out here with you, didn't I?" she said finally.

"I suppose so."

"I mean with no ground rules or anything."

"Uh-huh."

"I mean, I don't know you from Adam, right?"

"That's right."

Rodrigue diced the conch meat very carefully. He had never in his life wanted a woman as much as he wanted this one.

"I was scared, John. I really thought I was going to die up there. It's made me just want to live, you know?"

He nodded, not taking his eyes from his work.

"*You* live," she said. "I could tell that about you—you really know how to live. I guess you've been through your share of tight spots, huh?"

He stopped cutting and looked at her seriously. "I never thought I'd make it to New Orleans."

She laughed, then looked at him for a long time again, chewing on her lower lip. It made him uncomfortable. He started squeezing limes over the white cubes of meat.

"I may have stumbled upon the last of the real gentlemen," she said. "You wouldn't touch a hair of my head unless I made the first move, would you?"

"I certainly would not rape you, if that's what you mean."

"No, that's not what I mean. If I had thought there was even a slight chance of that, I never would have come. No, I mean you're not even hitting on me. You're treating me like a sister. I think it's because I'm sort of treating you like a brother."

"A sister?" said Rodrigue, laughing.

She fidgeted in the sand, taking a deep breath. "This is really wild, but what I wonder is, what if I wanted something different—I mean *really* different, and I made it very plain. I—I wonder if you would be as accommodating."

"Probably," he said, still playing it cool.

Okay, so she had mentioned the lack of a toilet seat—Nicky could pick up a toilet seat at the Western Auto.

She'd want ice when it got hot. And if the wind died, the mosquito repellent might not keep the no-see-ums from driving them back to the air-conditioned rooms of the Fort George.

Rodrigue didn't care. He was feeling a lust so deep, he

must've inherited it from an ancestor. What was she talking about, wanting something *really* different—? It didn't matter. Whatever she wanted, Rodrigue was prepared to give it to her.

And probably that was the way it should be. It was plain to him that all the heavy evils of the world arose directly from civilization. Pollution. Corruption. *Commerce.* Yes, and technology that ran amok like cancer. And it was just as plain that women were the cause of it all. Men made it, but only because women wanted it.

God had created an emerald paradise primordial. . . .

But then He turned right around and created woman.

You had to figure He knew what He was doing.